NVK

NVK

永

TEMPLE DRAKE

OTHER PRESS / NEW YORK

Poetry excerpt on page 235 by Hsiang Kao, and poetry excerpt on
page 238 by Po Chu-I. Translated by N.L. Smith and R.H. Kotewall
in *A Book of Chinese Verse*, 1962. Bilingual English-Chinese edition
copyright © Hong Kong University Press, 1990. Poetry excerpt on
page 316 from "Elsewhere" by David Harsent, from the collection *Night*
(London: Faber & Faber, 2011). Copyright © David Harsent, 2011.
Published with permission of Faber and Faber Ltd.

Production editor: Yvonne E. Cárdenas
Text designer: Jennifer Daddio / Bookmark Design & Media Inc.
This book was set in Bembo by
Alpha Design & Composition of Pittsfield, NH

1 3 5 7 9 10 8 6 4 2

Library of Congress Cataloging-in-Publication Data

Names: Drake, Temple, 1955- author.
Title: NVK : a novel / Temple Drake.
Description: New York : Other Press, 2019.
Identifiers: LCCN 2019002172 (print) | LCCN 2019006981 (ebook) |
ISBN 9781590519363 (ebook) | ISBN 9781590519356 (paperback)
Subjects: | BISAC: FICTION / Fantasy / Paranormal. | FICTION / Romance /
Gothic. | GSAFD: Occult fiction.
Classification: LCC PR6070.H685 (ebook) | LCC PR6070.H685 N88 2019 (print) |
DDC 823/.914—dc23
LC record available at https://lccn.loc.gov/2019002172

TO RORY

NVK

NORTH KARELIA

1579

AFTERWARDS, she couldn't remember how she came to be hiding. Did someone tell her to, or did she think of it herself? That piece of the past was missing. She was inside the walls of the house, a secret place her father had showed her when she was very young. No one knew about it, he had told her, not even her mother. She had seen it as a game until she looked into his face. His eyes as still as well water, his usual easy smile gone. It was only to be used in special circumstances, he went on, but he didn't say what those circumstances might be. She peered through a crack in the paneling and took in the rough floorboards and the half-open door that led out to the kitchen. It was a simple wooden house. Four rooms. A low window revealed the flat land to the west, the grass ruffled by a summer wind, the blue sky free of clouds. The roof above her creaked. The walls were creaking too. As a child, that rushing noise had made her glad. Even now, she would often run outside with her arms spread wide, her blonde hair wrapping round her face. She would feel caught up in something generous and wild, and she would lose all sense of time, and of herself. That day, though, she was older. Already in her twenties. She huddled in the dark and barely moved.

She might have slept because the world seemed to give beneath her. Some kind of slippage happened. The next thing she knew there were other sounds under the wind. Horses' hooves, men's voices. She couldn't think who might be visiting. They almost never had visitors. They lived too far from the village, and miles from the nearest thoroughfare. She thought about pushing the loose panel aside and stepping out into the room, but something prevented her. There was shouting, then coarse laughter. She couldn't hear her father. She couldn't hear her mother either, or her aunt. Footsteps crashed across the wooden boards. A pair of legs appeared. Boots that were damp and muddy. The man's hand had a club in it, which he swung and twirled, as if to entertain her. He cleared his throat and spat. When he moved to the window, she saw her mother's foot in the kitchen doorway, pointing at the ceiling. Her heart went still. She couldn't think why her mother might be lying on the floor. She couldn't come up with a single explanation. The man in the mud-stained boots had gone, but she could hear voices outside, at the back of the house, and a smell crept into the small space where she was, the smell of roasted meat. It wasn't enough to be crouching in the dark. She had to do something that would help her to deal with what was happening, something that would fix her in the moment but also lift her out of it. Raising her left arm towards her face, she bit into the inside of her elbow. The skin broke, and the flash of pain was like sheet lightning in an evening sky. Then the warm metallic taste of blood. An emptiness flowed into her, steady and remorseless, and she sank back, the crack in the panel no more than a long thin rip of light that showed her nothing.

More time passed.

It was the silence that woke her. The middle of the afternoon. She crawled out into the room and stood up. The wind was still blowing, though it had weakened. It would be hours before it drained out of the world. She crossed to the window and swung her legs over the sill and dropped lightly to the ground. She walked away from the house in a straight line, through grass that was calf-deep. On the horizon was a row of poplars. A fly buzzed past her ear and was gone. Summer in North Karelia.

At last, she turned and looked back. Smoke rose in a greasy column from the rear of the house, where the animals were kept. She could see a group of men on horses. They appeared to be riding east, towards the river. This was a place she loved, its water running calm and blue between low banks lined with orange reeds. She watched the men for a long time to make sure they were leaving. They would have come from Novgorod, she thought. The language she had heard had almost certainly been Russian. She waited where she was until they dissolved in the heat haze, melting to nothing, then she started back. This time she walked slowly, covering the distance with her eyes lowered. She came round the northwest corner of the house and stopped near the front steps. A man lay facedown on the ground, one arm beneath his body, the other flung out to one side. Only his hair was moving.

"Father?"

When she knelt beside him, she saw that the back of his head had been split open. Blood clogged his ear and ran in trickles down his neck. Blood soaked the grass.

The men had killed him.

They had also killed her aunt, who they had strung up on the edge of the property. Her wrists had been lashed together and tied to the lowest branch of a cherry tree. Her head hung forwards, her brown hair falling over her face. Her clothes had been torn from her body, and there was dried blood on her legs.

Inside the house she found her mother, still lying on the kitchen floor, her bare feet pointing at the ceiling. Most of her clothes were gone as well, and part of her ripped skirt had been used as a gag. She took the rag from her mother's mouth, then fetched a reindeer skin and laid it over her body, pulling it up to just below her chin. Kneeling on the floor, she kissed her mother's forehead, which was already cold.

"My darling…"

She said the words over and over. There were no others. As she spoke into the quiet of the house, dark circles appeared on her dress and on the floor. The inside of her body felt scraped with a blunt instrument.

She held her mother's hand and looked away towards the door, where the wind rummaged in the grass and the sky stood still and blue. She smelled the roasted meat again. The men must have killed some of the livestock too.

I'm all that's left, she thought.

She decided not to fetch help. The nearest neighbors lived half an hour's walk away, and she didn't want to leave her loved ones on their own. She stood up and took a knife from the drawer and went outdoors. Cutting the rope that bound her aunt, she half dragged, half carried her back to the house and laid her on the floor next to her mother. Outside again, she gripped her father under the arms. Like her, he was finely made, but it still took all her remaining strength to haul him across the grass and into the house. When her father, her mother, and her aunt were lying side by side, she sat on the steps facing north. She felt short of breath, as if a weight were on her chest. The wind had blown itself out, and the blue of the sky had dimmed. She could hear the flies gathering in the room behind her. Every now and then, she turned her eyes to the east, but there was no sign of the men.

She couldn't have said how long she sat there for. At that time of year there was almost no difference between afternoon and evening. The sky was never entirely dark, not even in the middle of the night. Finally, she rose to her feet and fetched a piece of rough cloth from inside the house and took it round to the back. The fire had burned down low, and the ground was covered with bones that had been stripped of their meat. A few clay jugs of *brännvin* lay scattered about, all of them empty. The doors to the sheds stood open. The men had cooked one of the goats on a makeshift spit, but the rest of the animals were gone. From the patch where the vegetables were grown, she collected several handfuls of rich dark earth and placed them on the piece of cloth, then she knotted the corners so it formed a kind of bag. Returning to the house, she packed the cloth bag into a knapsack, along with a few clothes and the knife, and set it down on the weathered boards of the porch. Stacked against the back of the house, under a lean-to, was the firewood they kept for the long winter months. She began to carry the logs inside, heaping them on the kitchen floor, then she went through the house opening all the doors and windows. She unscrewed the oil lamp that hung from an iron hook on the wall and poured its contents onto the pile of wood and onto the animal skins and blankets that covered the bodies of her family, then she took a small shovel from next to the stove and walked round to where the fire was and scooped up the last few embers. Back in the house again, she tipped the glowing embers onto the logs. There was a quick rush of sound, like an intake of breath, and the flames snaked across the room, fanned by the draft from the open doors and windows. Her family lay still beneath a shroud of bright dancing orange. Backing out of the house, she picked up the knapsack and ran down the steps and out onto the grass. At first, the flames were only visible through the doorway, but it wasn't long before they burst through the roof. Thick white smoke poured up into the sky.

She turned away and walked off across the meadow towards the distant line of trees. The inside of her elbow stung, and she still had the taste of her own blood in her mouth. She could hear the house burning behind her. Her past was burning too. Later, she would imagine there had been a happy time, all those years growing up with her family, all that love, but she couldn't find it in her memory. The happiness wasn't something that could be proved. It was a matter of belief, or faith. Like God.

She spent the first night in the forest, at the base of a tree, in the sheltered space between two roots. On the second night, she found a woodsman's hut, a floor of beaten earth, its roof half gone. She had been troubled by the prospect of sleep, fearful of the dreams that might be lying in wait for her, but every morning when she woke the inside of her head was bare, like a room emptied of all its furniture. As she walked, she recited spells and incantations that were part of her heritage, and came naturally to her. *There are strangers at every gate, and enemies round every corner, and in the forest there are sorcerers, but I am not alarmed. I am not in the least afraid.*

The weather was in her favor, warm and dry.

One evening, after walking for six or seven days, she came to a smallholding. Two children ran out to meet her. They tugged at her skirts, begging her to join in with the game they were playing. One of them brandished a doll made from bleached bones, a torn rag, and a piece of string. Their father stood watching from a darkened doorway. He was a tall man. His left hand lacked a finger.

"Have you come far?" he asked. "Where are you from?"

She began to cough, as if smoke from the torched house had forced its way into her lungs. As if she too had been soaked in lamp oil and set on fire.

The man's wife brought her cool water in a wooden scoop. She drank it all. The taste was of pine needles, fallen leaves.

"Tell us your story," the man said.

He was only asking what anyone might ask, and his eyes, though narrow, were not suspicious or unkind. A story was a passport, after all. Something that allowed people to place you. Trust you. But her story had been hidden from her, and she found she couldn't speak. When she looked behind her, there was nothing but trees and more trees, and then perhaps a meadow, and in the distance, at the very limits of her remembering, a house consumed by flames. She seemed, even to herself, to have emerged from nothing. She was like a boat that leaves no wake.

"Don't pay any attention to him," the man's wife said, pushing him away. "You can stay if you like. You'll be safe here."

The woman's promise seemed rash, and born of a profound and dangerous innocence, and she didn't believe it. She would never be safe again. Nonetheless, she let herself be taken to a woodshed at the back of the house, where there was a simple bed of straw. That evening, she lay down and rested, but she couldn't sleep. There were things just out of sight inside her head. She had to keep herself from looking.

She was gone before the people woke, while all the stars were still out, dusting the sky like flour spilled from a sack. Once again, she murmured as she moved among the trees. *May I pass unnoticed through this world and leave no trace. For if I am not seen, I will not come to any harm.* That she might cast off her life like this wasn't something that had ever occurred to her. Before, she would walk to the river, where she would dream or swim or fish, or to a neighbor's house, to see Agata, her friend, returning after many hours, but this was movement in one direction only, and it felt hazardous, as if she might outstrip herself, unravel. Cease to be. She wanted the miles to open up behind her, though. She wanted to keep going and never reach the end. She supposed that was impossible, but she couldn't be sure.

Sometimes at night she bit into her arm, opening the wound. Or sometimes she used the knife she had brought with her. There was the bright flash of pain and the metal taste of blood. There was the calmness that flowed through her afterwards. It became a habit. A necessity. It helped her to remember, and to forget. But there was no sense, in those early days of exile, that she was undergoing a transformation, no sense that she might be changing into somebody who did not change.

That came later.

SHANGHAI

2012

1

IT WAS CLOSE TO MIDNIGHT, and Zhang Guo Xing was thinking of going home. He was in a club on Fuzhou Road, twenty-four floors up, the Shanghai skyline in the window. There were private tables sealed off with scarlet ropes, and bottles of champagne in silver buckets. The DJ had been flown in from Brazil. Zhang's guests were the usual European businessmen. Most of them were middle-aged, and most were drunk. They would try to pick up the go-go dancers, aloof and graceful on their cubes, or the Russian models who were in town for photo shoots or runway shows, but they would almost certainly be unsuccessful. They would take taxis back to their hotels. Wake up jet-lagged, dehydrated, and alone. Excusing himself, Zhang stood up and left the table.

The walls in the bathroom were black, and the lighting was so dim that an attendant had to guide him to the urinal. Afterwards, as he washed his hands, a small man appeared beside him. The man was wearing a pale blue suit and white patent leather shoes. The suitcase he had with him was also pale blue. Looking straight ahead, into the smoked-glass mirror, he began to talk.

"You think you have everything under control," he said, "but then something happens. Something you didn't see coming."

Zhang looked sidelong at the man, but didn't speak.

"Suddenly, you're in a whole new world," the man went on. "Things have a different smell, a different taste." He bent close to the mirror and picked at his teeth, then smoothed his oily hair down flat. "All the familiar parameters are gone. You lose your bearings." He paused. "Fear rushes through you, like a gust of wind."

Zhang was still looking at the man. His voice, so eerily objective and detached. His head thrust forward, like a turtle's. The suitcase on the floor next to his leg.

"Did you just arrive," Zhang asked, "or are you about to leave?"

The man chuckled and nodded, as if this was exactly the question he had been expecting.

Zhang took a towel from the attendant and dried his hands. When he glanced round, the man with the suitcase had disappeared. Dropping the towel into a basket,

Zhang left the bathroom. Out in the corridor again, he looked both ways. There was no sign of the man. He shrugged, then moved back towards the main part of the club.

His guests had forgotten all about him. Many were on the dance floor, their jackets undone or tossed aside, their faces wide and loose with alcohol. The music was louder than before, a constant pulse that pushed up through the soles of his shoes. He stood still, watching people dance. It was then that he noticed her, over by the bar. A light round her, a kind of shimmer. Something he could feel rather than see. He walked up to the bar and asked for a cognac. Now he was beside her, the effect was even stronger. Like standing beneath a pylon, or next to an electric fence. The angle of her head had altered, and her eyes drifted across his face. He felt her intensity, and her indifference.

Though she looked European, he decided to speak to her in his own language. "What kind of person brings a suitcase to a nightclub?"

"You saw him too?" Her Chinese was unfaltering, and almost without accent.

"In the men's room. He spoke to me."

"What did he say?"

"It was strange. He was talking about the way your life can change, in unexpected ways."

"You don't actually know him, though."

"No."

"What else did he say?"

"Something about change being scary."

"It was his suit that was scary."

Zhang smiled.

When he first walked up to her, she'd had her back to the bar, the points of both elbows resting on its gold surface. Now, though, she turned towards him. Her eyes were dark, almost black, but her hair was like a fall of light.

"Your Chinese is excellent," he said. "Have you been in Shanghai long?"

"I like learning languages. I've always been good at them."

"How old are you?"

"How old do you think?"

He looked at her for several long seconds, and she met his gaze, unblinking.

"Twenty-four." He hesitated. "An old twenty-four, though."

"Meaning what?" Her look had tightened. He had said something that interested her.

"You were born old. It's there in your face. How do they put it in English? *An old soul.*"

"And you?" she said. "How old are you?"

"Forty-two."

"Are you married?"

"Of course."

"But your wife lives in another city, and you hardly ever see her."

He smiled, then glanced at his phone. Three new messages, but nothing that couldn't wait. "Are you with anyone?"

"No," she said. "What about you?"

"I came here with some business colleagues. They wanted to see Shanghai at night—the bars, the girls..."

She was watching him, amused. Her teeth were white and even.

"Can I buy you a drink?" he asked.

"Let's go somewhere else," she said. "This place is getting loud."

He finished his cognac, then followed her through the crowd. Black leather jacket, short black skirt. Black ankle boots with chunky heels. Everything she wore seemed a setting for the blonde hair that fell in gleaming tangles to her shoulders. She turned down a narrow passageway. The left-hand wall was lined with floor-to-ceiling fish tanks, and small sharks swam this way and that, their sinuous gray bodies gliding through the brightly lit blue water.

"Your colleagues won't miss you?" she said.

"They've been drinking all evening," he told her. "They won't even realize I've gone."

They took a lift to the ground floor.

Out on the narrow street it was dark and warm and clammy, and the air smelled of cabbage that had been boiling for hours. September in Shanghai was still a kind of summer. As they crossed the pavement, a white Lamborghini pulled up outside the club. Its doors lifted like insect wings, and three Chinese girls in knee-length boots and miniskirts got out. She glanced at him. He kept his face expressionless. Upstairs, in the air-conditioned air, the whites of their eyes glowing in the ultraviolet, it had almost felt as if they had met before. As if they knew each other. Down here, in the murk and steam, they were strangers.

"Should we get a taxi?" she said.

He took out his phone. "I have a car."

He called Lu Chun Tao, his driver. Seconds later, the black Jaguar drew level. Chun Tao was twenty-six, with a pearl stud in his left ear and hair that was shaved at the sides and swept back on top, and he had been in

Zhang's employ for almost a year. So far, he had proved himself reliable.

They climbed into the back, and Zhang gave Chun Tao an address. He looked out of his window, and she looked out of hers, but the gap between them was so charged that it seemed they were already touching. The city slid past, the molded concrete sides of flyovers floodlit by pale green or lilac neon, the hundred-story buildings topped with horns or spikes or balls. She didn't appear to be impressed by any of the usual things—or even by Shanghai itself. His chauffeured Jaguar would not be enough, nor would his $2,000 Prada suit. No, it would be something else, something he did not intend. A phrase he used. A gesture. Some look that came and went in his eyes. He had been stripped of all his advantages, but it didn't bother him. He liked having to rely on chance and intuition. He liked the not-knowing. He shouldn't talk too much, though. He should make her talk.

"Did you go to the club by yourself?" he asked.

"I was there with a friend," she said. "He left early. He met someone."

Her face was still angled away from him, and he could only see the bright gold hair, one cheekbone. The edge of her mouth.

"But you stayed on," he said.

"Yes."

"It didn't worry you, to be alone?"

She gave a little shrug. "Shanghai's safe enough."

"Even so. Men can be annoying."

She turned to him, and as they held each other's gaze mauve light washed through the car's interior. The whites of her eyes seemed silver then.

"Where are we going?" she asked.

"Somewhere quiet," he said.

The car eased down off the Yan'an elevated highway and into the dark tree-lined streets of the French Concession. She opened the window. Stagnant air flowed in.

"Do you mind?" she said. "The city smells so good at night."

"If you like drains," he said.

She smiled.

The chatter of cicadas came in waves, louder and louder, like something that might explode.

The Jaguar dipped down a steep concrete slope and into an underground car park, where the shiny dark green floor was slick with water. The car's tires squealed as Chun Tao turned right, past a pillar.

"This is where you live?"

For the first time, she sounded wary, and Zhang felt he should reassure her.

"No," he said. "This is a private members' club."

Private members' clubs were places where politicians and entrepreneurs could meet discreetly, without being interrupted or observed, places where gifts could be exchanged and deals could be done. There was no entrance as such, only an unmarked lift.

Zhang asked Chun Tao to wait. He didn't say how long they would be.

"I thought private members' clubs were only for men," she said as they stood by the lift.

He nodded. "Usually."

Once upstairs, they were shown to a room that was at the end of a long, hushed corridor. There were vases of fresh lilies and cedarwood armchairs upholstered in gold brocade. Traditional lute music tinkled out of hidden speakers. A picture window framed a little spotlit forest of bamboo and a wall of rough brown bricks with water running down it. At the foot of the wall was a rectangular pond filled with carp. He sat down on one of the chairs and watched her move towards the window.

"This is perfect," she said.

"Not too quiet?"

"No."

Two glasses of Hennessy X.O arrived. As she stood with her back to him, looking out, he once again sensed the force field that surrounded her, invisible, magnetic.

He asked what her name was.

"Naemi," she said.

"Where are you from?" He was aware of the need to keep his questions simple. His unpredictability would come from somewhere else.

"I'm Finnish," she said. "My mother was Sami."

Zhang wasn't familiar with the word.

"The Sami are nomads," she told him. "They can be found in the northernmost parts of Norway, Sweden, and Finland, and also on the Kola Peninsula in northwest Russia. Sami people used to make a living from herding and hunting reindeer. From fishing too. They were believed to be skilled in the art of magic. Laplanders, they're sometimes called."

Zhang tasted his cognac. "But you grew up in Finland?"

She nodded.

"I've never met anyone from Finland," he said. "What are Finnish people like?"

"We're supposed to be undemonstrative. Reserved. There's a myth about us—the myth of the silent Finn."

"But it's not true?"

"I don't think you can generalize." She turned from the window. "Are Chinese people really inscrutable?"

Zhang smiled.

"And your family?" he said. "Are they still there, in Finland?"

She shook her head. "My parents are both dead."

"Do you have any brothers or sisters?"

"No."

"You're alone," Zhang said. "I'm sorry."

She was suddenly next to his chair, and leaning over him. The heat of her mouth came as a surprise, almost as if she had a temperature. She didn't seem ill, though, not in the least. His heart speeding up, he put his hands under her jacket and drew her closer.

Later, she moved back to the window and looked out into the garden.

"I like the wall with the water running down it," she said. "I grew up near the water."

He joined her at the window.

She used to swim in a river, she told him, about half an hour's walk from her parents' house. The river was cold, even in the summer. The shock of it tightened your skin against your bones. But afterwards you felt so alert, so alive. They had lived in the country—the middle of nowhere, really. Her eyes lost their focus, and she seemed to swallow.

"You were a child, then," he said.

She nodded slowly. "Yes."

There was a stillness, and he thought he could hear water trickling, like the sound you make when you run your tongue over your teeth without opening your mouth. He couldn't have, though. The window was closed. And anyway, soft music was being piped into the room.

"I should go," she said.

"Already?"

"I have to be up early, for work."

"You work?"

"Doesn't everyone?"

He touched her cheek with his fingertips. "I didn't see you as everyone."

She was standing so close that he could feel her breath against his face. There was a single faint line at the edge of her left eye. Otherwise, her skin was unblemished, clear. He moved his hand to the back of her neck, beneath her hair. Then they were kissing. Once again, he noticed the heat of her mouth. Once again, the wild racing of his heart.

As they took the lift to the basement, they stood against opposing walls, looking at each other, the space between them charged and tingling, just as it had been earlier, in the car.

Everything they hadn't done as yet.

Everything they might still do.

When the door opened and the car park lay before them, vast and warm and windowless, he asked if she wanted a lift back to where she lived.

"I'll take a taxi," she said. "It's not so far."

His car was waiting, engine running, but he turned his back on it and walked her up to the street.

"I'd like to see you again." He reached into his jacket pocket. "Can I give you my card?"

"No need," she said.

"How will you find me? You know nothing about me—" He bit his lip. He hadn't meant to say so much.

"I found you tonight," she said. "I'll find you again."

In a city of more than twenty million, he thought. How was that possible?

A green light appeared.

He waved the taxi down and opened the door for her. She climbed in. One hand on the top of the door, he gazed at her. The night smelled of cordite and sulfur, as if people had been letting off fireworks. As if there had been a wedding.

"Was I right when I said you were twenty-four?" he asked.

"In a way," she said.

"You like riddles, don't you."

"It's not a matter of liking them. We live with them." She looked up at him, her lips black in the yellow light of the streetlamps. "We're all riddles, aren't we, even to ourselves."

He closed the door. As he watched the taxi pull away, he felt oddly torn between regret and relief, and had no idea why.

By the time Zhang reached his apartment complex, it was raining hard. The security gate lifted, and Chun Tao drove through the landscaped grounds and down into the car park in the basement of Zhang's building. It was almost three thirty in the morning. He asked Chun Tao to pick him up at ten. Chun Tao would probably park outside the complex and sleep in the car, though Zhang didn't encourage it. He didn't like the smell of slept-in clothes and exhaled breath. He was particular about such things. But it was hard to see what other option Chun

Tao had, given that he lived more than an hour's drive away, near Hongqiao airport.

Zhang climbed out of the car and closed the door. It was hot in the car park, but the white lights in the ceiling gave off a muted chilly glow, like ice cubes. The Jaguar moved smoothly away. All was still. A dripping at the edge of his hearing again. The frosted lights unblinking. His phone vibrated, letting him know he had a message. His heart flared like a struck match. *Naemi*. But it was just a text from one of the European businessmen he had been entertaining earlier. *What a night, Mr. Zhang! Thank you.* The lift door opened. He stepped inside and pressed 39.

Once in his apartment, he poured himself a glass of water and stood at the floor-to-ceiling window in his living room. In a neighboring tower, a window clicked from dark to light. Far below, Puming Road was deserted. How could Naemi have texted him? He hadn't given her his number. She hadn't given him her number either. She had told him she would find him, though, and he knew he wanted to be found. It reminded him of a game he used to play at school. You stood with your feet together and your arms folded over your chest, then you closed your eyes and let yourself fall backwards. The idea was, someone caught you before you hit the ground. He had always been slender, and his classmate, Wang Jun Wei, who was almost twice his size, would squat behind him, only catching him when he was inches from the ground. He liked to imagine that he was standing on a precipice, his heels on the very edge, a thousand-meter drop behind him. When he let himself fall backwards, he would sometimes have the feeling that he might fall forever.

2

IT WAS YEARS since something like this had happened. How many, she couldn't have said. She leaned against a pillar in her living room, all the lights still off. A glow from the streetlamps fell across the varnished floorboards, the burnt orange broken into blocks by thin black lines. Cool air closing round her. The smell of rich dark earth.

Zhang Guo Xing.

She had seen him first, standing at the edge of the dance floor in his dark suit and his crisp, open-necked white shirt. He watched people dancing the way you might watch cars passing on a road, his face relaxed, attentive. She wanted him immediately. Even before he noticed her, she wanted him.

When he approached her, as she had felt he might, he underwent a kind of change. It was subtle, like the lights dimming in a fancy restaurant. His expression became more subdued, more intimate. He hadn't imagined he would meet anyone that evening—that wasn't why he had come out—but he adjusted to her presence in an instant. The unexpected didn't trouble him. Then he did something that took her by surprise. He spoke to her in his own language. In that moment, he appeared to know things about her that he shouldn't have known. Things he shouldn't even have been able to guess.

She pushed away from the pillar. Moving across the living room and on into the small room she used as a study, she opened her laptop. She typed Zhang's name into Baidu, the main Chinese search engine, and was able, in the space of an hour and a half, to assemble a rough outline of his life. Born into a privileged family in Beijing—his father was a high-ranking Party member—he had studied economics at the university. After graduating, he relocated to Vancouver, where he took a master's degree in business. On his return, he worked for various financial institutions in Hong Kong. In 1998, his mother had a severe stroke that left her incapacitated, and the family put her in a nursing home. At the age of twenty-nine, Zhang moved to Shanghai. At present, he was the senior vice president of a Chinese-owned private equity firm that was based in Pudong. He was married, with one son.

She clicked Sleep and sat back in her chair. It was almost five in the morning. The rain on the window blurred the city skyline, one shade of neon bleeding into another. If only I wasn't attracted to anyone, she thought. If only there was no such thing as desire. But she got lonely. She was only human. She smiled to herself. A wistful smile, not much humor in it. Still, she felt reassured by the information she had unearthed. It would be normal for a Chinese man of Zhang's wealth and privilege to have lovers. He would understand the rules, namely that affairs should be clandestine, finite. He would be adept at dividing his life into self-contained compartments, accustomed to the subterfuge involved. Perhaps, after all, she could afford to take the risk.

In the bathroom, she removed her photochromic lenses. She knew how her irises must look, the green so pale it was almost colorless. Over the years, her eyes had become more light-sensitive, and there had been a time—decades, in fact—when she'd had no choice but to live at night. Recent developments in science had liberated her, though. Opening the mirror door on the cabinet above the sink, she placed the contact lenses in a small plastic receptacle. Slowly, she closed the door again. The mirror stayed blank as it swung back into position in front of her. She liked the fact that she did not appear. It was a virtue, not a lack or a deficiency. Other people seemed to need the validation a reflection brings, even if that validation was deceptive, illusory, but she wasn't in any need of proof that she existed.

She took off her clothes, then walked into the living room and used a remote to drop the blackout blinds. Back in the bedroom, she lay down on the bed of earth that she had shipped at great expense from North Karelia.

The earth of her homeland.

Turning onto her left side, the side where her heart was still beating, even after six or seven lifetimes, she slowed her breathing. Let her eyelids close.

3

DURING THE WEEK THAT FOLLOWED, it rained every morning, from dawn until midday. In the afternoons, the sun came out. The city steamed. Zhang worked late every night. Shanghai's economy was booming, with foreign direct investment up 21 percent year-over-year and annual growth in the double digits. There were business opportunities everywhere you looked. Sitting in his office with his chair turned to face some of the tallest buildings in the world, he realized he was waiting for Naemi to contact him, but the days went by and he heard nothing. *I found you tonight. I'll find you again.* How would she do that exactly?

When he called Beijing on Wednesday and spoke to Xuan Xuan, his wife, she asked if something was wrong. He told her he was fine. He was just calling to see how she was. But she insisted that he sounded different.

"Different?" he said. "How?"

"Impatient," she said. "Like you're standing in a queue and it's not moving."

On Thursday he spoke to a friend of his father's, a man who happened to be the director of the Shanghai Museum. He asked if a brief after-hours visit could be arranged.

"Twice in a month," the director said. "You're addicted."

"There are worse addictions," Zhang said.

The director laughed. "That's true."

It was just after six in the evening when Zhang's Jaguar stopped on the south side of People's Square. He told Chun Tao he would be about forty-five minutes, then he walked round to the side entrance of the museum and pressed the bell. A security guard buzzed him in. The deserted interior had an air of peace and dignity it never had during the day, when it was crowded with schoolchildren and tour parties. It was as if the whole building had breathed a huge sigh of relief. His footsteps echoed as he climbed the marble stairs to the second floor. Otherwise, the only sound was the deep, hushed roar of the climate control.

He was drawn, time and again, by the Yue ceramics that had been made during the T'ang dynasty. Some of them were celebrated for their moon-white glaze, which experts likened to snow or silver. Others were a grayish shade of green known as "celadon," a color whose secret had died with the craftsmen working in the Gangyao kilns at Shanglinhu. To stand before a white Yue vase, with its simple lines, its smooth texture, and its calm but eerie lack of pigment, was to be taken far away from yourself. It was like looking at a blank face, and yet he always felt there was something to be learned. The emptiness seemed charged with wisdom. The director was right. He was addicted. Though created by men, the ceramics existed in a realm beyond man's understanding. He might, if he spent long enough in contemplation, be afforded some small epiphany, but he would never fool himself into thinking it wasn't limited or partial. There were other layers, hidden meanings. Infinite possibilities. The fact that the mystery couldn't be exhausted was a source of comfort to him. Not everything could be known.

For almost a quarter of an hour he gazed at a white oblate pot with a subtle or veiled design, two delicate handles protruding from the neck, and when he left the museum his mind felt depthless, unencumbered. Those moments on the second floor had given him sufficient equilibrium, he felt, to last for days. As he crossed the paved area in front of the museum, a gust of wind lifted his jacket away from his body, as if to search him, and it was then that he became aware of someone standing to the west of the main entrance, under the trees. *Naemi*. He knew her by the darkness of her clothes, and by her air of attentiveness, as if she was listening to music she had heard before but couldn't quite identify. He knew her by the gold of her hair, that twisted and gleaming gold—like happiness, if happiness were visible. Strange thoughts. She was just a girl he had run into in a club, a girl he had taken for a drink . . .

As he continued to look at her, she moved towards him slowly, haltingly, as if the distance between them was hard to negotiate, or perilous. Time spilled sideways, like a river that had burst its banks, the flow no longer linear, but vague, diffuse. It took her two minutes to close the gap from fifty feet to five, then half a second to close it to nothing. Suddenly she was up against him, and her mouth was on his mouth, even before a word was spoken, her hands under his jacket, pulling him against her, the black trees above their heads, the dull brown sky.

"I wondered how long it would take," he murmured.

"How long what would take?" She spoke in the same low register.

"For you to find me."

"I could have done it quicker." Her phone rang, but she ignored it. "I wasn't sure it was a good idea. Even now, I'm not sure."

"But you're here."

"Perhaps it was a mistake." She leaned back and looked at him, her face all ivory and shadows, like the moon. She was more beautiful than he remembered.

"It doesn't feel like a mistake," he said.

"Where's your car?"

"Over there." He moved his eyes beyond her, to the row of parked cars on the south side of the square.

"Can we go somewhere?"

"Not right now. I have a dinner."

"You can't cancel it?"

"No. But I could meet you later." The wind circled them, and the dark trees stirred, a sound that was like someone with a hosepipe watering a lawn. "Shall I tell you where," he said, "or do you already know?"

She curled a strand of hair behind her ear, the faintest of smiles at one corner of her mouth.

"The bar in the Park Hyatt," he said. "Ten o'clock."

He didn't kiss her again, though he wanted to. Instead, he touched the side of her face, once, gently, then turned and walked away. The calmness was still with him, the calmness of all that ancient porcelain. Only when he was in the Jaguar did he look back. She was standing where he had left her, and she was looking in his direction. She wouldn't be able to see him, though, not through the tinted windows.

Chun Tao glanced at him in the rearview mirror. "Straight to the restaurant, Mr. Zhang?"

"Yes."

He was scheduled to meet two commodity brokers from London, and he would have to drink more wine than he was used to, but at least there was the thought of Naemi at the end of it.

If she turned up, that is.

At a quarter to ten, Zhang's Jaguar pulled up at the foot of the Shanghai World Financial Center, also known as the "Vertical Complex City." The Park Hyatt, which was the highest hotel in the world, occupied floors 79 to 93. The cloud cover had lowered, and the sheer, curving facade of the building, edged in light that was electric blue, seemed to sink bladelike into the soft mass of the sky. Chun Tao asked if he should wait.

Zhang shook his head. "You can go."

"You're sure?"

"Go home. Get some sleep."

"What time tomorrow?"

"I'll text you."

Zhang stepped out of the car. The rain was fine and weightless, like face mist, and the air smelled of mustard seeds and soy sauce. Opening an umbrella, a valet hurried over and accompanied him to the hotel entrance.

Walking into the lobby, with its towering ceiling, its blind turnings, and its unadorned dark brown walls, he felt he was passing through some kind of portal, entering a new dimension. The lighting was dim, the atmosphere mysterious, subversive. By the lifts was a Gao Xiao Wu sculpture of three old men standing side by side, and leaning out from the wall, as if to offer a service or a favor. Made from a shiny white ceramic, they were the size of children, with eyes that looked sightless and expressions that were obsequious or craven. As he placed a hand on top of one of their smooth bald heads, a lift arrived, its door sliding open to reveal the deceptively affable, pockmarked face of Wang Jun Wei.

"Guo Xing!" A smile bubbled under Jun Wei's skin, like soup under a lid. "Still as handsome as ever."

Zhang smiled back. "My brother."

The two men shook hands.

"Nice suit," Zhang said.

Jun Wei's eyes widened, as if Zhang had just insulted him, then he grinned. "I'm off to a new KTV place. Like to join me?"

"I can't. I'm meeting someone."

"A woman, I suppose."

Zhang held Jun Wei's gaze, but said nothing.

"All right." Jun Wei looked off to one side, then back again. "Call me tomorrow. There's something I need your help with."

Zhang stepped into a waiting lift and pressed 87.

On reaching the hotel's reception desk, he picked up a key to the suite he had reserved, then he transferred to the lift that would take him to the bar. A jazz band was playing when he walked in. The singer was a young black woman in a yellow dress. He scanned the people sitting at the tables. Naemi had not arrived as yet. In his mind he saw her passing Wang Jun Wei in the dim, clandestine lobby, ninety-two floors down.

He found a table for two and ordered a glass of champagne. *There's something I need your help with.* He knew what that meant. Jun Wei wanted to rope him into some business deal or other. At school, they had been in the same class. Jun Wei was lazy and delinquent, and Zhang used to help him with his homework. When Jun Wei was suspected of cheating, Zhang had vouched for him. Without Zhang, Jun Wei would never have graduated. Brothers, Jun Wei had said at the time, draping one heavy arm round Zhang's shoulders. Brothers for life. Even back then, Zhang wondered what he had let himself in for. When he went to Canada to study, he lost touch with

Jun Wei. In the early 2000s, though, after a gap of many years, the two men met up again in Shanghai. Now a wealthy and successful property developer, Jun Wei had consulted Zhang on various construction projects that he was pushing through. These days, he was in charge of a whole platform of companies, not all of which were necessarily legitimate, and Zhang had been careful to minimize his involvement.

"Have you been waiting long?"

Zhang glanced up.

Naemi was standing in front of him. She had changed, though she was still dressed in black. On her feet she wore a pair of chrome-colored Converse All Stars.

"I just arrived." He gestured at his drink, which he had yet to touch. "Have a seat. What can I get you?"

"Whatever you're having."

He stopped a passing waitress and ordered another glass of champagne. Turning back to Naemi, he watched her slip her phone into her pocket. He found that he couldn't conceive of who her contacts might be, or what her browsing history might look like. When he imagined accessing her phone, it was empty, blank. Nothing there at all. That was a quality she seemed to have, of being brand-new, as if she had come into being at that very moment, fully formed.

"How was dinner?" she asked.

"It was just business," he told her. "If I hadn't known I was meeting you afterwards, I might never have got through it."

Her champagne arrived, and they touched glasses.

"You don't seem like the kind of man who would go in for compliments," she said.

"I don't?"

She shook her head.

"What kind of man am I, then, do you think?"

"You're asking me to guess?"

"Why not?"

She put down her glass. "I detect a sense of entitlement," she said. "As if you were—how do you say it in Chinese?—born with a golden key in your mouth."

He smiled. "Very good."

"You're used to getting what you want," she went on. "You're not spoiled, though." Sitting back, she looked at him steadily. "Your job doesn't fulfill you. There's more to you than that."

"I didn't realize I was so transparent." He drank a little champagne. "I have something for you." Taking out the key to the hotel suite, he placed it on the table in front of her.

"What's that?" she said.

"Who knows? Maybe it's the golden key."

Still watching him, she reached for her drink again.

"I booked you a room," he said. "I thought you might find it relaxing. It might make a change—from where you live."

"You don't know where I live."

He cast a light, theatrical look around the bar. "Is it like this?"

"I didn't bring my toothbrush," she said.

"Call room service," he said. "Housekeeping."

Leaving the key where it was, she looked away from him. For a while, she watched the band, who were playing a cover of the Sarah Vaughan classic "Whatever Lola Wants." When the song ended, she turned back to him.

"You were in the museum," she said, "even though it was closed."

"That's right."

"You don't work there, do you?"

He laughed. "No. But I might be more fulfilled, as you put it, if I did."

"So what were you doing?"

"I can't tell you." He finished his champagne. "I've never told anyone. Secrets lose their power if you share them."

In that moment, there was a dark and oddly covetous aspect to the look she gave him. Perhaps, without knowing it, he had passed some sort of test. She reached for the key.

"It's not a room, actually," he said. "It's a suite."

"Would you show me?"

"Of course." He signaled for the check.

Once he had paid, he followed her between the tables. Her black skirt clung to her hips. Her legs were bare. Something fizzed and crackled through him, a fork of lightning that zigzagged from his heart down to his belly. The set had ended, and everyone was clapping.

Near the lifts that were reserved for hotel guests was a wall of soft white lights, like snowflakes trapped under glass. She stood against it, backlit and in shadow, her hands behind her.

"I'm so glad you came," he said.

She looked down and smiled, her hair falling across her face. She used the spread fingers of one hand to push it back.

Once inside the lift, he pressed 88. He was aware of the shaft beneath them—the tall column of dark air, the smell of oil and warm dust, the long drop to the ground.

The lift door opened.

They walked along a dimly lit taupe-colored corridor, a huge red abstract painting on the left-hand wall. There was no noise from the other rooms. It was as if they were under a bell jar, or in a vacuum. Cut off from the world. He thought this was something she might appreciate.

When she unlocked the double doors that led to 8801, they opened onto a small rectangular area of artificial grass. Arranged on this fake lawn were three gray-and-white ceramic animals with big, pointed ears. The sculptures resembled rabbits crossed with cats. All three had their eyes turned soulfully towards the ceiling.

"Oh." She laughed softly.

To the right was a living room with chrome-and-leather furniture that looked Milanese and a long window framing neon-tinted clouds. There was a kitchen too, he had been told. Even a dining area. He followed her into the bedroom, choosing to leave the lights off. Two king-sized beds faced another long window. As they entered, the clouds swirled and thinned, revealing the top of the Jinmao Tower. It was closer than he had imagined it would be, its steel-gray turrets and crenellations tapering to a long needle, like part of some immense and dangerous machine.

She went and stood by the window.

"It feels strange to be looking down on it," he said. "It's still one of the tallest buildings in the world."

She turned to face him. While they were kissing, she let the key drop to the floor. As always, he was aware of the heat of her mouth, a sensation so at odds with the coolness of her appearance that he doubted himself each time he noticed it. Their clothes coming away, they moved to the nearest bed. The aliveness of every inch of his skin. The beat of his blood in the dark. He had never been with anyone like her. What was so different? It was her elusiveness, perhaps. Her unapproachability. He had thought that if they made love she would become less of a mystery, but he was touching her, and then inside her, and she still escaped him. Her head tipped over the edge of the bed, as if she had abandoned her body. Her throat silvered by the neon that filtered through the window. He felt drawn into a void, swallowed up by it. He felt he might cease to exist. He didn't care. The sex was so vivid that he forgot where he was.

Later, as he lay back, the air vibrated above him, seemingly made up of thousands of tiny moving particles. She was pressed close to him, her head against his shoulder, her body dark against the crisp white sheet. The world came back to him. The room came back. Not all at once, but gradually, like water soaking up into a paper towel. The air con's exhalations, the low-level buzz of the flat-screen TV. The muted squawk and rumble of traffic eighty-eight floors below.

"I knew it would be good," she said.

"When did you know?"

"When I first saw you, in the club."

"You knew right away?"

"Before you even noticed me." She turned to face him, her head propped on one hand. "I saw you first."

"What was I doing?"

"Watching people dance."

He had been thinking about the small man with the suitcase. Wondering who he was. Where he had gone.

"Then you walked up to me," she went on, "and you had a kind of serenity about you." Her face seemed to empty out as she thought back. "You were afraid of boring me—not like all the others..." She smiled. "I liked your eyes."

Not like all the others.

He had known she would be used to being looked at, to being wanted. How could she not be? Still lying on his back, he pulled her closer, his left hand on her rib cage, below her breast. She drew up one of her knees until it rested on his thigh. Her hair smelled of a perfume he didn't recognize.

"That small man with the suitcase," he said. "Didn't you say you saw him too?"

"Yes, but it was earlier. He was in the round bar, next to the restaurant."

He had been sitting on a cowhide sofa, she said. He had a drink in front of him that looked like a piña colada. He seemed to be on first-name terms with several of the staff.

"Perhaps he works for the club as well," Zhang said.

"You think?"

"I don't know." Zhang remembered how the man had appeared beside him as he was washing his hands. He remembered the darkness in the men's room, the kind of darkness out of which almost anything might feasibly emerge.

"It's strange," he said, "but when I talk about him I feel as if I made him up."

"If you'd made him up, I wouldn't have seen him."

He was losing the feeling in his arm and had to move it out from under her. Drowsily, she turned away from him, onto her side. He turned with her. As he held her from behind, he thought he felt a ridge or roughness in the skin on the inside of her elbow.

"What are you doing?" she murmured.

"Nothing," he said.

"It's late. We should get some sleep."

He kissed her shoulder, then leaned over her and kissed her on the lips. "You're very beautiful."

"So are you," she said.

When he woke, he was alone in the bed. He glanced at the other bed. It was empty, undisturbed. The blind on the long window had been lowered, but a soft white glow came from the living room, where it looked as if a light was on. He remembered Naemi standing beneath the trees in People's Square, and how time seemed to become suspended as she walked towards him. It wasn't that she had been walking slowly. It was more as if the distance between them was greater than he had realized. As if she had been farther away than he had thought. He was still turning those moments over in his mind when she appeared in the room, already dressed. He glanced at his watch. It was 6:44. They had slept for less than three hours.

"Sorry if I woke you," she said.

"Are you leaving?"

She came and stood next to the bed. He put an arm round the back of her thighs and pulled her close, his face pushed against her skirt. It smelled of the night before—perfume, alcohol, the faint trace of a cigar. He felt her rest a hand on his head, then she stepped back.

"Don't you want breakfast?" he said.

She seemed to hesitate.

"Go to the restaurant," he said. "I'll join you."

He thought she might say something else, but she only nodded and turned away. The door to the suite opened and closed. He got out of bed and crossed the room. He wanted to tell her that he would be twenty minutes at the most, but when he opened the door and looked down the corridor, towards the lifts, there was only the huge red painting and the beige walls and the intense, almost supernatural hush.

He had a shower and pulled on his clothes, then he texted Chun Tao, telling him to be outside the Park Hyatt at eight o'clock. As he traveled up to the 91st floor, he remembered waking in the night to see Naemi kneeling at the window, naked, looking at the view. Had she slept at all? He stepped out of the lift and checked his watch: 7:06. He wasn't hurrying. There was no need. He didn't believe that she'd be there.

But she was.

She had taken a table against the slanting window, next to a white pillar that soared up to the roof of the atrium two floors above. She was writing something on her phone. The city sprawled below her, the Huangpu River wide and mud-colored, and winding lazily through a mass of tall buildings. The sky was a flawless blue. Small puffs of white cloud lay close to the horizon.

"That was quick." She placed her phone facedown next to a half-full glass of water.

He stopped a passing waiter. "Would you like coffee?"

"I'm fine, thank you."

"Are you hungry?"

"I don't eat breakfast."

He ordered a cappuccino—very strong, very hot.

"That room..." She shook her head.

"The Chairman Suite," he said. "It's supposed to be the best room in the hotel."

He had paid 40,000 RMB for the night, but in November, which was the beginning of peak season, the tariff would more than double.

"Did you reserve it in advance?" she asked.

He nodded. "Yes."

"So you knew I was going to sleep with you?"

"How could I know that?" He adjusted the position of the cutlery in front of him.

"What would have happened if I'd said no? Would you have stayed there by yourself?"

"No. I would have offered it to you."

"And you would have driven off into the night, alone?"

"Yes, of course."

But he didn't want to talk about what might or might not have happened. They had spent the night together, as he had hoped, and he was still under the spell of it. Her cool concealed nature. The sudden blood-heat of her mouth. Her body like a dancer's, somehow both voluptuous and lean. Sitting across from him, she seemed remote, though. Disengaged. As if she hadn't been to bed with him at all. As if he had slept with someone else entirely. Was this discretion on her part, or was it the tip of some deeper determination not to become involved? His cappuccino arrived. He took a sip. Just right. He nodded at the waitress, and she left.

Naemi was looking at her phone again. "I'm sorry," she said. "I don't have long. I have a meeting."

"What do you do? I never asked."

"I work for a gallery."

"A gallery?"

"We specialize in Chinese art, from the late twentieth century onwards."

It was the first time he had seen her in daylight, and there was something unusual about her appearance. To begin with, he couldn't work out what it was. Then he realized. Her irises were almost exactly the same color as her pupils, so much so that it was hard to tell the difference between the two.

"You're staring at me," she said.

"It's your eyes," he said. "They're black."

"Oh that." She smiled at him. "I suffer from photophobia. I have to wear special contact lenses." Her phone rang, but she declined the call. "I should go—"

"Nina?"

Naemi's head swiveled, the response so swift and primal that Zhang was startled. His shock registered at a deeper level too. In most relationships, there is a moment when you glimpse something the person you're with has been trying to suppress, and this revelation, no matter how trivial or minor, tends to signal the beginning of the end. But he and Naemi had only slept together once... Still watching her, he saw her cover up that aspect of herself, and it was accomplished so smoothly and slickly that he was reminded of the way a membrane slides across a snake's eye, to protect or moisten it. Who had spoken, though? He turned to look. A man stood next to their table. He had the kind of face that softens as it ages, with pouches beneath the eyes and jaw, and cheeks that sagged. His thick brown hair was generously dusted with gray. He appeared to be in his early sixties.

"I'm sorry," Naemi said, switching to English. "Do I know you?"

"Nina." The man seemed transfixed by her, and also paralyzed. "It's me. Torben."

"You must be confusing me with someone else. My name's not Nina—"

"It's uncanny. You haven't changed at all."

"You're making a mistake."

The man gave an astonished laugh. "You're Nina. You have to be." He looked around, as if for support, and then looked back at her, the fingers of his right hand moving nervously against his thigh. "There's no one else who looks like you."

Naemi glanced at her phone. "I really have to go." Getting to her feet, she turned her back on the man and kissed Zhang on the cheek. "Thank you for everything. I'll call you."

Zhang watched her leave. How could she call him? She didn't have his number. The man was also watching her. He clearly felt the urge to run after her and plead with her, but she didn't offer him the chance. She was too decisive. All he could do was stand there haplessly.

"Do you know her?" Zhang asked.

"Yes. I mean—I'm not sure..." One hand clutching the back of his neck, the man looked at Zhang with a dazed expression. "I'm sorry. It's a bit of a shock. I haven't seen Nina for forty years."

"Forty years?" Zhang stared at the man. "But that's impossible."

"I know." The man looked away again, towards the entrance to the restaurant. "I feel like I've just seen a ghost."

Zhang was still staring. "Perhaps you'd like a coffee."

"I'm disturbing you."

"Sit down," Zhang said. "Please."

The man sat where Naemi had been sitting moments earlier, and when the waiter came he ordered a double espresso. "The name's Gulsvig. Torben Gulsvig." He took a business card from his wallet and handed it to Zhang.

Zhang studied the card. Gulsvig was a professor at Helsinki University, with a long list of letters after his name. So he was Finnish. Like Naemi.

He looked up. "I'm Victor Zhang."

Victor was the name he had adopted while studying abroad in the early '90s. He still used it when he met foreigners who couldn't speak Chinese. It made things easier.

"Pleased to meet you." As Gulsvig reached across the table to shake hands, his sleeve caught a small vase of flowers and it toppled over. Water spilled onto the tablecloth.

He said something in his own language—a swear word presumably—then switched back to English. "That was clumsy. I'm so sorry."

The waiter came and cleared up the mess. Gulsvig apologized again.

"That woman you were with," he said. "She looked exactly like someone I used to know."

"Someone called Nina?"

"Yes." Gulsvig's double espresso arrived. He leaned forwards and brought the cup to his lips, but put it down again without drinking. "Is she a colleague of yours?"

"Yes," Zhang said.

"I'm sorry," Gulsvig said. "It's none of my business. I hope I didn't upset her."

"She had to leave in any case. She had a meeting."

Gulsvig shook his head. "Extraordinary, the resemblance." He brought his cup to his lips again. This time he drank. Letting out a sigh, he put down the cup. "You don't forget someone like Nina. Can I tell you a story?"

"Of course."

Once, Gulsvig said, he had met Nina in a pub near the British Museum. This was in London, in the '70s. A man came over to where they were sitting. He was drunk. He told Nina she was the most beautiful girl he had ever seen. He wanted to buy her a drink. He wanted her to go out with him that evening. He wouldn't leave her alone. In the end, he—Gulsvig—interrupted. He told the man that Nina was his wife. The man lurched backwards, shocked. He wanted to know how long they had been married. We got married yesterday, Gulsvig said. We're very happy.

"Nina thought that was hilarious." Gulsvig paused, thinking back. "I was always braver when I was with her."

"You were just friends, though," Zhang said.

"That wasn't my point—but yes, just friends." Gulsvig nodded to himself, head lowered, his smile embarrassed, wistful. "She was out of my league."

Zhang finished his coffee, then glanced at his watch.

"I'm sorry," Gulsvig said. "I've taken up too much of your time."

Something suddenly occurred to Zhang. What if Naemi was *related* to Nina? What if she was Nina's daughter, for instance? If that was the case, though, surely she would have recognized the name? And why would she have reacted with such unease?

"I still can't get over the resemblance," Gulsvig was saying.

Zhang rose from the table. "Our memories play all kinds of tricks on us."

"You're right." Gulsvig let out another sigh and shook his head. "It's probably the jet lag. I only arrived last night."

"Well, it was nice to meet you."

Gulsvig shook hands with him again and thanked him for the coffee. "You have my card?"

"Yes, I do," Zhang said. "And here's mine." He put his business card on Gulsvig's side plate. "Enjoy Shanghai."

4

ONCE IN THE TAXI, Naemi leaned forwards, her elbows on her knees, her hands covering her face. She was
sweating, and her brain whined and crackled like a radio
stuck between stations.

"You're not going to throw up, are you?" The driver
was eyeing her in the rearview mirror.

"I'm fine," she said. "Just drive."

He muttered a few derogatory words, then shifted
into gear and pulled away from the hotel.

She hadn't wanted breakfast in the first place, but
Zhang had talked her into it. And it had gone well, she
thought. Then, just as she was about to leave, she heard a
name she hadn't heard in almost half a century.

Nina.

If Torben hadn't told her who he was, would she have
guessed? She doubted it. Unless, perhaps, she had closed
her eyes and listened to his voice, which was tentative

and candid, exactly as she remembered it. To look at him, though? No. He was just a middle-aged man in a crumpled beige suit. She had a sudden, sickening realization. The world was full of such people. Since they looked older, they could stand right in front of her, and she'd be none the wiser. It was as if they were in disguise. To them, though, she was instantly recognizable. She corresponded to the memories they had of her—*because she hadn't changed at all*. Time had rendered her conspicuous, like a rock exposed by an ebbing tide, there for everyone to see.

She ought to have had a strategy in place, but she had been caught off guard. In a panic, she had done the only thing she could think of doing. She held on to the genuine bewilderment she had felt when he said, "Nina." She pretended she had no idea who he was. Then she fled. Through the restaurant, down in the lift, and out into the sunlight, trembling...

The bars on Changyi Road slid by, their exteriors sleepy, shut-eyed, unsuited to the daylight. In her mind she traveled back to London. June 1974. She was in the Students' Union with friends when a young man came over, an empty beer glass in his hand. He stood in front of her in his maroon velvet loon pants, his hair unfashionably short.

"They tell me you're Finnish," he said.

"Do they?" Her voice was lightly mocking, but she already knew that he posed no threat to her, and that she could be kind.

He nodded. "Yes."

She lit a cigarette. "I'm from North Karelia, originally."

"I was born in Helsinki."

"Ah," she said. "The sophisticated type."

He grinned.

"Can I buy you a drink?" he asked.

"I don't drink."

"What kind of Finn are you?"

He was joking, or half joking, but this was a question she had often asked herself, a question she had no answer to, and she looked at him steadily, no longer smiling. He didn't understand the look—how could he have done?—and yet it didn't seem to bother him. He was a little drunk, of course. He told her later that he had been wanting to talk to her for months, but had never dared.

"Am I so frightening?" she asked.

"Yes," he said. "You are."

Was it that same night that she and Torben set off through the streets of Bloomsbury? When they came to Coram's Fields he spread his raincoat on the ground and they sat down. They smoked roll-ups and talked, with London all around them, murmuring and mumbling under a warm charcoal sky...He seemed oddly familiar to her. It was as though she already knew him, or had known him before. As though he belonged to the part of her life that she thought of as the happy time, the life that had come to such a sudden end on that day of sun and wind, when the world went dark while she wasn't looking. Perhaps he reminded her of somebody she had been close to as a child—or perhaps it was simply that he was gentle.

They began to seek each other out. They drank endless cups of coffee in cheap cafés. They went to art galleries, and to the cinema. They walked for hours—through the West End, in Richmond Park, on Hampstead Heath. Since they shared a secret language—Finnish—they could talk about people without them knowing. They laughed a lot. Once she had Torben as a friend, it became clear to her how lonely she had been before. And there was something about his company that rekindled the innocence in her. The youth. He helped her to be the age she appeared to be. The age she was *supposed* to be. Up until then, she had felt like an actor in a spotlight, delivering a monologue. Now, suddenly, she had someone on stage with her who she could play off, someone who could give her cues. Also, she was able to unburden herself without arousing suspicion or being judged.

Once or twice, she came close to telling him the truth. Since she couldn't make sense of it herself, though, she doubted she could explain it to him, despite the fact that he was intensely loyal, and would want to believe her. At times, the temptation was almost irresistible, but she never quite gave in.

Though she realized he might want something from her, and that he might, at certain moments, long for that, she also realized he was in no position to insist. In other circumstances, this might have caused him pain, and yet it seemed to her that theirs was a relationship from which both parties stood to benefit. No, she wouldn't sleep with him, but he gained in confidence and stature just by being in her company. They were both able to inhabit themselves more fully. Like balloons that were filled with air, almost to bursting, they became lighter, and more joyous. And perhaps, in the end, she thought, it came as a relief to him that he couldn't entertain the possibility of sex with her. As much of a relief as a regret, at least. Not to have to win her, or risk losing her. As it was, he could have it all—or almost...

Back in her apartment, she stood at the window, staring down at the murky, polluted waters of Suzhou Creek. She took out her phone and called the gallery, saying she would be late. She still couldn't quite believe that Torben had appeared—and in Shanghai, of all places... But what could he do, really? He was on a business trip, or on holiday, and he would be gone again in a few days. There was little chance of a second meeting. She'd had a fright, nothing more. Shaking her head, she walked into the bathroom and turned on the shower.

Later, as she dressed for work, the sense of being threatened was replaced by a feeling of nostalgia. She could see the young man in the old one—the halting quality, the persistence. He had loved her, and she, in her own way, had loved him too. She wished she could have sat down with him and asked him about his life. Had it gone the way he thought it would? Had he been happy? And later, perhaps, when they had got over the shock of running into each other after so many years, when they were laughing again, just as they used to, she would ask him, half jokingly, if he had missed her...

But what was she thinking? Torben would expect her to be in her sixties, as he was. The fact that she hadn't aged would render any normal conversation quite impossible. She wondered what had happened after she walked out of the restaurant. Had he apologized to Zhang and then staggered off, his mind in a daze, only half believing what he had seen? Or had the two men fallen into conversation? If they talked, what would Torben have said?

How *much* would he have said? And what effect would the whole episode have had on Zhang? She took out one of his business cards, which she had stolen from his jacket pocket while he was sleeping. Perhaps she should call him and find out.

5

WHEN ZHANG LEFT THE PARK HYATT, the Jaguar was already waiting, parked in a sharp wedge of shadow. Fastening his seat belt, he told Chun Tao he had a meeting on the Bund. Chun Tao said there was gridlock in Lujiazui. It might be best if they took the Renmin Road Tunnel.

"You decide," Zhang said.

While he was answering e-mails on his iPad, his phone rang. He glanced at the screen and hesitated, then pressed Accept. "How are you, Father?"

"You sound tired."

"I didn't get much sleep last night."

"Out carousing, I suppose."

Zhang turned his eyes to the window. Outside, everything looked whitish, almost dusty, the city bleached by sunlight.

"Who were you with?" his father asked.

"I'm about to go into a tunnel," Zhang said, though they were nowhere near.

Ignoring him, his father began to lecture him about his lifestyle. He ended the call, and when his phone rang again he pressed Decline, then put it away. Passing a hand over his face, he thought he smelled Naemi's perfume, despite the fact that he had showered. Why did she guard her privacy so fiercely? Who was she, really? He took out the card Gulsvig had given him and stared at it. But it was only at five o'clock that evening, when he was sitting in the Bamboo Lounge, a cocktail bar in the French Concession, that he realized what he should do. He scrolled through his contacts and put in a call.

"How are you, boss?" Johnny said.

Johnny Yu was skinny, with narrow shoulders, and he wore cheap suits from Hong Kong and a porkpie hat with a brown ribbon. When you were with him, his eyes were always sliding past you or away from you, checking out the bigger picture. If he was at home in the gutters and alleyways, with the chicken feet in buckets and the blocked drains and the men in soiled white undershirts scratching their bellies, he was just as familiar with high-end restaurants and nightspots. Like Zhang, he was in his forties, but he had been many things in his life—accountant, taxi driver, journalist, croupier, detective.

"I'm fine," Zhang said. "How are you?"

"*All things beyond the body are an encumbrance.*" Johnny was fond of quoting poets from the seventeenth and eighteenth centuries, which he saw as a golden era in Chinese literary culture. His hands might be dirty, as he liked to say, but his soul was lyrical.

"Who wrote that?" Zhang asked.

"Wang Chi-Wu."

The lights flickered, and Zhang looked around. The girl who had served him wore a clinging plum-colored dress, and she was drawing circles with her forefinger in the moisture on the surface of the bar. It was still early, and he was the only customer in the place. Outside, a heavy, steel-gray rain was coming down.

"I feel bad, Johnny," Zhang said. "This thing I'm going to ask of you, it's too easy. It's beneath you, really. But I don't know who else I can trust with it."

He pictured Johnny's smile, which had always borne a close resemblance to a wince.

"What is this thing," Johnny said, "that is beneath me?"

"I need you to find someone. I want to know where she lives and where she works. I want her phone numbers. I want her e-mail."

Zhang told Johnny everything he knew about Naemi.

"Blonde hair, black contact lenses," Johnny said. "A woman like that must stand out in Shanghai."

"She'd stand out anywhere."

"How long have I got?"

"A week."

"That isn't long."

"Don't tell me you're busy."

"I've got a couple of irons in the fire." Johnny sounded wounded, defensive. He would be sitting in the back room of his uncle's bar, his feet up on the desk, an open bottle of beer in his hand. The girls still asleep upstairs, the balls on the pool table motionless and gleaming. There was a whole row of bars on the north side of Changyi Road: Hot Lips, Spicy Girl, Blue Angel, Naughty Beaver...

"Something I forgot to mention," Zhang said. "She has scar tissue on the inside of her left arm."

"What are you telling me? She's a junkie?"

"I don't think so. I don't know." Zhang finished his drink. "Call me when you have the information."

Pocketing his phone, he walked over to the bar, sat down on a stool, and asked the girl in the plum-colored dress for another whiskey. He asked if she would like a drink as well.

She looked at him. "It's not that kind of bar."

"I know," he said. "It's just a drink." He glanced around at the empty chairs and tables. "You've nothing else to do."

"All right. Thank you."

She poured his whiskey and put it in front of him, then she reached for a bottle of Malibu. He smiled to himself, since he felt this was a choice he could have predicted.

"What's your story?" he asked.

"My story?" Her full lips twisted, and she looked towards the window. "Nothing's happened yet."

She was twenty, she told him, and she came from a village in Anhui Province. Her father was a minor government official. He drank too much *baijiu*. If they were lucky, it sent him to sleep. If not, he shouted and broke things. Her mother sat in front of the TV. She didn't care what she watched. She only stopped if there was a meal to cook or washing to be done.

"It doesn't sound like much of a life," Zhang said.

"No," she said. "But maybe I learned a lesson."

"Don't live in the countryside?"

She shook her head. "Don't live with somebody who drinks."

"That's a good lesson to learn." He paused. "Strange you ended up working in a bar."

"I know. How stupid is that."

The door opened, and two foreigners in suits walked in, shaking the rain from their umbrellas. Zhang put a few notes on the bar.

"Thank you," the girl said. "Have a nice evening."

The next morning, Zhang's alarm woke him at six, and he sat on the edge of his bed, studying his phone. There were e-mails from Hong Kong, London, and New York. Nothing from Naemi, though. He walked to the window and opened the floor-to-ceiling curtains. The city was plunged deep in a milky fog. The other forty-story towers in the compound were visible, but the high-rise buildings to the north and west looked insubstantial, featureless. She was out there somewhere. He had no idea where. Just as screen savers are triggered by periods of inactivity, so images of her would float into his mind whenever he relaxed. Naemi with her elbows on a gold-topped bar, Naemi at a distance, beneath dark trees. Naemi kneeling by the window in the Chairman Suite, staring at the view. He was still wondering about her detachment, her apparent self-sufficiency. She had told him Finnish people were known to be reserved, but this was reserve taken to extremes—and anyway, she had gone on to say that she didn't believe in generalizations. Was she trying to cultivate an air of mystery? Was it all a game? Whatever lay behind the facade she had built up, he had no regrets about asking Johnny to look for her. He wanted the information, even if he didn't use it.

In the kitchen area, he switched on the TV. As he waited for his yellow tea to brew, his phone rang. It was Wang Jun Wei.

"So did you sleep with her?" Jun Wei said.

"Sleep with who?"

"The Park Hyatt girl."

Zhang reached for the remote and turned the volume down. "You're up early."

"I haven't been to bed yet. Are you hungry?"

"I could eat."

Jun Wei gave him an address on the north side of the Yangpu Bridge. Zhang knew those streets. They were dark and pungent, the creeks jammed with rubbish, the wooden houses patched with corrugated iron and sheets of colored plastic. Pet shops selling fish and snakes. Foot massage. Karaoke. Though Jun Wei drove a Maserati and owned several blue-chip properties, it seemed fitting that he would be drawn to such areas. He had made a fortune from the flattening of old Shanghai. History? he'd once said to Zhang. I piss on it. Nostalgia too.

Zhang finished his tea. It would be hot again, the weather girl was saying. There was an orange alert for rainstorms in southern China later in the day. He switched off the TV, picked up his keys, his wallet, and his phone, and left the apartment. He took a lift to the underground car park, where Chun Tao was leaning against the front wing of the Jaguar, smoking. When he saw Zhang approaching, he dropped his cigarette and trod on it.

"Where to?" he said.

Zhang gave him an address.

They arrived half an hour later, pulling in behind the black Mercedes Vito Tourer that Jun Wei often used on his nights out. Zhang told Chun Tao to wait, then entered the restaurant.

Usually, when Jun Wei had been partying, he had a woman with him. Sometimes two. Not today. Sitting alone, facing the door, he was hunched over a bowl of noodles. Lined up on the table next to his left hand were a packet of Chunghwa cigarettes, a lighter, his gold iPhone, and an ice-blue charger.

Zhang sat down. "There are some nice restaurants round here. This isn't one of them." He looked around. "I'm probably going to get diarrhea."

"Only a bit." Jun Wei's head tipped back, and his mouth opened wide. His laughter was almost always silent, which Zhang found unnerving, even after a quarter of a century.

He scanned the menu, then ordered braised fish belly and a pot of green tea.

"You should have gone for the noodles," Jun Wei said. "You don't know what you're missing."

"Yes, I do."

"What about a beer? Or a plum brandy?"

"No." Zhang closed the menu.

Jun Wei sat back. The whites of his eyes were pink, and his forehead shone. "You didn't answer my question."

"I didn't need to."

"Who is she?"

"She's called Naemi. She's Finnish."

"Finnish? What's that?"

Zhang explained.

Jun Wei's phone rang. He glanced at the screen, but didn't take the call. "Sounds exotic," he said. "But foreigners—I don't know. More trouble than they're worth." He reached for his beer. "What's wrong with Chinese girls?"

"You sound like my father." Zhang drained his cup of green tea and poured himself another.

His food arrived.

"You wanted my help," he said as he picked up his chopsticks.

Jun Wei used a paper napkin to wipe his forehead and the back of his neck, then he crumpled it into a ball and dropped it in his empty noodle bowl. He shook a Chunghwa out of its red packet and reached for his lighter. Jun Wei had a reputation as something of a gangster— things had been done by him, or in his name, which were questionable, to say the least—but he had been careful never to compromise his friend. Whether Jun Wei was driven by consideration or by a lack of faith, Zhang couldn't have said. He was grateful nonetheless.

"HDPE." Jun Wei leaned back in his chair. "Do you know what that is?"

Zhang shook his head.

"High-density polyethylene. It's used in the manufacture of plastic lumber and corrosion-resistant piping."

"Crucial in construction, then."

"Crucial in all kinds of areas. Globally, it's a billion-dollar industry." Jun Wei flicked ash onto the floor. "I'm looking to import large quantities of HDPE from Iran, and I want you on board as a consultant."

"Iran?" Zhang said. "What about sanctions?"

Jun Wei crushed out his cigarette, smoke streaming from his nostrils. "That," he said, "is why it's such a good opportunity."

As Zhang finished his breakfast, Jun Wei expanded on certain aspects of the deal. He was having trouble with pricing mechanisms, he said, and with delivery routes, but these were difficulties that Zhang—or Zhang's business contacts—would be able to resolve.

"Let me think about it." Zhang signaled for the bill.

"My treat," Jun Wei said.

The door opened, and two girls walked in. One had a boy's haircut and a mole on her upper lip. Her heart-shaped silver earrings were the size of a man's hand. The other one wore a tight pink T-shirt that said DREAM BIG.

"Over here, you two," Jun Wei called out, waving an arm. "I want you to meet a friend of mine."

The phone call Zhang had been waiting for came on a Tuesday evening. After returning from work, he had showered, and he was standing at his living-room window with wet hair and a towel around his waist. The temperature had dropped, and the sky was a stormy greenish gray. He thought he could hear thunder behind the rain.

When his phone rang, Unknown appeared on the screen.

"Hello?" he said.

"It's Naemi."

"How did you get my number?"

She didn't answer.

"You call me," he said, "but I can't call you. The traffic's a bit one-way, don't you think?"

"I suppose you're usually the one who behaves like that."

It was true that he usually conducted his affairs on his own terms. He had never been confronted with it, though, and he wasn't sure quite how to respond. Opening the sliding doors, he stepped out onto the terrace and leaned on the railing, his phone still pressed against his ear, the rain falling just beyond his face. To his surprise, he found that he was smiling. Far below, the compound's outdoor swimming pool was neat as a pale blue tile.

"How long has it been?" he said. "A week?"

"I'm sorry," she said. "I had to travel. It was work."

"Sure," he said. "Okay."

"Also, I'm a very private person. I have issues with trust." She paused. "I have to protect myself."

"What from?"

She sighed.

"It's all right," he said. "You don't have to explain."

"Thank you."

Her relief sounded heartfelt, genuine.

She also wanted to thank him for the wonderful night at the Park Hyatt, she went on. She was sorry if she left abruptly. The man in the beige suit had thrown her.

Zhang told her not to worry.

"What happened after I left?" she asked. "He seemed very confused." She paused again. "I hope he didn't bother you."

"I got rid of him."

"Was that difficult?"

"No, not at all."

He wondered why he was misleading her. Perhaps because he felt it was what she wanted to hear. How would she react if he told her he had sat down with Torben Gulsvig and bought him a coffee? What would she say if she knew the professor's business card was in his wallet?

"Are you free this evening?" she asked.

"Not really. I'm singing."

"Karaoke?"

"No," he said. "Not karaoke."

He played in a blues band, he told her, with Gong Shen and Fang Yuan, otherwise known as "Mad Dog" and "Laser." They called themselves the Gang of Three.

They got together most weekends, in a recording studio off Beijing East Road, but sometimes they played live, and this was one of those rare nights.

"Do you have a nickname too?" she asked.

He hesitated. "Flower Heart."

"Nice," she said. "What does it mean?"

"You don't know?"

"Tell me."

"I think it means I'm popular."

"With women?"

"With everyone."

She laughed.

"Mad Dog came up with it about ten years ago," Zhang said. "He has all kinds of strange ideas."

"I'd love to hear you sing," she said. "I saw B.B. King once, when I was in America."

"I'm not that good."

She laughed again.

The venue was Yu Yin Tang, he told her, and they would be on stage at about ten thirty.

"I'll be there," she said.

The moment she ended the call, Zhang rang her back. There was no reply. Just the flatline tone of a phone that was dead or a phone that had been switched off.

I have to protect myself.

An hour later, he was heading west on the Yan'an elevated highway with Mississippi John Hurt turned up loud on the Jaguar's sound system, the night's sticky blackness piled high on either side.

Situated between a metro station and a park, Yu Yin Tang was a small place that held about one hundred people. Above the entrance was a sign that showed a polar bear playing an electric guitar. The ground floor had a distressed black ceiling and brick walls that were painted red. Between the stage and the bar was a door leading to a modest terrace that overlooked the park. Upstairs were two or three more rooms. There were brown plastic sofas, and the walls were defaced with graffiti. On one wall was a poster listing drinks. A cocktail called Fuck Me Friday cost 65 RMB.

When Zhang walked in, there was no sign of Naemi, but his band members were already at the bar. They made an unlikely pair. Gong Shen, aka Mad Dog, would be seventy in a few months' time. He was wearing a waistcoat and pinstripe trousers, and his shoulder-length gray hair was tucked back behind his ears. He drank too much, and though it never seemed to interfere with his playing he often had trouble getting home. Once, the police found him outside a restaurant near where he lived, passed out on a heap of oyster shells. Another time, he fell asleep in an alley. When he woke up, his boots were gone. He played the double bass and the harmonica. Fang Yuan, who answered to Laser, was a drummer. Young enough to be Mad Dog's grandson, he had dropped out of university, and he supported himself by working in a record shop that specialized in vinyl. He also played drums for a speed metal outfit called the Dense Haloes. Zhang had seen them live. It was three days before he could hear properly again.

Mad Dog saw him first. "Flower Heart! Over here."

Laser was too deferential to call Zhang "Flower Heart." He called him "Laoban"—boss—or "Lao Zhang."

"What are we drinking?" Zhang asked.

"Beer," Laser said.

"And whiskey," said Mad Dog.

There was a girl in a red sweater behind the bar. Zhang caught her eye and ordered three whiskeys and three Tiger beers.

They took the stage at a quarter to eleven. As Zhang was tuning his 1964 Gibson, he saw Naemi in the crowd. Denim jacket, smudged black eye shadow. Her blonde hair messier than usual. She gave him a thumbs-up, then looked away towards the bar.

They began with "Stormy Monday," very slow and jaded, the vocals not sung so much as muttered, and followed it with a sinister brush-drum version of the Howlin' Wolf classic "Killing Floor." By the time they finished the second number, Naemi was near the front of the stage and off to one side, leaning against a pillar that was papered with flyers. Zhang decided to play one of his own compositions, a song called "Red Rope Blues." It told the story of a man who becomes obsessed with a girl in a massage parlor. He meets her in a bleak anonymous apartment building near Hongqiao airport after a night of heavy drinking. It is almost four in the morning. He takes off his clothes and lies down on a bed. A girl hangs above him on a length of scarlet silk that is suspended from the ceiling. She is also naked. To start with, there is distance between them as she twists and turns on the red rope, but gradually, artfully, she begins to close the gap. As she descends, he falls for her. It is her hair that touches him first. Her long black hair. She brushes his body lightly with it. Later, she uses her mouth. She is still suspended above him, though the gap has closed to a few inches. He has never seen anyone more beautiful... The next day, he thinks of her dancing in the air above him, pale as a star. He thinks about her all the time. But it is a week or two before he is able to return to the apartment building in Hongqiao, and when he asks for the girl he is told that she has left. He is offered another girl. He turns away. The red rope dangles above an empty bed. Outside, a siren wails. The early-autumn rain is coming down.

When they left the stage, they sat on the terrace with Naemi, and she told them how much she had enjoyed the set.

"You're really good musicians," she said, "all of you."

Mad Dog watched her, but said nothing.

Laser asked about B.B. King, and soon Naemi was talking about how she had stayed at the Peabody hotel in Memphis, and then driven down Highway 61, stopping at famous blues towns like Clarksdale and Greenville. They were so deep in conversation that Zhang left the terrace to go to the toilet. Once he had climbed the stairs to the first floor, he stopped and looked out of a small window that was half open. A fine rain was falling through the light of a nearby streetlamp, like the last line of his song.

On his way back to the bar he met Mad Dog, who surprised him by pushing him up against the wall. Mad Dog's mouth had widened and straightened, and he had gritted his teeth. This was a look he got when he was on his way to being very drunk. He always appeared to be bracing himself for some kind of impact.

"Listen." Mad Dog glanced left and right to check nobody was around. "That girl you're with..."

"What about her?" Zhang said.

"Stay away from her."

Mad Dog's face was only inches away, and though his eyes had narrowed they had a sudden fierce clarity, which kept Zhang from mocking him or making a joke.

"What's got into you?" he asked.

"Something isn't right." Mad Dog looked at Zhang for a moment longer, then let go of him, muttered a few derogatory words, and pushed past him, towards the toilets.

The old fool, Zhang thought. He was probably just jealous. Either that or he was prejudiced, like a lot of Chinese men his age. Zhang straightened his clothes and set off down the stairs.

When he reached the bottom, he saw that Naemi and Laser were sitting at the bar.

"We came back in," Laser said. "It started raining."

"I know," Zhang said.

Naemi gave him a tilted look, half challenging, half mischievous. "That song you sang," she said. "The one about the rope. Was it autobiographical?"

It was after midnight, and the streets had the gleam of patent leather. The air smelled of wet cement. Standing under the soaring concrete pillars of the Yan'an highway, Zhang and Naemi watched as Mad Dog set off in an easterly direction, bent over under the weight of the double bass that was strapped to his back.

"Isn't he too old to be doing that?" Naemi said.

"Probably," Zhang said. "But he won't have it any other way."

If he ever offered Mad Dog a lift, he went on, or money for a taxi, Mad Dog always refused. The old man prided himself on not accepting any favors, not even from his friends, and if he had been drinking his pride tended to redouble. After a session at the recording studio, it would take him two hours to walk home. Once, when a moped ran into him and he had to go to hospital, it took three days.

Naemi asked if he would be all right.

"He's staying with family tonight," Zhang said. "His cousin lives half an hour away." He looked off down Kaixuan Road. By now, Mad Dog was a small hunched figure in the distance. "He's pretty indestructible."

"I'm not tired yet," Naemi said. "How about a drink?"

"I have an early start tomorrow."

"One drink?"

Zhang signaled to Chun Tao, who was waiting nearby with the Jaguar.

As they drove east, lightning crazed the sky up ahead, like cracks in a dark glaze. He had yet to talk to her about his passion for Yue ceramics—he hadn't even told her why he visited the museum after hours—but he would in time, he thought, despite what he had said about the power of a secret. He instinctively felt that she would experience what he experienced.

"I don't think Mad Dog likes me," she said suddenly.

"He doesn't like anybody." Zhang remembered how Mad Dog had shoved him against the wall outside the toilets. *Stay away from her.* "Did he say something to you?"

She hesitated. "Not exactly. It was more the way he looked at me."

"Don't worry about it. He's a bit unhinged." He looked across at her. "Hence the nickname."

"I don't understand."

"He wanders the streets on his own. Sometimes he bites."

"Right." She leaned back, her head against the headrest. Light passed over her face. Blue, then yellow. Blue again. It was smooth, and it kept happening. Like watching someone stroke a cat. "What about you?" she said after a while. "Do you bite?"

Not long after they ordered their drinks, Zhang looked up and saw his sister, Qi Jing, at the bar. She was sitting with a man who seemed familiar.

Naemi leaned close. "Do you know them?"

"That's my sister," Zhang said.

He stood up and walked over. Qi Jing was dressed in a miniskirt and a black gauzy blouse that showed the black bra she was wearing underneath, and her hair was dyed dark brown, with waves in it where it fell below her shoulders. Born just before the one-child policy came in, Qi Jing was eight years younger than Zhang, and she had always been something of a rebel.

She lifted her eyes to his as he approached. "Long time, no see."

The man on the stool glanced round. He had prominent cheekbones and close-cropped hair, and a chain of gold links hung around his neck, inside his shirt. Zhang couldn't place him.

"What do you want?" the man said.

Qi Jing told him that Zhang was her brother.

The man stared at Zhang, then nodded and hunched over his cocktail again. He didn't bother to introduce himself. He didn't even shake Zhang's hand.

Zhang asked Qi Jing how she was. She said she was fine.

"You're sure?" he said.

There was a sudden stubbornness in her face, around the mouth and jaw, and he knew her well enough to realize she wouldn't admit to anything—at least, not while that man was sitting next to her.

But he persisted. "Are you sure?"

"You heard her," the man said.

Zhang let his eyes drift out across the room. Deep pink lighting, like an old-fashioned whorehouse. Holograms of green rats on the walls. The Glamour Bar.

He spoke to Qi Jing again. "If you need me, I'm over there." He gestured towards his table.

"Who's the blonde?" Qi Jing asked.

"A friend."

She gave him a knowing look.

"She's beautiful, your sister," Naemi said when he sat down again.

"She's trouble too," he said. "Sometimes."

"Do you feel like a game of pool? I know a place that isn't far from here."

He smiled. "I need to go to bed. Why don't you come back to my place?"

"Where's that?"

He pointed through the window at the Oriental Pearl Tower, the huge sphere halfway up the building glowing purple. "Over there. Pudong."

While Naemi was reaching for her jacket, he glanced over his shoulder. Qi Jing and the man with the gold chain had left. He should stop worrying, he told himself. After all, she was thirty-four years old. Probably she could take care of herself.

"Come in," Zhang said.

He held the door open for Naemi, and she moved past him, into the apartment.

"Something to drink?"

She shook her head. "I'm fine."

He leaned his Gibson against the wall, then went over to the sound system and put an LP on. The Mexican release of Gloria Estefan's *Cuts Both Ways*.

"I thought you would live in an old place," she said as she stood at the living-room window, looking out over the city. "Somewhere traditional."

He was pouring himself a nightcap. "Are you disappointed?"

"Not disappointed. Just surprised." She turned back into the room. "Would you dance with me?"

He put down his drink and took her in his arms and held her close. She had removed her denim jacket. Her arms were bare. Under his right hand, he could feel the slender muscles that flanked her spine.

"I never dance," he murmured. "I must be drunk."

"You're not bad," she told him later. "You don't try too hard."

By then, they were scarcely moving at all, his right hand lower down, near her coccyx, his cheek against her hair. He had asked her what fragrance she was wearing. The Sacred Tears of Thebes, she said. She had bought it in Paris. She refused to tell him how much it had cost. His mouth found hers. The kiss lasted as long as one entire song. "Si Voy a Perderte." He led her into the bedroom, where one dim lamp was burning. The record finished, and the low roar of the air conditioning took over.

Once inside her, he seemed to leave the room. He found he was skimming, birdlike, over level countryside.

Beneath him were acres of wild grass that was scoured and flattened by the wind, and punctuated, here and there, by smooth gray rocks. Sometimes there was a small wooden house on its own, sometimes a few huddled dwellings, but people had made little or no impression on the landscape. It was unspoiled. In its natural state. He had no idea where he was—it wasn't somewhere he had ever been—but that didn't bother him. All that mattered was the flying. How happy it made him, how effortless it was.

I didn't know I could do this, he thought.

He was filled with an elation that seemed to have something to do with innocence. He felt like a child, but ageless too.

On he flew.

His whole body jerked, like a penknife snapping open. It was dark in the bedroom, and Naemi was leaning over him.

"You fell asleep," she said.

"Not while we were—"

Her white teeth showed. "No, afterwards."

She was lying on her stomach, her hair disheveled, half covering her eyes.

"Zhang?"

"I'm here." He liked the way she called him by his family name. It was so formal that it created, paradoxically, a whole new level of intimacy.

"I think I'm being followed," she said.

Fully awake now, he stared at her, but didn't speak.

She told him that a man in a green suit and a porkpie hat had come to the gallery where she worked. Even from where she was sitting, at her desk on the first floor of the office, she could tell that his interest was feigned. He might be looking at the paintings, but his mind was elsewhere. As she stared down at him, he seemed to sense her presence, and glanced sideways and upwards. Their eyes met. Though he only held her gaze for a split second, there was something in his face that told her he had seen what he needed to see, that he had come not for the art but for her. She watched as one of her colleagues—Kevin—approached the man. They had a brief exchange. Kevin walked away, returning moments later with a program of upcoming events and shows. The next time she looked the man was gone.

Zhang propped himself on his pillow. "You don't think you're reading too much into that one quick glance?"

"Then it happened again," she said.

Two days later, in the evening, she looked out of her

living-room window. Seven floors below, on the narrow promenade that bordered the creek, stood the man she had noticed in the gallery. He was dressed in the same suit and hat, which made him seem either careless or dangerously confident. Hands in his pockets, one ankle crossed over the other, he was leaning against the painted metal railing that separated the promenade from the creek below. His eyes were fixed on the front of her building. She stepped back from the window. The lights weren't on, and her window was one of many. She doubted he had seen her. Thinking fast, she pulled on a T-shirt, some leggings, and a pair of trainers, tied her hair back, and let herself out of the apartment. Once on the ground floor, she exited through the rear of the building. In less than five minutes, she was jogging along the promenade, back towards the place where the man had been standing.

Zhang laughed in anticipation, though he was silently cursing Johnny Yu for having been so indiscreet.

When she drew level with the entrance she usually used, she said, she slowed to a walk, pretending to be out of breath. Elbows propped on the top of the railing, hands dangling, the man was still staring up at the building. Staring, if she had it right, in the rough direction of some windows on the seventh floor. *Her* floor.

"Great building, isn't it," she said.

He turned and looked at her, and his face seemed to open wide. "I've seen you before."

She had to admire the coolness of his response. It was canny. Sly. But she could tell that he was lying. Of course he had seen her before. He was spying on her. Stalking her.

"In a gallery on Moganshan Road," she said. "Two days ago."

"You have a good memory." His sudden smile revealed stained teeth. "You fancied me, perhaps."

"I don't think it was that."

"Oh." Adopting a wounded look, he took out a packet of cigarettes and offered her one.

She shook her head. "Are you interested in art?"

"I'm interested in art, in poetry—in culture generally." He gestured with the cigarette he had just lit. "I'm not a collector, though. I don't have that kind of money."

"Do you live round here?"

"Not really." Turning lazily, he leaned back against the railing. He held his cigarette below his chin, with his thumb against the filter, and watched her through the smoke that coiled upwards, past his face. "What about you?"

This, too, was sly.

"I live there." She pointed at her own dark windows.

"Sir Victor Sassoon built it," he said. "In 1934."

"That's right."

"Apparently, it's constructed in a loose S shape—a subtle reference to his initial."

"I didn't know that."

"You'd need to see it from above, of course. From the air." He smiled, his stained teeth showing once again. "Anyway," he said, and he took a deep final drag on his cigarette and flicked the butt into the soupy waters of the creek, "I should be getting along." He brushed a few flakes of ash from the arm of his jacket, then looked at her sidelong. "Have a nice evening."

She watched as he set off along the promenade. Just before the bridge, he climbed down a flight of steps and signaled to a taxi that happened to be passing. He didn't look back, not even once.

"Strange encounter," Zhang said.

"Twice in a matter of two days, and in two completely different locations." She pushed the hair out of her eyes. "It seems an unlikely coincidence."

Zhang agreed that it seemed unlikely.

"It's not you, is it," she said, "spying on me?"

He held her gaze, though his heart was beating fast. "Why would I spy on you?"

She didn't answer.

"If you see the man again," he said, "tell me. Maybe I can do something."

"Like what?"

"I know people. I might be able to sort it out."

She looked at him for a long moment. Finally, she nodded. "All right," she said.

"It's late," he told her. "I should get some rest."

He woke again to see her standing naked at the bedroom window. Her back to him, she appeared as a silhouette, slender triangles of daylight showing on either side of her, between her elbows and her waist.

"Can't you sleep?" he said.

She turned from the window. "I have trouble sleeping."

"Are you worried about that man?"

"It's not that." She glanced at her watch. "I should go. I have a busy day."

"Would you like a lift somewhere? Chun Tao could drive you."

She leaned over him and kissed him, her hair falling across his face. "That's sweet of you, but there's no need."

He heard the hiss of the shower, but didn't hear her leave.

When he woke an hour and a half later, at seven thirty, he rolled over in the bed and lay where she had been lying. Her pillow smelled costly, exquisite. *The Sacred Tears of Thebes*. He smiled. As he washed and dressed, he remembered how he had flown over windswept grass, and he remembered the exhilaration, a heart-bursting feeling that seemed to belong to childhood. *I didn't know I could do this.* He could see the landscape even now—the quaint wooden houses, the river, the distant line of trees. They were no less vivid in daylight than they had been in the dream—except that it hadn't been a dream at all, since he hadn't been asleep. Why had he imagined such a place? What did it mean?

Once in his office, a Starbucks Frappuccino next to his laptop, he put in a call to Mad Dog.

"What?" Mad Dog sounded tetchy and listless, the legacy of too much whiskey and Tiger beer. In the background, Zhang could hear the chatter of cartoons. Mad Dog lived with Ling Ling, a woman half his age, and Ling Ling had a five-year-old daughter.

"You got home all right, then," Zhang said.

"No thanks to you."

"Any damage?"

Mad Dog's chuckle was dry and humorless. "Unscathed."

"Do you remember what you said when we were upstairs," Zhang said, "by the toilets?"

"I was drunk. Forget it."

Zhang checked his watch. He had a meeting in five minutes. "Will you be at home at lunchtime?"

"I'm retired," Mad Dog said. "Where else would I be?"

When Zhang stepped out of the building at half past twelve, the sky was blue, and a fierce and abrasive heat pressed down on everything. A young woman in a red dress and sunglasses walked past, her head protected by a red umbrella. It was a relief to climb into the Jaguar—its tinted windows, its chilly leather seats. Chun Tao drove north through Lujiazui. Men lay on plastic loungers in the shade. The parks were empty. The sun no longer felt like something that was good for you. His thoughts drifted back to his time in Vancouver. Driving to the beach in a convertible. The fresh salt sting of the air, the glitter of the waves. He had done his best to fit in—he learned English, and started wearing T-shirts and jeans—but his life never seemed entirely normal or natural. Even the sex was different. The girls he slept with were always putting things into words. *What do you like? Should I blow you? Did you come?* So many questions...They sped down into the Dalian Road Tunnel, emerging a few minutes later on the north side of the river. The dappled streets, the toxic sunlight. More women with umbrellas. When they approached the junction of Anguo Road and Tangshan Road, he told Chun Tao to pull over.

"I shouldn't be more than an hour," he said.

In the alley where Mad Dog lived, all the doors and windows were open. Men stood about in their underwear, with plastic slippers on their feet, talking or smoking or simply staring at the sky. Zhang pushed on the door that led to Mad Dog's yard. Mad Dog was sitting by the wall in a white undershirt and a pair of stained tan trousers. On the Formica table next to him was a packet of Shanghai Gold, a lighter, a teapot standing on a newspaper, and a half-drunk glass of tea. A sloping sheet of pale green corrugated plastic jutted from one side of the house, shielding him from the sun and rain. Strung across the yard behind him was a washing line hung with children's clothes and two faded pink bras.

"Bit of a nip in the air today." Mad Dog bared his teeth, which was the closest he ever came to smiling. The air under the lean-to was solid, humid. Thick as soup.

Zhang pulled a dishcloth off the washing line, spread it over the dusty seat of a white plastic chair, and sat down in the shade. Mad Dog pushed the packet of Shanghai Gold towards him.

"I don't smoke," Zhang said, "remember?"

"You used to smoke. You used to smoke more than all the rest of us put together."

"That's why I stopped."

"So now you're going to live forever?"

"Longer than you, anyway."

Mad Dog reached for the packet and shook out a cigarette and lit it. The flame coming from the lighter and the glowing tip of the cigarette seemed to add to the heat of the day.

"It must be important," he said, "for you to come all the way out here."

All the way out here. Zhang smiled. Mad Dog might live in an alley no wider than a hotel corridor, but if you got on the metro it was only four stops to the city center. It was just that he liked to think of himself as marginal, alternative.

"It's because of what I said to you," Mad Dog went on, "isn't it."

Zhang didn't respond. He remembered a brief exchange with Naemi as they drove back into town after

the gig at Yu Yin Tang. *I don't think Mad Dog likes me.*
He had tried to reassure her. *He doesn't like anyone.*
Which was true, actually. Mad Dog was often caustic,
and even, sometimes, violent—especially if he had been
drinking.

Selecting a glass from the narrow shelf behind him,
Mad Dog poured Zhang a glass of tea. "I meant every
word."

"Why would you say something like that?"

"There are things you don't know about me." Mad
Dog studied the end of his cigarette, took one last drag,
then flicked it away from him, into the yard. "I wrote a
book once."

"Really? What about?"

"Ah, I surprised you." Mad Dog allowed himself a
small, sour smile. "It was a history of ghost culture in
China, from ancient times to the present day."

Zhang stared at his friend. Mad Dog a writer? He
would never have guessed.

"I studied the subject for many years," Mad Dog went
on. "I even taught at the university."

"What's this got to do with Naemi?"

"Let me tell you a story."

Sipping his tea, Zhang felt a bead of sweat slide down
the middle of his chest.

"A woman who had died in childbirth walked into a grocery shop one morning," Mad Dog began.

"Good opening," Zhang said.

Mad Dog gave him a look that meant, Don't interrupt.

"She bought the kind of food a mother and baby would need," he went on. "As always, the shopkeeper admired her looks, but kept his eyes lowered, out of respect. She paid for the groceries and left.

"When she had gone, the shopkeeper noticed that the money she had given him had turned to ashes in his hand. He ran out into the street and looked around. The woman was already some distance away. It was raining, and she had no umbrella. Her black hair grew blacker, and her wet dress stuck to her back, and to her bottom. The shopkeeper was struck more than ever by her beauty.

"After following the woman to the gates of the cemetery, he lost sight of her. Not knowing what else to do, he wandered among the graves. The rain eased. A weak sun shone.

"When he finally found her, she was lying in a coffin, dead. On her breast was the baby she had given birth to. Waving its arms. Crying out as the rain tickled its face."

Mad Dog finished his tea.

"Have a think about that," he said, "while I make us some lunch."

As Mad Dog disappeared indoors, Zhang's phone rang. It was Wang Jun Wei. He wanted to know if Zhang had reached a decision about the Iran deal.

"There's a meeting tomorrow," he said, "in my office. It would mean a lot to me if you were there."

Zhang said he would do his best.

After finishing with Jun Wei, Zhang called Sebastian, a German commodities trader who he had worked with before. He asked Sebastian if he could attend a meeting the following day. He apologized for the short notice.

By the time he had talked Sebastian into it, proposing a fifty-fifty split on fees, Mad Dog had appeared again, with two steaming bowls of noodles. The two men began to eat.

"The broth is excellent," Zhang said after a while.

Mad Dog nodded. "I'm a good cook. Better than Ling Ling."

"So that's why she stays with you."

The gums above Mad Dog's top teeth showed. "What did you think of the story?"

Zhang shrugged. "It's a ghost story, like a thousand others." The hot food was making him sweat even more.

Did he have a fresh shirt back at the office? He couldn't remember.

Mad Dog put down his chopsticks and lit a Shanghai Gold. "When I met your blonde friend the other night, I felt uneasy. At first, I thought it was because she was foreign. But I've met foreigners before—obviously. I get irritated sometimes, confused as well, but uneasy? Never. So I watched her." He brought his cigarette up to his lips and took a deep drag on it. "I watched her all evening."

Pushing his bowl away, Zhang sat back. A breath of air moved through the yard. He had a sudden craving for one of Mad Dog's Shanghai Golds.

"And?" he said.

In the light that filtered down through the corrugated plastic, Mad Dog's face looked pale and sickly.

"There's a moment in the story," he said, "when the shopkeeper realizes that he is dealing with a ghost."

"When the money turns to ashes?"

"Yes." Mad Dog reached sideways, past the end of the table, dislodging the ash from his cigarette by flicking the filter with his thumb. "There was a moment, also, with your friend."

Zhang was watching Mad Dog closely now.

"We were sitting on the terrace, just the two of us," Mad Dog went on. "You'd gone inside, and Laser was over by the door, talking to someone. She wouldn't meet my gaze—she was staring out into the park—but I didn't take my eyes off her. Then, all of a sudden, she turned her head and looked at me, and that was when I saw her."

"*Saw* her? What do you mean?"

"She was ancient," Mad Dog said. "Her hair was gone, and her fingernails and teeth were black. Her eyes shone with a strange, cold light." He paused. "She opened her mouth, as if to speak, and her tongue stretched out towards me, much longer than a human—"

"Stop," Zhang said. "That's horrible."

Mad Dog shrugged, then dropped his cigarette butt on the ground and trod on it.

"You were drunk," Zhang went on. "You said so yourself."

Mad Dog slowly moved his head from side to side. "I looked and looked, and in the end I saw."

Zhang shook himself, then checked his phone. Seventeen new e-mails, including two from Sebastian, and one from his wife. "I should be getting back."

"Suit yourself."

"Thanks for the lunch." Zhang stood up and lifted his jacket off the back of the chair.

As he walked to the door that led out to the alley, Mad Dog called after him.

"What are you going to do?"

6

TO AROUSE HOSTILITY IN PEOPLE was nothing new. All her life, Naemi had encountered it, and almost always from men. But she was thinking of the first time, which had happened in a past so deep it felt invented. Her name was Netu then. After her family was killed, she had taken a random path through countryside laid waste by years of conflict. In an attempt to escape the violence, she had found her way at last to the coast of Finnmark, that acid-eaten edge of the world, all inlets and islands, which many believed to be the entrance to hell itself. In those days, hell was seen as a cold place, and no place was colder than Vardø, though she arrived on a summer's day, when sea and sky were a matching blue, and the light breeze smelled of the pine tar used for caulking boats.

In time, she met and married a fisherman called Halgard, and went to live with him in a turf hut belonging to Elsebe, his mother. One of the richest people in the village, Elsebe owned a wooden shack down by the shoreline, a boathouse, and half a dozen racks for drying fish, but her husband had died of a fever not long after Halgard was born, and then she lost her left eye to an infection. Something in her had corroded, and she was always bemoaning her fate, rebuking a world she thought of as conniving and malevolent. She took against Netu from the beginning. It is possible she would have taken against anyone who came between her and her son. Some mothers are like that.

Halgard was tall, square-shouldered, and easygoing, with a ready grin that put Netu in mind of her father, but he was often away for twenty or thirty days in a row, hunting seal and walrus in the Barents Sea, or fishing for cod. The moment he was gone, Elsebe would begin to find fault with her. Not until the early spring, when the light returned, would Netu be able to get away. While the snow was still on the ground, she would strap on skis made from the shinbones of reindeer and leave the village, losing herself in the eerie magic of the tundra. In the summer, she would go for long walks up the smooth green slopes of Domen, or out towards the Kibergsneset peninsula. It might not have been safe to wander off alone, unarmed—by August, the polar bears were desperate for any sort of food—but that didn't stop her. For those few hours, she could escape her mother-in-law's constant insinuations and complaints. The old woman would be waiting for her when she came back, though. *Shirking your duties again, I see. Doing as you please. I suppose you think you're too good for us.* By the time Halgard returned after a long stint at sea, exhausted and elated, she would be at her wits' end. Halgard assumed it was because she had missed him—and she had, though that was only part of the story. When she attempted to explain what she had been through, he found it difficult to believe, since his mother was careful to hide that side of her nature from him. Also, he didn't like to hear his mother criticized. She tried a different approach, asking if they might perhaps live elsewhere, but her entreaties usually coincided with his homecoming, when he was happy to be alive and back among his people. He had no desire to move, he told her. He belonged in Vardø. And besides, how could he leave his mother all alone, with no one to look after her?

There was another source of tension. Halgard wanted a family, but the years went by and no child came. Children were vital in a small community like Vardø—without children, it would die out—and barrenness was seen both as a failure and as a selfish or hostile act, a kind of withholding. *Where are all my grandchildren?* Elsebe was always muttering, which did nothing to dispel the pressure.

One June morning, Netu and Halgard walked out along the shore and sat on the flat rocks to the south of the village. The sea lay calm as a lake, the water silver gray, like the belly of a fish. The moon was half a chalky thumbprint high up in the sky.

"Is something wrong with you?" Halgard asked.

She had been asking herself the same question. When she first began to drink her own blood, her monthly cycles had become irregular. Then she stopped menstruating altogether. She had told no one, not even the women in the village. *Especially* not the women in the village. Instead, she faked her periods, using blood from slaughtered pigs and deer. She needed to prove she was the same as everybody else. Inside, though, she realized she was in the process of turning into someone—or some*thing*—unfathomable, and it occurred to her that she might have forfeited her fertility as a result. It was part of a bargain, perhaps—a bargain that had somehow been struck without her knowledge, a bargain in which she had had no say. She was as troubled by her inability to conceive as he was.

After all, aside from any longing or frustration she might feel, it was a threat to her.

She rested her head against Halgard's shoulder. "Let's keep trying," she murmured. "I'm sure we'll be blessed before too long." But she knew she was lying, and that more questions lay ahead, questions she would have no answer to.

Then disaster struck. Vardø's small fishing fleet was caught in a summer storm in the waters off Skaldenes, and three of the four boats sank. Halgard survived, but many of his companions were lost. Good men, who would be sorely missed. On Halgard's return, there was talk of bad luck descending on the community. An evil eye. Netu was an outsider, one of the few who had not been born and raised in the place. During the weeks of mourning that followed the drownings, she became the object of malicious gossip and suspicion, and the fact that her husband had been spared was used as evidence against her. Elsebe redoubled her attacks. Finally, she had the sort of ammunition she had been looking for.

One evening, while Halgard was out fetching wood, she asked Netu how long she had been in Vardø.

"You know how long," Netu said.

Elsebe's one eye seemed to gleam, like something that had recently been polished. "Remind me."

"Nine years."

"And yet you haven't changed at all."

Netu didn't know how to respond.

"My son has aged," Elsebe went on. "Little lines at the edges of his eyes, a few white flecks in his beard. But you—you're like a freshly minted coin…"

Again, Netu had no answer.

By this time, Halgard had returned with the firewood. "Are you saying I look old, Mother?" He wore his usual easy smile.

But Elsebe was still staring at Netu. "You're not a Sami by any chance, are you?"

With Elsebe, no question was ever straightforward, but this, Netu immediately understood, was intended as a calumny, since Sami people were sorcerers who had been known to sell favorable winds to foreign traders arriving by ship. Their spell-casting and enchantments could be lethal, both to people and to animals, and they were often persecuted, or hunted down and killed. She wasn't about to admit she had Sami blood—and certainly not to someone like Elsebe.

"Mother," Halgard was saying, "she's *blonde*."

"They can be blonde." Lurching forwards, Elsebe grasped a fistful of Netu's hair. "So beautiful—like a völva."

Netu twisted free. "Völva? What's that?"

Elsebe's good eye glittered. "It means 'witch.'"

"That's a slander," Netu said. "I know nothing of their craft—"

Once again, the old woman leaned forwards in her chair. This time, she seized Netu's left hand and pointed at the scar between her thumb and her forefinger. "What's this, then?"

"I burned myself—baking the flatbread..."

Elsebe dropped the hand and sat back with a self-righteous, knowing smile. "The Devil pinched you with his claws."

"Mother," Halgard said.

"You come out of nowhere with your red mouth and your yellow hair," Elsebe said. "You cast your spells, and you ensnare my son—"

"That's not how it happened," Netu said.

"And now some of the finest men in the community are dead, and this whole place is cursed—"

"What's that to do with me?"

"Yes," the old woman said, still as a snake. "That is the question."

Netu turned to Halgard, appealing to him to intervene.

"Leave her alone, Mother," Halgard said.

But his tone was weary and grudging, and there was no force or conviction in his words. He hadn't taken sides. He was just trying to keep the peace.

A few days later, while Halgard was out hunting, Elsebe and Netu attended a meeting of the village elders. To Netu's horror, Elsebe began to speak out against her, castigating her for her beauty and her barrenness. She tried to leave, but two or three of Elsebe's close friends held her back. She disturbed the heart of any man who saw her, Elsebe was saying. Yet nothing grew in her. She was a girl who would never become a woman. They had been harboring an aberration in their midst. Elsebe's words were like whips, goading everyone who listened. How was it they hadn't realized? How could they have been so blind?

"I, too, was blind." The old woman's voice had lifted, and she struck her chest with one closed hand. "I took her in and gave her everything I had—including my son."

They needed somebody to blame for the loss of their menfolk. They were looking for a murderer.

"Look no further," Elsebe cried.

Later that day, the people of the village put her in a cart that was like a cage and drove her towards Vardøhus Castle. Though it was still light, they carried torches soaked in seal fat, the smoke soiling a sky that was the luminous gray white of a pearl. She was in no doubt as to what they had in mind. The new district governor, a Scotsman by the name of Cunningham, had moved into the castle, and he had made it his business to cleanse the land of witches. Apparently, he thought of little else. She would be taken before him and required to confess. If she failed to cooperate, she would be tortured. She already knew what instruments he favored. Arm chains, heated sulfur on the skin. The rack. Later, she would be bound hand and foot and dropped in deep water. If she sank, she would be considered innocent. If she floated, she would be found guilty and burned to a cinder at the stake. Either way, she was done for. In those days, in Finnmark, that passed for justice.

As the cart jolted along the shore, the jeering faces of Vardø women all around her, she squatted behind the bars. She began to talk to herself, her voice pitched low. She was calling on the spirits of those who had come before her. Her ancestors. *If I exert myself, let five exert themselves. For I am alone.* Did the words come from inside her or from somewhere beyond? She couldn't have said. When she first left her parents' house, she would, at any given moment, name what surrounded her—the plants, the rocks, the trees, the animals, the water. If you describe something, you have a chance of controlling it.

Whatever is well-disposed towards you can be enlisted. Whatever is hostile can be disarmed. There is great power in naming. Crouching on the cart's unsteady floor, words came to her unpremeditated, as though rising from some dark place where they had been waiting. *If I appear with five, let ten rise up to side with me, for I have no one. Let them stand before me and behind me, and deliver me from harm.*

When they were just a mile from Cunningham's headquarters, a miracle took place. Mist stole in off the sea, growing thicker as it passed over the land. The women were swallowed up. Snuffed out. Their faces, their torches. Even their harsh voices. The mist came up close and wrapped itself around her as she shivered in the rocking prison of the cart. She seemed to become one with it, made of something other than blood and bone, made of soft gray air. Though the gaps between the wooden staves that held her were no wider than a hand's span, she slipped clean through, and off she went, across the burnt-orange, furze-like grass, not walking, not flying, somewhere between the two. She didn't worry that she might lose her way, spill off the edge of the world. She had been delivered. There were cries of *She's escaped!* and *Where the devil is she?* There was a distant howl of rage. Her mother-in-law, perhaps. No one would ever know what became of her. She would be a story that was told to children. A cautionary tale. A fable.

Sometime later, she found herself on the white dirt road that led southwest, and after several days of traveling she reached a small town on the river Tana. She would like to have said goodbye to Halgard. She would like to have explained, if such a thing were possible. In her absence, she assumed he would take sides against her. He would have no choice. It saddened her to think he might lose that easy grin. That he might turn bitter, like his mother. Given the way things had gone, she viewed her infertility as a necessity, or even as a blessing. How could she have children when she might be forced to disappear at a moment's notice, never to return? Leaving a husband was one thing. Leaving a child would be something else entirely.

After Vardø, a time of wandering...

She climbed the mountain at Koli, its rounded slopes once used for human sacrifice, and still haunted, so people told her, by the spirits of the dead. She spent a spring and summer on the island of Läpisyöksy, where the north wind blew through the holes in the rocks, making them moan and wail like organ pipes. Years passed. Decades. Decades she shouldn't have had. Somehow she didn't question it. She would sink her teeth into the soft skin of her arm—or sometimes she would use a knife. She was comforting herself, and also punishing herself, perhaps. She was paying homage to her family. It was a sacrament. A kind of mass.

What she did became a reflex, a habit. A ritual. She would break the circle in her body, the loop of her own blood, and then she would repair it. The feeling was like a sigh, but also like a rush. A slowing down, a speeding up. The pleasure chasing the pain. But people began to notice what was happening to her. Elsebe was the first. Later, there were others. She was like a clock in a catastrophe. Her hands had stuck. Her face no longer told the time. While everyone around her grew older, she held on to her youth. People who knew her became intrigued, and then suspicious. They began to ask questions. Always the same questions. *How is it that you never change? What's your secret?*

Tell me your story.

She realized she couldn't stay in one place for too long. Ten years. Fifteen at the most. After that, she would have to leave, and when she left the break would have to be decisive, absolute. The person she turned into could have no contact with the person she had been before. Nothing could be allowed to compromise the new life she was embarking on. At first, she kept her name, and chose not to venture beyond the borders of her own land. In time, that became unsustainable. She moved farther afield, setting her course for the ends of the earth. She acquired new languages, new customs. She altered her appearance. Short hair, long hair, black hair, red hair—no hair at all. Once or twice, she masqueraded as a boy, but it was more of an experiment than anything else, and it carried its own inherent dangers. There were times when she couldn't have said if she was alive or dead. All she knew was that she didn't age. Was it because she drank her own blood? Was she an auto-vampire, if such a thing might be said to exist? Or was it fueled by rage at what her family had suffered? Was it a weird, unexpected by-product of violent emotion? She had no idea. And there was no one she could ask either—though there had been years when she searched the world for somebody who might be qualified to speculate. But in the end it was probably better not to know. Thinking about it only made her squeamish. It was like being too acutely aware of the heart beating in your chest. Why not just accept it and be grateful? After all, most people dreamed of living forever, and she often had to pinch herself when she considered all the possibilities that lay before her. There was nowhere she couldn't go, nothing she couldn't do...Elation doesn't last, though. You can have too much of a good thing. The feeling that crept up on her in the wake of all that euphoria was like a hollowness. A kind of dread. She began to feel trapped in something endless. Immortality is claustrophobic.

At some point in her travels, it occurred to her that she could circle back and live where she had lived before, since all those who might have recognized her would now be dead. It was such a relief to be able to return—not to a person she had loved, admittedly, but to a place. She would revisit North Karelia, sometimes spending months there, sometimes years. Or she would pass through, on her way to somewhere else. She needed the green trees and the blue water. She needed the earth. What an uncanny feeling it was to walk among the grandchildren and great-grandchildren of people she had known! By then, she had become accustomed to departure. Adept at it. That was the lesson she had learned. She had also resolved that there would be one aspect of herself that she would not renounce, one element that all her many lives would have in common. Her initials. NVK. There had to be something to hold on to, some faint trace of continuity, or she would fall apart.

And now, in Shanghai, it was happening again...

She sat on the floor of her apartment, facing the window, the light from the street arranged in orange blocks in front of her, and she began to speak. Her voice was as it always was, monotonous yet also musical, like plainsong, but the language she was using was new language. *You think you know what I am. You have no idea. I'm not in any of your books. You try to catch me. Your hands grasp empty air. I'm not a story you can tell. My blood leaves my body. My blood returns. Like breath. I am between two deaths. The day goes dark. I walk over your grave.*

7

WHILE ZHANG WAS ON HIS WAY BACK to the office after lunch at Mad Dog's house, he received a call from Johnny Yu.

"I've got what you need," Johnny said.

Something in Zhang's mind tightened a notch. "Can you meet me at six?" He gave Johnny the address of the Bamboo Lounge, the cocktail bar he had visited a few nights earlier.

When he walked into the bar that evening, the same girl was working, only this time she was wearing a green dress, and her hair was pinned up in a chignon. The place wasn't empty, but business was slow. She smiled at Zhang as he approached. He ordered a whiskey, then asked if she would like a Malibu.

"Not tonight," she said. "The owner's here." She tilted her head in the direction of two men sitting in the corner. "But thank you."

He carried his whiskey to a table by the window. Parting the wooden blinds, he peered out. Since the bar was on the second floor, he had a good view of the street. The yellow light seeping from a neon sign on the restaurant below slid over the cars that passed. He sipped his drink. The whiskey burned a line of glowing gold down the middle of his body.

Taking out his phone, he called his wife, Xuan Xuan. She picked up, but told him that she couldn't talk as she was about to leave the house. Her best friend was taking her to a spa. He asked if he could have a word with his son. There was a muted discussion on the other end, most of which he couldn't hear. Hai Long was in the middle of doing his homework, she said at last. He didn't want to be interrupted. Zhang told her that he would ring back another time, when it was more convenient, then he ended the call.

Johnny arrived ten minutes later, with his chin lowered and his hat brim pulled down at the front, as if he was a celebrity, and was afraid he might be recognized. He was wearing a bronze-colored suit and a black shirt. He shook hands with Zhang and sat down opposite. When the waitress came over, he ordered a beer. His eyes traveled up and down her body as she took his order, and he kept looking at her as she moved away.

"I playfully sniff and finger the plum blossom," he said, *"and there, at the branch tip, is all the fullness of Spring!"* He turned to Zhang with a sly grin. "Author unknown."

Zhang sighed. "What have you got for me?"

Johnny took out a folded sheet of paper and handed it to Zhang. "Everything you asked for—and more."

Zhang began to read.

Her name was Naemi Vieno Kuusela, and she had been born on September 19, 1979. He smiled. All those nines. In China, it was considered a good omen, since the word for "nine" sounded like the word for "everlasting." But she had lied about her age—or rather, she had allowed him to think she was twenty-four when in fact she was already in her early thirties. She worked for Art Island, a prestigious gallery housed in the complex on Moganshan Road, where her principal role was artist liaison. She lived alone on the seventh floor of the Embankment Building on Suzhou North Road. Apartment 710. Zhang knew the place. It was popular with foreigners, especially those who were looking for history and atmosphere. The monthly rent on a decent-sized apartment with a view of downtown would be somewhere between 30,000 and 40,000 RMB. Either Naemi was being paid a generous salary or she had money of her own. Included with her home address and the address of the gallery were two e-mail addresses and a phone number. As Zhang scanned the sheet of paper for a second time, he was aware of the girl bringing Johnny his beer and Johnny staring at her, as before.

"Anything missing?" Johnny spoke with the cockiness of someone who already knows the answer to his question.

"Not a thing," Zhang said, folding the sheet of paper and slipping it into his pocket, "though I can't say I'm entirely happy."

Johnny's beer bottle hung in the air, halfway to his mouth. His smirk was gone.

"You were seen," Zhang said, "in your green suit. You were seen twice."

Johnny put down his drink. Eyes lowered, he seemed to be peering into the neck of the bottle. "I did the job," he muttered. "I got results."

"She *saw* you, Johnny."

"There's no way she could connect us."

"Why in that case would she mention it to me? Why would she ask if I was spying on her?"

"I'm sorry, boss."

Zhang took out an envelope and placed it on the table between them. "Be more careful in future, otherwise I won't be able to use you."

Eyeing the envelope, Johnny nodded.

"And don't get any ideas about the waitress," Zhang added.

Johnny looked at him. "I didn't know you were—"

"I'm not."

"So what's it to you if I take a crack at her?"

"She deserves better."

"She's only a bar girl."

"Get out of here," Zhang said, "before I lose my patience."

Apologizing again, Johnny picked up the envelope and tucked it into his jacket pocket, each movement deliberate, almost labored, as if to counter the impression that he was being summarily dismissed, then he stood up and drained his bottle of beer. After sending one swift, hunted look in the girl's direction, he turned and left the bar. She watched him go with blank, uninterested eyes.

Zhang parted the wooden blinds on the window. On the pavement below, Johnny glanced left and right, like someone trying to decide what to do next. In the yellow neon light his bronze-colored suit looked charred. *I playfully sniff and finger the plum blossom...* Shaking his head, Zhang finished his drink and walked up to the bar.

The girl smiled at him. "Would you like another?"

"No. Just the check."

"I already told you what my life is like," she said. "Maybe one day you'll tell me a little about yours."

"Maybe," he said.

Back in his apartment, Zhang couldn't seem to settle. He poured himself a tumbler of bourbon and took his twelve-string acoustic guitar out of its case. Sitting on the sofa, facing out into the night, he began to play a basic instrumental blues. Gradually, words came to him. It was dusk, and he was in the country. The smell of mud and leaves. Then he heard a soft roaring sound, like a gust of wind, but the air was still and the trees weren't moving. He turned around. A woman stood behind him, on the path. She was the woman he loved. He scarcely recognized her, though, since all her hair was gone and her teeth and fingernails were black. He used the line the small man in the pale blue suit had used: *Fear rushed through me.* In less than half an hour, the song was done. He called Mad Dog and played it to him on the speakerphone. When he finished, there was silence. He could hear a child crying in the background. Ling Ling's daughter.

He asked Mad Dog what he thought.

"What I told you at lunchtime the other day seems to have had quite an effect on you," Mad Dog said.

"It's not just about that," Zhang said. "I'm drawing on all sorts of things."

Mad Dog let out a small, derisory chuckle. "In any case, you're probably right to be afraid."

"You think the song's about Naemi?"

"Don't you?"

Zhang played a minor chord, but didn't speak.

"That night at Yu Yin Tang," Mad Dog went on, "when I sat with her on the terrace, I wasn't imagining things."

Putting his guitar aside, Zhang picked up the phone and moved out onto the terrace. The night was humid and musty. He had the uncanny feeling, suddenly, that the city that lay before him was a huge, dark lake in which all kinds of mysterious objects were floating. "What are you saying?"

"She's a ghost."

Zhang's laughter was brief, incredulous. "You can't expect me to believe that."

"Believe what you like."

"Are you serious?"

"I know what you're thinking," Mad Dog said. "She seems as real as you or me. And she's beautiful, of course. You're probably besotted with her. That's all entirely predictable—"

Zhang tried to interrupt, but his friend talked over him.

"In the Chinese imagination, ghosts have always been closely associated with sex, and that's particularly true of female ghosts. When they appear, they tend to appear in an erotic context. They're seductive. Irresistible. They lure you in. What you see is what you want to see. But it's not the truth. It's an illusion."

"You're the one with the illusion," Zhang said. "You're basing this whole hypothesis on something you thought you saw when you were drunk."

"Ghosts are devious," Mad Dog continued, quite undeterred by Zhang's objections. "They don't tend to reveal much. They can't afford to. They know that if they're recognized they could be destroyed." He paused. "If you were honest with yourself," he went on, "if you were seeing *clearly*, you'd be able to supply me with evidence that would support my argument. I know you would. You're in denial, though."

Zhang shook his head, but inside he felt a certain agitation or disquiet, the sense of something coming loose. He was thinking of Naemi's restlessness at night, the way she never appeared to sleep, and how she seemed much older than her years. He thought of her impenetrability. *Was* he in denial, as Mad Dog claimed?

"How do you know all this?" he said finally.

"I told you. I wrote a book. Don't you ever listen?"

"You seem a bit obsessed."

"Obsessions are what make people exceptional." There was a quick, scratchy noise from Mad Dog's lighter as he lit a cigarette. "My knowledge hasn't come in especially useful, though—at least, not until now."

"So what would you advise?" Zhang said. "I should stop seeing her?"

"Yes."

"And if I can't—or won't?"

Mad Dog fell quiet for a few moments.

"Be careful," he said at last. "And tell me if anything happens that seems out of the ordinary."

Zhang was aware that he was keeping things from Mad Dog, but he couldn't bear to provide him with any ammunition.

"By the way," Mad Dog said, "that song of yours. It's not so bad."

Zhang smiled faintly. "We'll work on it next time we meet."

"Saturday?"

"Yes. See you then."

Only seconds after Zhang ended the call, his phone started to ring. He pressed Accept.

"Naemi?" he said.

"How did you know it was me?" She sounded warm and slightly blurred, as if she had been drinking.

"I don't know. I just did."

They listened to each other breathe.

"I've been thinking about you," he said. "I want to see you."

"I want to see you too."

"Can you come over?" The words were out of his mouth before he knew it, despite everything Mad Dog had said.

"I wish I could. I'm in Hong Kong."

He thought about throwing a few things in a bag and taking a taxi to the airport—Shanghai to Hong Kong was only a two-hour flight—but it would be four in the morning by the time he reached her, and he had a midday meeting with Jun Wei.

"When are you back?" he asked.

"Tomorrow. I have to be at work in the afternoon."

"What about tomorrow evening?"

An awkward silence fell.

"I can't," she said eventually. "I have plans."

They agreed to see each other the day after, at lunchtime.

Once the phone call was over, he showered, then went to bed. Lying in the dark, though, he found he couldn't sleep. Perhaps it was because he had been thinking of flying to Hong Kong to see her. Or perhaps it was her influence: just speaking to her had unsettled him. Usually, when he felt restless, he would take a taxi to Wing Mei's apartment in the French Concession. When he arrived, she would remove his clothes and wash him with fragrant soaps and oils. Afterwards, they would make love on an opium bed that had belonged to her great-grandfather. Once he was inside her, she would hum a tune, and he would know she was approaching orgasm because she would look away, into the corner of the room, and she would bite her bottom lip, as if nervous or apprehensive. Later, she would cook for him. Something delicate, delicious. He could predict almost every aspect of an evening with Wing Mei, and there were times when that familiarity would excite or comfort him. But things were different now...

Turning onto his side, he saw himself arriving at the Embankment Building on Suzhou North Road. He had been there once before, for drinks with a French economist, and he remembered how shabby and run-down the lobby was, with a rudimentary Art Deco floor and a wall crowded with hundreds of small, dark green mailboxes. At the rear of the building was a flight of stairs, the dull brown wood furred with dust. Cobwebs hung high up on the pale walls. He remembered thinking it would make a good location for a horror film. If Johnny was to be believed, Naemi lived in apartment 710. He took a lift up to the seventh floor and stepped out into a corridor that stretched away in both directions. As in a nightmare, though, he couldn't find a door with 710 on it.

Outside again, he stood on the promenade that followed the curve of the creek. Was it here that Naemi had confronted Johnny in his porkpie hat and his green suit? He found the idea that they had met unlikely—they were such very different characters—though he knew Johnny well enough to know that he wouldn't have given anything away, despite having been caught red-handed.

Leaning against the railing, with the creek at his back, he looked up at the building's intricate brown facade. The place was vast—it occupied an entire block—and yet it managed to be secretive. Ambiguous.

Like her...

At last he felt himself sinking into sleep.

After his lunchtime meeting with Jun Wei and Sebastian in north Shanghai, Zhang would normally have returned to the office. Instead, he asked Chun Tao to drive him to 50 Moganshan Road. It was five o'clock when they stopped outside. The cluster of old industrial buildings backing onto Suzhou Creek had been converted into galleries and artists' studios that were now famous the world over. Zhang told Chun Tao to pull into the residential car park opposite. It was probably illegal to wait there—Zhang wasn't a resident—but if they parked on the road Naemi might recognize the car. He kept his eyes trained on the main entrance. When she told him she couldn't see him that evening because she had plans, he had noticed a shift in her voice, a kind of wariness or caution, as if she had said more than she meant to. He wondered if he was about to learn something he would rather not know. Hopefully not. Hopefully, it would turn out to be something innocuous—a doctor's appointment, dinner with an old friend.

A security guard stood near the entrance, beneath a dark red parasol. He seemed to be asleep on his feet, like a horse. Ten meters to his left, in front of a gallery called Fish Studio, a parking attendant sat slumped on a plastic chair. Dressed in a pale blue uniform and black sandals, she was staring at an iPad. A bag of plums hung from the arm of the chair. Farther along, towards the main road, was a street vendor who was probably there for the foreign tourists. His wooden handcart was cluttered with bric-a-brac. Old teakettles. Pieces of mud-colored jade.

The minutes passed.

Five forty. Five fifty-five. Six o'clock.

Every now and then, a taxi pulled up, and someone would get in or out. Otherwise, the street was quiet.

He hoped he hadn't missed her.

When the clock in the car was showing 6:19, the security guard suddenly turned his head. Naemi had appeared. She was conservatively dressed, in a black blouse, a gray skirt, and a fawn raincoat with a belt, and she was pulling the small overnight case she must have taken to Hong Kong with her. It was dusk by now, and there were no taxis. She exchanged a few words with the guard, who smiled and nodded, then she set off towards the junction with Changhua Road. Zhang told Chun Tao to start the engine. He should leave the headlights off, though.

The street vendor gestured at Naemi as she passed by. She shook her head and kept walking.

She didn't even glance in their direction.

When she was out of sight, Zhang told Chun Tao to turn the lights on and drive slowly towards the main road. He should park fifty meters short of the junction. Under no circumstances, he said, could they allow themselves to be spotted.

As they edged out into Moganshan Road, he could see Naemi ahead of them, her blonde hair and pale coat showing up clearly in the dark. On reaching the junction, she stood still, facing to the right, then she lifted a hand. She was hailing a taxi, as he had thought she would.

"Follow her," Zhang said, "but stay well back."

Chun Tao eased the Jaguar into the heavy rush-hour traffic on Changhua Road. The mass of brake- and taillights in the windscreen filled with car's interior with an incandescent scarlet glow. Afraid they might lose her, Zhang leaned forwards and gave Chun Tao the taxi's number plate, but Chun Tao said he had already made a note of it.

They drove south, then east. Where was she going? Zhang couldn't even begin to guess.

After half an hour, Naemi's taxi pulled over and she got out. They were at a crossroads, not far from the Westin Bund hotel. Chun Tao parked nearby. Through the rear window, Zhang watched Naemi vanish into a huge gray-and-brown building that occupied the southeast corner of the crossroads. The naturalness with which she approached the building suggested that this was not the first time she had visited. The sign above the entrance said MEDICAL SUPPLIES.

She was inside for about five minutes, and when she emerged she didn't appear to be carrying anything she hadn't been carrying before. She stood on the curb with her suitcase, looking away from him, into the oncoming traffic. A taxi stopped for her, and she climbed in.

"Should I follow?" Chun Tao asked as the taxi cruised past.

"Stay where you are." Zhang opened the car door. "I'll be right back."

He crossed the pavement and entered the building. Inside, it reminded him of a showroom, with glass cabinets containing everything from the clamps and scalpels used in surgery to uniforms for doctors, nurses, and paramedics. This was a wholesale outlet, he realized. Apart from the middle-aged man behind the counter and two young saleswomen on the shop floor, he was the only person in the place.

He approached the counter. "There was a blonde woman in here just now," he said. "A foreigner."

The man looked at him and blinked.

Zhang put a folded 100 RMB note on the glass counter and covered it with his hand. "I need to know why she was here."

"Are you the police?"

"If I was the police, would I be paying you?"

"I don't know." The man looked at the two salesgirls. One of them was giggling at what the other had just said. They hadn't noticed anything. "Is she in trouble?"

"No."

Zhang produced a second note.

The man studied Zhang's hand, which was flat on the counter, then he looked at Zhang again. Though his expression had not altered, something was different underneath. A decision had been reached. There was a feeling of compliance.

"What did she come here for?" Zhang asked, pushing the two notes across the counter. "What did she buy?"

The man's shoulders sagged. He glanced at the two young women again, then swiftly pocketed the money. "Okay," he said. "She bought a multipack of syringes and a cannula."

"A what?"

"A cannula. It's used in hospitals, for a drip."

"Show me."

The man led him to a display case and pointed.

"Did she take them with her?" Zhang asked.

The man shook his head. "This is the place where you pay. You have to go to another building to pick up your order."

"Where's the other building?"

"Hongkou district."

Zhang remembered what Johnny had said when he mentioned the scarring on Naemi's arm. *What are you telling me? She's a junkie?*

"What would she do with the items she bought," he asked, "if you had to make an educated guess?"

The man shrugged. "I suppose she works with sick people."

"Have you ever seen a nurse who looks like her?"

The man poked a finger into his ear and wiggled it around. He didn't seem to know how to answer the question.

Zhang tried a different angle. "How often does she come here?"

"I don't know. About every six months."

"Does she talk to you?"

"Sometimes she asks me how I am."

"Nothing about herself?"

"Only the usual things. How busy she is—" He stopped to think. "Her Chinese is very good—for a foreigner."

"Next time she appears," Zhang said, "don't mention me. I was never here."

"Okay." The man gritted his teeth, as if determined, or in pain.

One of the young saleswomen came and stood beside him. All her fingernails were painted green except for the little one, which was yellow.

"Why is one of your nails yellow?" Zhang asked.

She giggled. "I don't know."

Outside, he stood on the pavement, thinking. Syringes, a cannula—the scar tissue on the inside of her elbow...All the evidence seemed to support Johnny's suggestion that Naemi was some sort of addict. But she didn't look like any addict that he had ever seen.

What should he do? Confront her?

Or keep quiet and observe?

At half past ten that evening, as Zhang was preparing for bed, the concierge called from downstairs. Someone by the name of Gong Shen was in the lobby, asking to see him. Zhang told the concierge to pass Gong Shen the phone.

"Are you alone?" Mad Dog asked.

"Yes," Zhang said. "What do you want?"

"We need to talk."

"Can't it wait? I was about to go to bed."

"If it could wait, I wouldn't be here."

Zhang sighed.

"Come downstairs," Mad Dog said. "I think we should go for a walk."

Five minutes later, when Zhang stepped out of the lift, Mad Dog took him by the arm and steered him out of the main entrance and into the grounds. Mad Dog's hair hung in greasy strands, and his jacket was loose on him, as if it had been borrowed from a much larger man. He had been drinking—Zhang could smell the alcohol on him—but he wasn't drunk.

"I've been doing some reading," Mad Dog said. "Some thinking too."

It was a warm night, and the sky was an oily brown, sticky too somehow, like the inside of an oven that hadn't been cleaned in years. The two men followed a curving path that led past the outdoor swimming pool and on through a modest forest of bamboo. Mad Dog was talking about female ghosts, and how they appear in all manner of forms and guises. He gave examples. As Zhang listened, he felt he was beginning to see the teacher his friend must once have been.

"Take the *nu gui*," Mad Dog was saying. "A *nu gui* is the spirit of a woman who has been mistreated. She might have committed suicide. She might even have been murdered. Or she might just have led a miserable life. The *nu gui* generally returns to the place where she experienced the abuse. What she is seeking is not revenge but justice. She tends to frighten women, but rarely does them any harm. With men, however, she behaves like a femme fatale..." He gave Zhang a knowing look.

"If you go back in time," he continued, "women's lives were harder than men's. Their voices were seldom heard.

They were more likely to have grievances. Perhaps that's still the case, even today…" He paused under a streetlamp to light a cigarette, and then moved on. "It follows that female ghosts are more plentiful. They have the best stories too—the most poignant stories. In a typical *zhiguai*, a mode of expression now viewed as giving a voice to the voiceless, one finds countless instances of female ghosts."

The two men passed through the compound's eastern gate. Binjiang Avenue was almost deserted, just the occasional goods van or taxi. They crossed the road, their shadows slanting away from them, over the sodium-lit tarmac. Entering Dongchang Riverside Greenland, a strip of park that bordered the river, they set off along a wide path that would lead, eventually, to the bus station on Lujiazui West Road.

Mad Dog picked up where he had left off. "Ghosts aren't necessarily evil," he said, "or even disruptive. Of course, there are ghosts who seem determined to cause trouble, but that's probably because they misbehaved when they were alive. More often than not, though, ghosts are personifications of misfortune or distress."

The two men passed a huge iron grapple bucket that was mounted on a plinth, like a sculpture. Until the late eighties, a coal-processing plant had stood on the land where the park now was.

"In ancient Chinese," Mad Dog went on, "the character for 'ghost' has its root in the character for 'to return'—and there are many reasons for returning, life being so infinitely preferable to death, despite all the suffering and boredom that go with it." Letting out one of his typically humorless chuckles, he flicked his cigarette butt into the bushes. "In the final analysis, ghosts are manifestations of something that is incomplete. That's what a ghost is: someone who still has something to resolve."

Out on the river, a tug surged past. Mud swirled beneath the surface of the water. A faint breeze blew, carrying a sweet, rotten smell that reminded Zhang of chicken feed.

He walked on, with Mad Dog following behind. A few moments later, Mad Dog stopped him by pulling on his arm.

"What is it now?" Zhang asked.

Mad Dog pointed. "Look."

Next to the path, and overgrown with climbing shrubs and creepers, stood a rain-stained concrete structure that had been preserved from the old mining plant, and perched on the high girder that ran horizontally across the front was a large brown owl.

Stepping closer, Mad Dog clapped his hands.

Zhang asked what he was doing, but Mad Dog ignored him.

"Go away," Mad Dog shouted. "Leave us be."

"Mad Dog?" Zhang said.

But Mad Dog kept shouting and clapping and jumping up and down.

Zhang turned his attention to the owl. Though it was gazing at Mad Dog, the old man's antics didn't seem to have any effect on it whatsoever. Its indifference was absolute, disdainful. Otherworldly. Mad Dog whirled off across the path and scavenged in a nearby wastebin, returning with an empty soft drink can. He took aim and flung it at the owl. It missed by at least a foot. The owl didn't even flinch. The same flat platelike face, the same unblinking eyes.

And then, when they were least expecting it, the huge bird shook itself, unfolded its wide wings, and soared off into the darkness over the river. To Zhang, it appeared to have departed on its own terms, as if obeying some decree or summons to which it alone was privy. He found that he was a little in awe of it.

"Did you see that?" Mad Dog said in a low voice.

"An owl." Zhang shrugged.

"Yes, but did you *see*?" Mad Dog turned to him, and his eyes were glittery and wild. "It was *her*."

Zhang stared at his friend. "What? You think—"

"I don't think. I *know*." Mad Dog went and leaned on the railing that bordered the west side of the path. "Some ghosts have the ability to turn themselves into animals, or objects—even into weather. It is believed that they gain strength from such mutations. They don't observe the usual boundaries, you see. Time, space—identity... The skin is not as big a barrier as people think it is. And with female ghosts, there's an extra level of significance. When they transform themselves, it represents a protest or a rebellion. They're challenging all the old patriarchal notions of logic and law."

Zhang joined Mad Dog at the railing. "You're not going to let this go, are you?"

"What I find odd," Mad Dog said, "is that they usually transform themselves into something that seems ordinary or natural, something suited to the environment. You'd think she would have appeared as a duck, or a dog. A gust of wind. Much more unobtrusive. But no. Obviously, she wanted to stand out. She *wanted* me to notice her. In deciding to be an owl, which is a rare sight in these parts, she was signaling her presence."

He bared his teeth as he stared out into the dark.

"And the significance of that particular bird is not lost on me," he continued after a moment. "The owl flies in absolute silence and hunts in the pitch-black. During the Shang dynasty, people used to think of it as the god of night or dreams. They also believed it carried messages between this world and the next. For that reason, the owl appears repeatedly in Shang ritual art. From the sixth century onwards, however, there was a shift in how the owl was viewed. It was no longer seen as benign or helpful. Instead, it became a bad omen. A harbinger of doom. In certain dialects, there is a striking resemblance between the sound an owl makes and the word for 'to dig,' as in 'to dig a grave.' When you hear an owl hooting, you should prepare for a death. Your own, or someone else's. Someone close to you. It's no accident that owls appear on the Han dynasty's burial ceramics."

Zhang was shaking his head, but Mad Dog hadn't finished.

"It was for my benefit. Don't you see? She was telling me she knows I'm onto her." Mad Dog's teeth were gritted now. "It was a warning—a threat..."

"I'm sorry," Zhang said, "but you're blowing this whole thing out of proportion." He glanced at his watch. "It's late. I'm going home."

"Before you go." Reaching into his jacket pocket, Mad Dog produced a small square mirror, a gnarled twig, and a red envelope. "Take these," he said, "and keep them on your person at all times—especially when you're with her."

"What for?"

"They might help to protect you."

Zhang held the twig up to the light.

"It's from a peach tree," Mad Dog said. "Peach trees are often used in exorcism rituals."

Zhang studied the other objects. The mirror had a cheap tin surround that was speckled with rust. He opened the red envelope and peered inside. All it contained was a circular piece of orange peel.

"Humor me," Mad Dog said.

"Well," Zhang said, "it'll hardly be the first time I've done that."

Mad Dog stood facing him, a stooped but dogged figure, the river at his back. "You know something? Sooner or later, you're going to have to start taking me seriously."

"Am I?" Zhang shook his head again and turned away.

At lunchtime the next day, Zhang took a lift to the ground floor of his office building and walked out through the revolving doors. Naemi was already waiting in the pickup area, in a taxi. She was dressed simply, in a short black dress and trainers. A pair of '70s-style sunglasses hid her eyes.

"You're not wearing your contact lenses," he said.

She adjusted her sunglasses. "Yes, I am," she said. "This is just fashion."

He smiled. "I missed you so much."

"I missed you too. How long has it been? Four days?"

"It feels longer."

They set off along Century Avenue. Under the trees that lined the road were groups of street cleaners in their baggy pale blue uniforms. The sky was grayish yellow.

"How was Hong Kong?" he asked.

She talked about a friend of hers, an artist called Kung Lan, who was in the final stages of preparing his new show. It was scheduled to open at her gallery in the first week of October.

"What kind of show?" Zhang asked.

The concept was simple, she told him. Kung had noticed that when young women looked at their phones the expression on their faces tended to be either contemplative or beatific. In his view, they bore a striking resemblance to medieval paintings of the Virgin Mary holding the Christ child. The stark white glow emitted by most phones only added to the atmosphere of reverence. Kung was in the process of creating a series of high-contrast color photographs, which were to be blown up to larger-than-life size. Some of the images were posed. Others had been taken surreptitiously—in the street, or on public transport. Kung had Daoist tendencies, she said. In his late fifties now, he belonged to a generation of artists whose disenchantment with politics was matched by its reservations about a society that was fast becoming materialistic. While his images would take their place in the tradition of Chinese portraiture, which was more than two thousand years old, they would also be seen as an attack on the new consumerism. He was calling the show *Modern Madonnas*.

"It's going to be wonderful," she said. "You should come."

"Maybe I will." Zhang glanced out of the window. They were still heading south. "Where are we going?"

"It's a surprise."

Ten minutes later, they pulled into the forecourt of the Kangqiao Holiday Inn. Zhang paid the driver, then stepped out on to the tarmac. On the other side of the road was a Muslim restaurant and an office that sold real estate. The sun felt hotter than it had in Lujiazui. There seemed to be less air.

Standing in the lobby, he watched as Naemi walked over to reception. He was surrounded by people in green plastic visors and pastel-colored leisure wear. A tour group from another part of China. Foreign tourists would never stay here. It was too far from the center.

When Naemi returned with a room key, they took a lift to the twenty-fourth floor. He wondered why she had chosen such an ordinary, out-of-the-way hotel. Was it anonymity that she was seeking? Did she want to avoid running into anyone they knew? Or was there a thrill to be found in places that were neutral, and characterless? What was happening between them was so vivid, perhaps, that it didn't need much of a backdrop.

He followed her out of the lift and down a corridor. Pink carpet, cream walls. He watched her bare legs, her blonde hair shifting against her shoulders. The small of her back. She seemed so youthful, so healthy. Everything he learned about her while she was elsewhere—the gloomy apartment building, the sinister medical supplies, Mad Dog's ghoulish visions—was undermined or contradicted the moment she appeared. He found it hard to equate one version with the other. In her hand was a white paper shopping bag he hadn't noticed while they were in the taxi.

They arrived in the pool area. Glass walls stretched from floor to ceiling on all sides, the white-and-orange apartment buildings of Kangqiao clustered below, only dimly visible through the milky veil of the heat haze. A silver sculpture stood at the shallow end, its curves reminding Zhang of seashells. The surface of the pool was perfectly smooth. No one else was there.

"Are we going swimming?" he asked.

"You are." She reached into the bag and handed him some trunks and a pair of goggles.

"You're not coming in?"

"I had an eye infection while I was in Hong Kong. I'm still recovering." Her gaze drifted away from him and out over the water. "I swam here for the first time in the spring. It's quite an experience."

A few minutes later, he was standing in the shallow end. Naemi was sitting on a white plastic sun lounger, her elbows on her knees. What did she mean—an *experience*?

"You'll need the goggles," she called out.

He wet the goggles and put them on, then he pushed gently out into the pool.

It wasn't until he was approaching the deep end that it happened. One moment, the bottom of the pool was lined with pale blue tiles, as most pools are, the lanes marked by slender strips of a much darker blue. The next moment, the tiles were replaced by glass, through which he could see the concrete side wall of the hotel dropping away, and the cars in the car park, small as toys. There was the feeling that he might fall, and he had the urge to hold on to something solid. He had stopped swimming, and was floating facedown, like someone snorkeling, and it felt unnatural, and miraculous, though the sense that he might be in danger hadn't gone away. His brain seemed

unable to choose between two equally compelling inter-
pretations of reality.

He started to swim again, keeping his eyes on the
ground twenty-four floors down. When he reached the
deep end, he realized that the last third of the pool ex-
tended horizontally from the side of an otherwise sheer
building, and that it must be visible from the street below.
He would also be visible, a tiny figure suspended in the
water, in the air.

Naemi called out to him again. He couldn't hear what
she was saying.

He swam back to the shallow end, then turned around.
Though he was prepared this time, there was still a part of
his brain that feared he might plummet to his death. But
there was another part that looked forward to the moment
when he swam out beyond the edge of the building, into
space. There was another part that couldn't wait.

Later, when he'd had enough, Naemi wrapped him in
a white bathrobe.

"What do you think?" she asked.

He pushed the hair back off his forehead. "It reminded
me of something that happened the last time we made love."

"Really?"

"I had a kind of fantasy or daydream," he said. "I was
flying over fields or meadows, the grass flattened by the

wind. I flew over some wooden houses too. A blue river. A row of trees. Then the ground dropped away, and there was just the air rushing in my ears, and all that green and blue a long way down..."

Naemi's enthusiasm for the pool had turned into something else—a strange blend of fascination and disquiet.

"That's what you saw?" she said.

"Yes." He looked at her. "Is something wrong?"

"No, nothing's wrong." She seemed to shake herself, and her mood changed again. "When you got into the taxi, I had to make sure you sat on the left side. I didn't want you to see the hotel—the way the pool sticks out from the side of it."

"How did you know I could swim?"

"I didn't."

"What would have happened if I couldn't?"

She smiled. "That would have ruined everything."

When Zhang arrived back at work, his secretary said that his father was waiting for him. It was a day of surprises, it seemed. But then his father made a habit of appearing unexpectedly. He had once told Zhang that unpredictability and the exercise of power were linked. Zhang consulted his watch. 4:25. His father might pride himself on being unpredictable, but Zhang already knew what he was going to say.

In his office, he found his father sitting at his desk, eyes lowered. He moved to the window and leaned on the sill, facing away from the view.

"Long lunch," his father said.

Zhang smiled.

After his swim, Naemi had taken him to a room on the eighteenth floor, where they had made love. Later, as they lay on the bed, half asleep, she asked if he had seen anything this time. Not this time, he said. You weren't too bored, I hope, she said. He laughed. No, he said. I wasn't bored.

His father looked at him and shook his head. "You lack focus. Drive. You always have."

"That's not what they told me at Sauder." Zhang had studied for his MBA at the Sauder School of Business in Vancouver.

"Are you going to contradict everything I say?"

"Only if I disagree with you."

His father pointed to the chair on the other side of Zhang's desk. "Sit down."

Zhang sighed, then took a seat.

For several long seconds, the two men eyed each other. Zhang's father's hair was cut brutally short, as always, and he wore a heavy gold signet ring on the little finger of his left hand. He was shorter than Zhang, and stockier, a physique that had been molded by decades of Sanshou. Unusually for someone of his generation, he didn't smoke. In fact, he had never smoked. Among his colleagues in the Party—he had worked for the ministry of foreign affairs, and had acted as adviser to two successive presidents, Yang Shangkun and Jiang Zemin—his nickname had been "Fresh Air." He was seventy-three, but looked fifteen years younger.

"Where were you?" he asked.

"I went for a swim in Kangqiao," Zhang said. "The traffic was bad on the way back."

His father didn't seem surprised, though Zhang knew he was. The old man never gave anything away. During the years when he moved in political circles, he had cultivated a look of blankness that masked every human emotion, including anger.

"Why Kangqiao?"

Zhang began to describe the pool at the Holiday Inn, but as he spoke he saw his father beginning to lose interest. He had always found it hard to hold his attention, even as a boy.

"Find somewhere closer to the office," his father said. "All the hotels round here have pools."

He didn't compliment Zhang on having taken exercise. Praise fed complacency. Or perhaps he thought Zhang was lying.

"I'm sure you didn't come here to discuss my fitness," Zhang said.

His father leaned forwards, his hands folded on the desk, his thumbs sticking up like chicken wings. "It's your sister."

"What's she done now?"

"She's seeing somebody who isn't suitable."

"That's hardly a first."

"I want you to intervene. She listens to you."

"Not always. Have you spoken to her?"

A smile that was faint and bitter came and went on his father's face. "If I were to speak to her, she'd probably marry him."

Zhang remembered the man Qi Jing had been drinking with in the Glamour Bar, and wondered if he was the "someone" his father was referring to.

"He's younger, I suppose," he said.

His father took out a photo and pushed it across the desk. Zhang nodded. Yes, it was the same man.

"His name is Chu En Li," his father said.

As Zhang studied the man's face, with its insolent expression, he remembered thinking that he seemed familiar, as if he had seen him somewhere before. In that moment, it came back to him. When he arrived at the noodle place in Yangpu district to have breakfast with Jun Wei, he had noticed a man slouching behind the wheel of the black Vito Tourer that was parked outside. Chu En Li was one of Jun Wei's drivers. He wondered if his father knew.

"Is something wrong?" his father asked.

"It's nothing," Zhang said. "I'll see what I can do." He slipped the photo into his jacket pocket. "It won't be easy, though. She's as stubborn as they come."

"Like her mother." The old man rose to his feet and made for the door. Halfway across the room, he stopped and looked at Zhang. "How's your wife? Have you seen her recently?"

"She's fine," Zhang said.

His father grunted, then left.

Zhang worked late into the evening, and it was ten thirty by the time he got home. He sat on his terrace with a whiskey, the living room in darkness behind him. As always, when his mind was empty, he began to think about Naemi. Something had occurred to him that afternoon, not long after his father walked out of the office. According-ing to Johnny Yu, Naemi had been born on September

19th. On the night of the 18th, Zhang had invited her to Yu Yin Tang, and at midnight, when her birthday started, they had been on their way to the Glamour Bar. They had one drink, then Chun Tao drove them to Pudong. Back in his apartment, they danced to a Gloria Estefan record. Later, they slept together, and she told him she was being followed. In the morning, she left early, before he was up. In other words, he had been with her for the first few hours of her birthday, and she hadn't so much as mentioned it. He didn't think it was because she was worried about her age, even though she was older than she had led him to believe. It was more as if her birthday didn't mean anything to her. As if it hadn't registered. *As if she wasn't even aware of it.* But what kind of person isn't aware of their own birthday?

He took out his wallet and found the card the Finnish academic had given him. *Professor Torben Gulsvig. Department of Mechanical, Electronic, and Chemical Engineering. University of Helsinki.* If it was eleven o'clock in southern China, it would be five in the afternoon in Finland. It was as good a time to try him as any. He called the university, and a woman answered. He asked to speak to Professor Gulsvig. The woman put him on hold, with a string quartet to listen to. While he waited, he went indoors and poured himself another whiskey, then he walked back out onto the terrace and leaned on the railing.

"Mr. Zhang," Gulsvig said at last.

The sound of his voice brought back his pale doughy face, his dusty gray-brown hair.

"We met at the Park Hyatt," Zhang said, "in Shanghai—"

"Yes, I remember. How are you?"

"I'm well, thank you." Zhang hesitated. "I have a question."

But where should he begin?

"Mr. Zhang?" Gulsvig said. "Are you still there?"

"When you saw the young woman I was having breakfast with," Zhang said, "you said you felt like you'd seen a ghost."

Gulsvig laughed. "I was terribly jet-lagged that morning. I'd only just arrived. I wasn't seeing straight."

"What if you *were* seeing straight?"

There was a silence on the line before Gulsvig spoke again. "I'm not sure what you're saying."

Zhang wasn't sure either.

"I'm a scientist," Gulsvig went on. "I have a scientific mind." He paused. "Clearly, the woman you were having breakfast with that morning couldn't have been the woman I used to know. I'm in my sixties, and your colleague looked like she was in her twenties."

"Yes, of course. You're right." Zhang decided to approach the subject from a different angle. "Tell me a little about the woman you used to know. Tell me about Nina."

"You want to hear about Nina?" Gulsvig sounded surprised.

"The way you spoke about her made a big impression on me," Zhang said.

"Well, if you insist…"

They had met in the Students' Union, he began, in the summer of 1974, though he had seen her on campus before that. Who could fail to notice a girl who looked like her? He let out a sigh. They were the only Finnish students in their year, which gave him an excuse to talk to her, though it was months before he summoned up the courage.

"Eight months, to be precise," he said, "and several pints of beer." He laughed. "I worshipped her, right from the beginning, but she didn't see me the same way. To her, I was just a friend."

"Did you ever sleep with her?"

Gulsvig laughed again. "You're very direct."

Zhang waited for an answer.

"It was my one great wish to know her intimately,"

Gulsvig said. "I would have given anything for that. But she was always able to keep me at a distance." He paused. "There was a kind of mystery about her. Everybody thought so."

"What was her last name?" Zhang asked.

"Kalman."

"How do you spell that?"

Gulsvig spelled it for him, and he wrote it down. *Nina Kalman*. A different name—but the same initials...

"Did she have a middle name?"

"Vilhelmina." Gulsvig chuckled. "I used to tease her about it."

Inside his chest, Zhang felt a sudden, fierce glow. Somehow he had known that Nina's middle name would begin with "V." What did it prove, though? He wasn't sure.

He asked Gulsvig when he last saw her.

"Ah, that was strange," Gulsvig said.

It was the summer of '76, he went on—the long, slow days after finals. A heat wave, and a sense of drift. No one knowing what the future held. In the middle of all that stillness, Nina's boyfriend, Peter, was found dead in a basement squat in Notting Hill. Rumor had it that he had overdosed, but the whole thing was hushed up. Peter's father was a peer of the realm.

"The next thing I knew, she was gone," Gulsvig said. "She didn't tell me she was going. She didn't even say goodbye. She just left."

"She was in shock, perhaps," Zhang said.

"Perhaps. In any case, I never heard from her again."

"Did you ever look for her?"

"No. It was too painful." Gulsvig paused, as if, for a split second, he had felt that exquisite pain again. "Someone told me she had flown to New York. I don't know if that's true." He paused once more. "The years passed, and in the end I managed to forget about her, I suppose— until, you know, the other day..."

Zhang nodded to himself, then asked Gulsvig if he would be prepared to try to find out what had happened to Nina.

"You really are interested in my story, aren't you, Mr. Zhang?"

"It seems that way," Zhang said.

"I'll do my best. Right now, though, I'm afraid I have to go. I have a class."

"Of course. Goodbye, Professor."

"Goodbye."

Zhang leaned on the balcony, his phone in his hand. Thirty-nine floors below, taillights slid along the curving length of Puming Road, their red glow softened by the fog. Going back over the conversations he'd had with Gulsvig, Zhang was struck by something odd. Whenever he listened to Gulsvig talking about Nina, he had imagined Naemi. In every scene—the meeting in the Students' Union, the drink in a pub near the British museum, the flight to New York—it was always Naemi who he had seen...

Just then, Zhang's doorbell rang. He went back inside.

On opening the door, he found Johnny Yu standing there. Blood ran down the side of his face and neck, some of it already dry and black.

"Johnny!" Zhang said. "What happened?"

Johnny grinned. "It's not as bad as it looks."

Zhang led him to the bathroom.

The cut was above the hairline, about three inches long. He asked Johnny if he had lost consciousness at any point. Johnny didn't think he had. Zhang cleaned the wound with iodine, which made Johnny suck his breath in through his teeth. When the bleeding had stopped, he gave Johnny a clean T-shirt, half a tumbler of whiskey, and a couple of painkillers, and showed him to the spare room. Johnny lay down on the bed. He was flooded with adrenaline, though, and wouldn't stop talking. His girlfriend had attacked him with a meat cleaver, he said. He had bought the cleaver the week before, in the market on

Fangbang Road. It had been her birthday present. She wanted to become a chef one day.

"I didn't know you had a girlfriend." Zhang was leaning against the wall, arms folded.

Johnny nodded. "We've been together for about two years."

"It doesn't seem to stop you chasing other women."

"That's why she was so angry. We'd had sex, and she said there was less sperm than usual. She thinks I've been seeing someone else."

"Wait a moment. She checks your sperm?"

"Only afterwards, when it comes out of her." Johnny stared up at the ceiling. "I always thought it was kind of romantic."

Zhang shook his head in disbelief.

"She could have killed me." Johnny was still gazing at the ceiling, as if his soul had already departed from his body and was floating in the air above him.

"You should go to the hospital," Zhang said. "You could do with some stitches."

Johnny drank a mouthful of whiskey. "I can't believe what she did to the apartment," he said. "She really trashed the place. It's going to cost me a fortune."

"You're sure you don't want me to take you to the hospital?"

"I'll just lie here for a while, if that's all right." Johnny closed his eyes, then opened them again. *"Unendurable is the night's length and a man's wakefulness, / As a few sounds in the moonlight pierce the screened casements."* He rolled his head sideways on the pillow and looked at Zhang. "Li Yu. My namesake."

Zhang said good night and left the room, and when he looked in on Johnny half an hour later Johnny was asleep and breathing through his mouth.

Not so unendurable after all.

8

As soon as Naemi saw Zhang's Jaguar pull up out-side MoCA in People's Park, she knew she had made a mistake. She should never have agreed to go out with him that evening. She should have gone straight home. There were times when she felt her true age was catching up with her, the process sickeningly graphic and speeded-up, like the fast-motion footage of a flower dying. It was a remorseless feeling, something like flu, and it seemed to present all over her body, in every bone and muscle, every cell. Her skin would feel damper, and less elastic, and her hair would seem to lose its luster. It wasn't painful exactly. It was more as if foreboding or dread had taken on a phys-ical form. And whatever appeared to be welling up inside her was all the more powerful for having been suppressed for so very long.

They headed east, towards the Peace Hotel. There was a gala dinner to celebrate the annual Business

Awards, and she was Zhang's guest. As they stopped at the lights on Fuzhou Road, he turned to her and asked if she was ill.

"No," she said. "Just tired."

"Would you rather forget about the dinner?"

She shook her head. "I don't want to spoil your evening."

Zhang's phone rang, and he took the call. As things tilted and she began to fall away, she heard his end of the conversation. *Ten minutes . . . Yes, of course . . . I also have something to discuss . . .*

When she came round, the car was parked at the side of the road, and Zhang and his driver were staring at her.

"I should take you home," Zhang said.

"No, no," she said. "I'm fine. Really." She hauled herself upright and tucked a loose, limp strand of hair behind her ear. "This happens all the time."

Zhang was still looking at her.

"It's all right. I'm not going to die." She let out a little laugh, which sounded strange, even to her. "Do you ever think that death—one's own, I mean—might actually come as a relief?"

She should not be saying such things—she was dropping hints, giving herself away—and yet the truth was so unlikely that she doubted he would ever guess.

Zhang told Chun Tao to drive on, then he turned to her again.

"I worry about you," he said.

"Please don't."

"There's something wrong—"

"It's my blood pressure. It fluctuates. Sometimes I pass out for no reason."

"You've seen doctors?"

"Yes."

"Good doctors?"

"The best."

They pulled up on Nanjing East Road, outside the entrance to the hotel. Someone opened the car door for her, and she got out. The air was cooler, almost refreshing. A briny drizzle fell.

Zhang took her arm as they walked up the steps and into the lobby. "How do you feel?"

"I need the bathroom," she murmured.

"I'll come with you."

"No." She had spoken more sharply than she meant to. With the last of her strength, she softened her voice. "Give me a few minutes on my own."

Watching her carefully, he nodded.

Once in the ladies', she entered a cubicle, locking the door behind her. She put down her bag and removed her jacket. Underneath, she was wearing a black silk top. Hanging the jacket on a hook on the back of the door, she lowered herself onto the closed seat of the toilet, reached into her bag, and took out a flat wooden box with brass catches. She laid it across her thighs, then thumbed the catches and lifted the lid. Snugly housed in velvet of a lustrous midnight blue was a cannula, two coiled lengths of tubing—one rubber, the other clear plastic—and several syringes, each inhabiting its own neat groove. She fastened the rubber tubing tightly round her left arm, above the elbow, then held it between her teeth. The cephalic vein rose into view. She removed the cannula from the box. With a series of deft movements, she attached the transparent plastic tubing to the cannula and unsheathed the needle. Avoiding the scar tissue on the inside of her elbow, she slid the needle into the vein, then used a strip of surgical tape to hold it in place. Once it was secure, she let the rubber tubing fall away and put the end of the plastic tubing to her lips. She turned a miniature tap on the cannula. Fresh dark blood slid up the tube and into her mouth.

When she had swallowed three or four times, she turned off the tap and sank slowly sideways, her head against the cubicle wall, her eyes half closed, the needle still stuck in her arm. The plastic tube fell from between her slightly parted lips. A drop of blood splashed onto her trousers, but since the trousers were black the blood didn't show. She remained in that position for perhaps a minute, then seemed to jerk awake. Sitting upright, she soaked a ball of cotton wool in white spirit, removed the cannula from her arm, and applied the cotton wool to the small hole left by the needle. She felt stronger suddenly, and more vivid. She felt renewed. It was like this every time.

Once the bleeding had stopped, she stuck a round Band-Aid over the wound, then packed the cannula and the lengths of tubing into the box. She would sterilize them later, when she got home. Fastening the catches, she slid the box back into her bag, then lifted the toilet seat, dropped the bloody cotton into the bowl, and flushed. She stepped out of the cubicle. There was nobody around. She stood at a row of spotless sinks and rinsed her mouth with mouthwash. She didn't look into the mirror. There was no point. It would show her nothing but the row of cubicles behind her. An empty room.

9

As Zhang waited in the lobby, the dinner guests paraded past, the men in black tie, the women in haute couture or traditional *qipao*. He was trying to imagine what Naemi was doing in the bathroom. Was she using one of her syringes? If so, what did it contain? Heroin? It would explain why she appeared not to eat—though he had never seen a junkie who looked so healthy. He wondered if he should he share his suspicions with Mad Dog. At the very least, it would put a stop to all his talk of ghosts and ghouls. He also wondered if being with Naemi would get him into trouble. It was just as well he had connections in the Shanghai police. The deputy commissioner's nephew worked for him, and had become a kind of protégé.

"My brother!"

Zhang looked up to see Jun Wei's pockmarked face, his swollen upper body crammed into a white tuxedo, his blue-black hair slicked back. Standing beside him was Xiang Jin, formerly known as Cherry, an ex–bar girl who he had installed in a modern one-bedroom apartment ten minutes' drive from his office.

"You were miles away," Jun Wei said.

The two men shook hands.

Jun Wei looked around. "No date?"

"She's in the bathroom—"

"Sorry to keep you waiting, Zhang."

He felt someone take his arm, and turned to see Naemi at his elbow, her eyes clear and dark, her hair all shining tangles. He stared at her in awe, but also in bewilderment. If it hadn't been for the small red mark near the edge of her right eye, where she had struck the window when she passed out, he would have found it hard to believe that anything untoward had happened.

Jun Wei was also staring, his mouth hanging open. Xiang Jin punched him in the ribs, but he didn't seem to feel it.

"What's wrong with you?" she said. "Have your batteries gone flat?"

Zhang smiled.

"This is the most beautiful foreign girl I have ever seen," Jun Wei said.

"That's very kind," Naemi said in Chinese, "though you do make me sound a bit like a painting or a vase."

Jun Wei stared for a moment longer, in shock, then his head tipped back, and he laughed his eerie, silent laughter.

Xiang Jin hit him again. This time he grunted.

"Show some respect," he said.

She stepped closer, tilting her face up to his. "*You* show some respect."

Jun Wei might act indignant, but Zhang knew that he found Xiang Jin's insolence and vulgarity provocative, in contrast to his wife, who had the build of a fridge, as Jun Wei liked to say, and the temperament as well, and who he kept in a gated residence on the outskirts of the city, along with his twelve-year-old son.

The two couples moved towards the lifts that would take them to Peace Hall, the grand dining room and ball-room on the eighth floor.

Towards the end of dinner, while coffee and liqueurs were being served, Zhang followed Jun Wei to the Nine Heaven Rooftop Terrace on the eleventh floor. Lighting a cigarette, Jun Wei told him Sebastian's contacts had proved excellent. Sebastian's Iranian supplier was government owned, and he was also on good terms with a prominent minister in Tehran. Between them, they ought to be able both to influence the bidding process and to agree on a pricing mechanism.

"I knew I could rely on you," Jun Wei said. "If this deal comes off, you'll stand to make $10,000 a month, which is more than enough to keep your new girlfriend happy—who is stunning, by the way."

"You're getting senile," Zhang said. "Repeating yourself."

Grinning, Jun Wei lit a new cigarette from the old one. "Wasn't there something you wanted to talk to me about?"

Zhang outlined the problem his father had raised with him the week before, then he showed Jun Wei the photo.

"I know this man," Jun Wei said. "He works for me."

"That's what I thought."

"Your father should have come to me directly."

"It's not the way he operates."

"I have great admiration for your father."

"Can you think of how we might resolve the situation?" Zhang asked.

Jun Wei leaned on the black metal railings and looked out over the city. The drizzle had stopped, but the high-rise buildings of Pudong were veiled, all the different-colored neon lights blurring into one another, like melting water-ice.

"There are perhaps ten or fifteen different ways," he said at last.

Zhang waited for him to elaborate.

"Probably we shouldn't kill him..." Jun Wei looked at Zhang across one shoulder, smoke trickling from his nose.

Though shocked, Zhang merely shook his head. "Probably not."

Jun Wei held his gaze for a moment longer, then turned his eyes back to the view. Taking one final drag on his cigarette, he flicked it away into the air. "I could send him to Beijing."

"Not far enough," Zhang said.

"Manila, then."

Zhang thought about that. "How soon could you do it?"

"Would the end of the week be soon enough?"

"You'd do that for me?"

"Of course." Jun Wei's voice seemed distant, almost misty, as if affected by the weather. "You're my brother."

Relieved to have been presented with such a neat solution, Zhang put a hand on Jun Wei's shoulder.

"Thank you," he said.

On returning to the eighth floor, he was approached by a local politician who had once worked with his father, and it was several minutes before he could extricate himself. When he looked for Naemi, he was surprised to see that she was deep in conversation with Jun Wei. What did they have to talk about? He couldn't possibly imagine.

"Were you terribly bored?" he asked her later, as they took a lift down to the lobby.

"No, not at all," she said.

He looked at her.

"And even if I *was* bored," she went on, "there was always the thought of being with you when it was over."

He smiled. She was reprising the remark he had made in the bar at the Park Hyatt.

Once outside, they stood on the promenade, looking towards Pudong. To Zhang, it felt like a place where the scale of things had gone awry. Though the river was about five hundred meters wide at that point, the ships looming out of the drizzle often seemed disproportionately large. He put an arm round Naemi's shoulders and drew her close as a tanker eased past, its hull vertiginous and grazed.

"Will you come back with me," he said, "or are you too tired?"

"I feel much better now," she told him.

"You look much better. We don't have to sleep to-gether, though, if you're not feeling up to it."

"Are you losing interest in me?"

He smiled again. "That's not possible."

Later, as they sat in the back of the Jaguar, he asked what she and Jun Wei had found to talk about.

"I don't remember," she said. "Nothing special."

He didn't believe her. He had seen Jun Wei lean in close to her, as if imparting a confidence, and a few moments later Jun Wei had laughed his strange, silent laughter. There had been an aspect to the conversation that seemed intimate, and secretive. It hadn't looked like "nothing special."

The double row of white lights on the roof of the Renmin Road Tunnel rushed towards them, like a zip unfastening. Like something coming undone. It wasn't late, but the road ahead of them was empty.

His eyes opened. For a few brief moments, he had no recollection of what had happened the night before.

Then he saw Naemi's clothes on the chair by the window, and he remembered. The Business Awards dinner. The Peace Hotel. Where was Naemi, though? He went to his bedroom door, which stood ajar. At the end of a windowless passage, at floor level, was a horizontal strip of light. Someone was in the bathroom. He began to walk. A pulse was beating in front of his eyes. He seemed to be looking through dark water that was being shaken by repeated, powerful explosions. He couldn't help remembering the state she had been in when he picked her up from the gallery in People's Park. What if she'd lost consciousness again? What if she was *dead*? His thoughts were melodramatic, and unlike him. He hardly recognized himself. Oddly, though, he didn't move any faster. When he reached the door, he didn't think to call her name or knock. Instead, he gripped the handle and threw it open.

Afterwards, he realized that what unnerved him about the moment when he appeared in the bathroom doorway was Naemi's reaction—or rather, her absolute failure to react. She didn't cry out, as most people would have done. She didn't even jump. She simply turned towards him, her face absorbed, trancelike. He had the impression that he had disturbed her in the middle of something, though he couldn't begin to guess what that might be. She was sitting on the edge of the bath, and there was blood on her teeth, and on her chin. Blood slid down her arm, towards her wrist. She was naked. Hunched over. He tried to say her name. Nothing came out.

"It's all right," she said. "It's only a nosebleed."

His spine curled, like a piece of paper tossed onto a fire. His skin felt cold. Her words fitted what he was looking at too loosely. Other words lurked behind them, in the shadows. He began to struggle for language of his own. It seemed important that he should speak.

"I woke up," he said. "You were gone."

"I felt it coming on. I should have told you." She used toilet paper to wipe her mouth and chin. "I'm sorry."

She stood up and walked to the sink, where she ran the cold tap and washed the blood off her arm. The scar tissue on the inside of her elbow looked infected. Her forehead was damp with sweat.

"I get nosebleeds all the time," she said. "I always have. For as long as I can remember." Her voice was calm and uninflected, like someone who was half asleep. She looked at him sidelong, across one shoulder. "Do I disgust you?"

"No. The opposite."

She moved towards him, her face seeming to darken as she blocked out the stark white light above the sink. There were no other lights on in the room.

"Kiss me," she said.

They kissed. There was the taste of blood in her mouth, warm and claustrophobic, and he began to feel giddy. The floor was tilting upwards. Either that, or she herself was tilting.

She broke away. "I think I need a shower. Do you mind?"

"No. Of course not."

"You go back to bed. I'm fine now."

In the bedroom he stood at the window, staring down at Puming Road. He watched the gaps between the cars, noticing how they kept widening and narrowing. He imagined the gaps as objects in themselves. Alternate beings. Hidden entities.

Somewhere far below, a siren ghosted through the night.

When Naemi climbed into bed, her hair still wet from the shower, she wanted to make love. She kept murmuring his name. Her lips burned his skin. She seemed feverish, and he wondered, once again, if she was ill.

Later, when he was dozing off, he thought he heard her say something else. "What was that?"

"I love you."

The words had come from nowhere, and he was too taken aback to respond.

"Did I say the wrong thing?" she murmured.

"No," he said.

She began to tremble.

He looked at her in the dark, but there was only the back of her head and the polished curve of her right shoulder. She was facing away from him. "Are you crying?"

"Could you hold me?"

He had imagined that he was beginning to get her measure—her insistence on privacy, her self-sufficiency—but this was a side of herself that she had not revealed, or even hinted at—until now. He took her in his arms and held her tight.

"It's all right," he murmured. "Everything's all right."

Her breathing slowed and deepened, as if she was sinking towards sleep. He had all kinds of questions for her, but they would have to wait.

Two days later, on Saturday morning, Naemi texted him to say that something had come up. She had to fly to London, she said. She would be gone for about a week, but he would be in her heart. He was disappointed, not least because it was almost Golden Week, which was a national holiday, and he had been hoping they might travel somewhere together—Lijiang, perhaps, with its magical Old Town and its complex history. He texted back, suggesting that he might visit her in London, but her response was not encouraging. It was a work trip, she said. She would have no time for him. He pictured her on the plane to London, the reading spotlight shining down on her, and people all around her in the darkness, sleeping.

Later, as Chun Tao drove him to the Athens Palace, the bathhouse in the center of Pudong, he read her text again. *You'll be in my heart.* He remembered how she had told him she loved him during the early hours of Thursday morning, and how she had asked him if he would hold her. She had seemed unlike herself, and he was still struggling to interpret her behavior as he walked up the wide steps of the bathhouse and through the lobby, with its faux-Greek statues, its ornate, gold-trimmed armchairs, and its ivory-colored grand piano.

While he was undressing, his phone rang. It was Laser, asking if their practice session was still on. He told Laser that it was. Mad Dog had canceled their session the previous weekend—he'd had flu—but he had called

Zhang earlier to say he was feeling better. For the next hour, Zhang moved between the Pool of General Flowers, which was heated to 44 degrees Celsius, and the cold plunge pool. Afterwards, he walked over to the massage tables, where a man with huge, muscular arms scrubbed him all over, removing the dead skin. Later, when he had showered, he went upstairs and lay on a bed in a darkened room. He slept for almost an hour. By the time he left the building, he felt much more relaxed, his mind cleansed of all anxiety and unease.

As they drove to the recording studio, Chun Tao asked Zhang for some advice. It was his girlfriend, he said. She wanted to get married and have a child, but he wasn't sure if he was ready.

"Do you love her?" Zhang asked.

Chun Tao nodded. "Yes."

"Then you have two choices. Either you give her what she wants, or you break up with her."

"I was hoping there might be another option."

"You can delay things, but only if you promise to give her what she wants in the end. If you stay with her, it'll probably happen anyway. She'll wear you down." Zhang paused. "It may be what you want too. You just don't know it yet."

Chun Tao nodded slowly.

Zhang looked out of the window. Sichuan Middle Road. Though there was still some gray light in the sky, it seemed dark at street level. A girl drew alongside on a moped. She wore a pink crash helmet, and a small dog lay between her feet on a piece of carpet.

"The trouble is, it's hard to keep saying no," Zhang went on. "'No' weighs a lot, like lead. It's hard to keep heaving it into your mouth. But 'yes'? It's light as air. What's more, there's the reward of how her face will change when you come out with it—how you'll suddenly be everything she hoped you'd be..."

They had stopped at a red light, and Chun Tao looked at Zhang in the rearview mirror. "That's amazing. Thank you."

In the silence that followed, Zhang felt a distaste for himself. Who was he to be offering advice? What did he know, really?

A few moments later, they pulled up outside the alley where the recording studio was. Mad Dog was already there, leaning against the wall by the entrance in an old gray suit and a green shirt. He was smoking. Zhang opened the car door, and the smell of the Shanghai afternoon flowed in. Warm tarmac, fermented fruit. And drains, always drains. He paused, with one foot on the pavement, the other still in the car.

"You know what, Chun Tao? Forget everything I said. It's always a mistake to generalize."

Chu Tao turned and looked at him.

"Except for the bit about yes and no. There might be some truth in that." Zhang took out his wallet, peeled off several 100 RMB notes and held them in the gap between the two front seats. "You can have the rest of the day off. Take your girlfriend to dinner. Go dancing."

"You're sure you don't need me later?"

"I'm sure."

Chun Tao got out of the car and opened the boot and handed Zhang his guitar. As Zhang walked over to where Mad Dog was standing, he heard the Jaguar pull away.

Mad Dog took his cigarette from between his lips and looked at it. "How's the girlfriend?"

"She's in London."

"Anything you want to tell me?"

"Maybe later."

"There's a kind of immortality that originates in trauma," Mad Dog said. "It's known as an 'awakening.' I've been thinking about this in relation to your friend. I've been wondering if something terrible happened to her. That's why she's still alive—or appears to be. She wants justice or retribution. She cannot rest." He looked at Zhang, then shrugged and threw his cigarette away.

Zhang followed Mad Dog through the open door and down a flight of gritty concrete steps into the basement. A couple of young musicians sprawled on the battered brown leather furniture with Cyborg, the sound engineer who ran the place. They were drinking cans of Tsingtao.

Cyborg looked around as Zhang and Mad Dog entered. "Your drummer's already here."

While Mad Dog fetched his double bass, which he kept in a storage cupboard at the back, Zhang opened the door of the studio they rented. Laser was sitting at his drum kit, playing a game on his phone.

"Lao Zhang," he said. "I hear you've written a new song."

Zhang nodded. "It needs some work."

As he snapped the catches on his guitar case, an idea occurred to him. He asked Laser if he was coming for a drink after the session.

"Of course he's coming for a drink," Mad Dog said, hauling his instrument into the room. "What kind of question's that?"

Laser grinned.

Leaving the studio again, Zhang went back up the stairs to a place where he had coverage and rang his sister. When she answered, he asked if she would like to meet that evening.

"I'm not sure I'm in the mood," she said.

And Zhang knew why. Jun Wei had been as good as his word. He had called Zhang to let him know that Qi Jing's boyfriend was on his way to Manila. Later, Zhang had checked social media. On WeChat, Qi Jing had made several references to Chu En Li's abrupt and unexpected departure. Zhang turned to face the stairwell wall. The white paintwork was grubby, defaced. Someone had written BEER & CHICKEN & ROCK & ROLL next to a heating pipe.

"You might feel better if you're out," he said. "Otherwise you'll just lie in bed eating sunflower seeds and watching bad TV."

"You're not going to lecture me, are you?"

"I'll leave that to our father."

"Right." Qi Jing sighed.

"Come and have a drink. It's nothing fancy—just me and a couple of musician friends." He gave her the address of the bar they always went to. "We won't be getting there till nine."

Four hours later, Zhang, Mad Dog, and Laser walked out into the night. A warm wind was blowing, and loose sheets of paper whirled about, trapped in the narrow, dead-end funnel of the alley. When they reached the main road, they turned right, past a fast-food outlet. Red sparks flew from the end of Mad Dog's cigarette.

"That was a good session," Laser said.

Mad Dog grunted.

They had started with some old favorites—"Love in Vain," "Champagne and Reefer," and John Lee Hooker's "Highway 13"—but they had spent at least half the time on Zhang's new song, which they were calling "Ghost Woman Blues."

Once in the bar, they climbed a flight of stairs and sat at their usual table, on a mezzanine. Their conversation drifted, punctuated by noise coming from the TV below.

They were already on their second drink when Qi Jing appeared. She was dressed in a black T-shirt and designer jeans, and a chunky Rolex encircled her slender wrist.

She looked at Zhang, then she looked around. "You weren't joking when you said it wasn't fancy."

Mad Dog and Laser grinned, as if she had paid them both a compliment.

"This is Qi Jing," Zhang said. "My sister."

He went downstairs and bought her a vodka and tonic, which was the only thing she ever drank. When he returned, she and Laser were talking about the recent Grand Prix in Shanghai. It seemed they were both motor-racing fans.

Mad Dog nudged Zhang in the ribs. "You didn't say your sister was coming."

"Let them talk," Zhang said.

"What are you up to?"

Zhang glanced at Laser, who was telling Qi Jing about his other band, the Dense Haloes, and how they had toured Korea and Japan.

"You should come and see us," he said.

Qi Jing was watching him, her right elbow on the table, her hand cupping her cheek and chin. "Why? Will it change my life?"

It was hard to believe that she was almost thirty-five. She looked—and behaved—like a much younger woman.

"About your blonde friend," Mad Dog said, staring down into his glass.

"What about her?" Zhang said.

"How long is she in London for?"

"A week."

Mad Dog knocked his whiskey back. "Something else to bear in mind about ghosts. They don't view time as we do. For a ghost, time is nonlinear. The present isn't a development of the past, but a palimpsest through which the past continues to assert itself. That's why the woman in the story I told you could be standing in a shop, buying groceries, and also lying dead in her grave. Both aspects of the story are true."

"They can appear in two places at once?"

"Yes."

Zhang drank from his bottle of beer.

"I told you to tell me if anything unusual happens," Mad Dog said. "Have you noticed anything?"

Zhang hesitated.

"You have, haven't you."

Zhang described what happened the last time he saw Naemi—the loss of consciousness, the miraculous recovery, the nosebleed in the middle of the night.

Mad Dog's whole body tensed. "This changes everything."

"How do you mean?" Zhang said.

"Get me another drink."

When Zhang returned with a double whiskey—Qi Jing and Laser didn't want anything—Mad Dog told him that blood-drinking ghosts were a breed apart. Another proposition altogether.

"I knew you'd jump to conclusions," Zhang said.

"When they drink someone's blood," Mad Dog went on, "they generally take on the appearance and energy of the person in question. Drinking blood allows them to be human. No, more than human. They're faster than ordinary people. Stronger too. They seem *enhanced*."

"This is all just superstition," Zhang said. "People out in the sticks might believe it, but not here, in Shanghai."

But the word his friend had used—*enhanced*—had triggered something. He thought of the way Naemi had moved towards him when she found him outside the museum, and the speed with which she had reached the lifts when she left the Chairman Suite after their first night together.

"The blood you mentioned," Mad Dog said. "Was it yours?"

"Of course not," Zhang said. "You think I wouldn't have noticed?"

"Whose was it, then?"

"I told you. She had a nosebleed."

"And you believed her?"

"Not exactly." Zhang hesitated again. "I felt she was lying, but I couldn't work out what the truth might be. I still can't."

Mad Dog took a Shanghai Gold from the packet on the table and rolled it pensively between his fingers. It was the first time Zhang had admitted that something might be wrong.

"Why did you feel she was lying?" Mad Dog asked.

"It was the position she was in when I appeared in the doorway. It was as if I had caught her doing something secret—or something intensely private." Zhang paused, thinking back. "What she was saying made perfect sense, but everything I was looking at seemed to contradict it. She wasn't *behaving* like someone with a nosebleed. There was a strange atmosphere in the room—"

Qi Jing reached across the table and touched his arm. "We're thinking of going somewhere else. Somewhere a little less—"

"I know," Zhang said. "This is a pretty awful place."

"You don't mind? We've hardly spoken."

"We'll catch up later. I'll call you."

She stood up and came round the table and spoke into his ear. "I like your friend."

Zhang smiled.

When Qi Jing and Laser had left, Zhang bought Mad Dog another whiskey and a beer. Mad Dog swallowed the whiskey and put the glass down carefully, as if he was making a move in a game of chess.

"Do your feet hurt?" he asked.

Zhang stared at him.

"Blood-drinking ghosts," Mad Dog said. "They draw your blood out through the soles of your feet. Usually at night, while you're asleep."

"My feet are fine."

"No sensitivity? No puncture holes?"

Zhang shook his head.

Mad Dog drank some beer, then he began again.

"This is what I know. When a ghost drinks someone's blood, he not only kills that person. He steals that person's identity. He becomes that person. He literally *takes the shape* of the person he has killed."

Zhang thought back to the breakfast at the Park Hyatt, and Gulsvig's face when he saw the young woman he had been in love with half a century before. It was a physical impossibility, of course—unless...

"You're not listening," Mad Dog said.

"Sorry. What did you say?"

"You can't judge by appearances." Eyes lowered, Mad Dog was turning his whiskey glass on the table, turning and turning it, his gray hair falling forwards, across his face. "On the outside, the ghost is the person he has killed. On the inside, he's a ghost. He's actually dead twice over.

A blood-drinking ghost is a murderer—by definition. At least, that's how it works in China."

Zhang thought about mentioning Gulsvig, but he was worried the story would only prove Mad Dog's theory. There was even a part of Zhang that wished he hadn't talked about the blood. Why? Because he wanted Naemi to be who she claimed to be. Because he couldn't contemplate the alternative. Because he loved her. That was what he realized in that moment, even though Mad Dog would tell him he wasn't thinking straight. You can't love a woman like that, Mad Dog would say. You can't love a *ghost*.

Zhang finished his beer. "I need to go."

"I'll come with you." Mad Dog stood up, swaying a little as he buttoned his suit jacket. "Is your car here?"

"Not tonight."

Outside the bar, they stood on the pavement, Mad Dog looking to the east, his hands clasped behind his back.

"Walk with me," he said.

Zhang wondered how many drinks Mad Dog had had. Six, at least. Maybe more.

They set off in the direction of Suzhou Creek. The warm wind had died down. They passed a small group of men on a street corner, sitting on upended crates and boxes, playing cards for money. A fruit shop was still open. A man in a T-shirt that said GRENADE dozed on a green plastic lounger by the entrance. Once, Mad Dog tripped on a tree root, but Zhang caught him before he fell. The smell he gave off was stale and bitter, like old bok choy.

"Are you angry with me?" Mad Dog asked.

"No," Zhang said. "I'm not angry."

"Blood-drinking ghosts aren't usually female. That's very rare. Unheard of, really." He stopped and turned to Zhang, a strained look on his face. "If what I suspect is true, then you're in danger."

"You're serious, aren't you."

"Do you still have the mirror I gave you," Mad Dog said, "and the little piece of peach wood?"

Zhang nodded.

They crossed Suzhou Creek. From the middle of the bridge, Zhang could just make out the Embankment Building, dark brown and bulky, almost brooding. Naemi would not be home tonight. She would be on her way to London—or perhaps she was already there...

They passed the New Asia Hotel, then turned right, onto Tanggu Road. It was darker suddenly, and there were fewer shops. After walking for another five minutes, Zhang noticed a paved area overhung with huge dark trees. A silver ghetto blaster stood on the ground, playing a waltz, and three or four young couples in T-shirts and jeans were dancing formally nearby. Mad Dog stopped to light a cigarette.

"All right," Zhang said. "Let's say, for the sake of argument, that she's a ghost. What's the worst that could happen?"

Mad Dog remained quite still—except for the hand holding the cigarette, which trembled slightly. "She could feed off you. Take you over."

"What would you do, if you were me?"

Mad Dog's eyes were on the dancers. "I'd have nothing to do with her. I'd cut off all contact." He paused. "I'd run a mile."

"It's not so easy."

"No. Probably not." Mad Dog glanced at Zhang and saw that he was smiling. "What's so funny?"

"The idea of you running."

A taxi's green light appeared up ahead, and Zhang held out an arm. As the taxi slowed and stopped, he asked Mad Dog if he would like a lift. Mad Dog pressed his lips together in a straight line and shook his head, as if Zhang had suggested they indulge in some unbelievable and slightly disgusting luxury.

"I'll walk," he said. "The night air will do me good."

"You're not too drunk?"

Mad Dog dropped his cigarette in the gutter, then moved off along the pavement, heading north, his right hand lifted in the air above his shoulder. Beyond him, the young couples danced beneath the overhanging trees.

Once in the taxi, Zhang checked his messages. He found a text from Qi Jing: *Your drummer's cute.* He nodded to himself. It seemed his ruse had worked. But there was nothing from Naemi. On a whim—and despite all Mad Dog's warnings—he rang the number Johnny Yu had given him, only half expecting it to work. She didn't answer. Five minutes later, he tried again, and there she was suddenly, so clear that she could have been sitting right beside him.

"Hello?"

"It's Zhang," he said. "Where are you?"

"I'm in London. On my way to an appointment."

"You sound so close."

"I wish." She laughed quickly. "How did you get my number?"

"I asked you the same thing once. You didn't answer."

There was a silence on the other end.

"Are you all right?" she said after a while. "Your voice is a bit peculiar."

Zhang looked through the window of the taxi. A man with no right arm stood outside a pet shop, smoking.

"I'm tired, that's all." He paused. "Sometimes it doesn't feel real, what's happening between us."

"How do you mean?"

"There's something I can't get hold of, even if we're in the same room. Even if we're in bed together."

"Is it because I'm not what you're used to?"

"I don't think it's that."

"What, then?"

"It's difficult. Mad Dog thinks—" Zhang bit his lip. He had been trying not to mention Mad Dog, but he'd had too many drinks, and it had just slipped out.

"What does Mad Dog think?" Her voice was light and curious, though he thought he could detect a hardness underneath, as if she was upset but pretending not to be.

"Nothing," he said. "I told you before. He has some pretty far-fetched ideas."

She fell silent again. In the background, he thought he heard a car go by. He checked his watch. In London, it would be rush hour.

"Naemi? Are you still there?"

"He drinks a lot," she said, "doesn't he."

Zhang nodded. "Yes."

"He should be careful." She seemed to be on the point of saying something else, but checked herself. "Listen, I'm about to go underground. I'm probably going to——"

Her voice cut out. He had lost her.

Taking his phone from his ear, he held it in his hand and stared straight ahead. The mouth of the Xinjian Road Tunnel filled the taxi's windscreen. He, too, was about to go underground.

10

THAT AFTERNOON, dressed in dark, nondescript clothing and wearing a black beanie over her hair, Naemi had
followed Zhang to a recording studio in an alley off Beijing East Road. Four hours later, she had followed him and
his two musician friends to a nearby bar. As she watched
the entrance from a position she had taken up on the far
side of the street, she was surprised to see Zhang's sister,
Qi Jing, appear. She left before they did—with Laser, the
drummer. It was almost midnight by the time Zhang and
Mad Dog emerged. This was the moment she had been
waiting for. But she had another surprise in store. The
two men didn't separate, as she had expected. Instead,
they moved off in the direction of Suzhou Creek. Once
again, she followed, but this time she was frowning. Was
Zhang going to walk Mad Dog home? She hoped not.

After an hour, the two men came to a halt. Duck-
ing into an unlit doorway, she watched as they stood at a

junction, talking. She was too far away to hear what was being said. Instead, the measured, jaunty notes of a waltz floated through the air to her. There were young people dancing in formal couples beneath the trees. It was oddly stately, quaint too, like a scene from another era. Turning her attention back to the two men, she saw Zhang raise an arm. A taxi pulled up beside him. Would they both get in? She held her breath. They exchanged a few more words, then Mad Dog walked away, leaving Zhang to climb into the taxi by himself.

"At last," she murmured.

She waited until the taxi turned the corner, then she followed Mad Dog down a wide road that led over a canal. She passed a man selling barbecued meat on bamboo skewers, and for a split second she was back near the beginning of her life, crouching behind a wooden panel in the dark...Just then, she felt her phone vibrate inside her pocket. She looked at the screen. Zhang was calling—from the taxi, presumably. But how had he got hold of her number? She certainly hadn't given it to him. She stared at his name, then pressed Decline. Putting her phone away, she looked up. Mad Dog had disappeared.

In a panic, she began to hurry along the pavement. The streetlamps gave off a dim brownish-yellow light, and there were long intervals between them. Could he be home already? She prayed this wasn't so. She passed an estate agent, which was still open. Who bought property at one in the morning? Even after a decade in the city, there were things that mystified her. Up ahead was a dingy restaurant. She slowed as she approached. Inside, Mad Dog was sitting on a chair upholstered in purple fabric with a large bottle of beer in front of him. He was the only customer.

Stepping back from the window, Naemi crossed the road and sat down on a bench. She would wait for Mad Dog to finish his beer. She didn't think it would take too long. While she was waiting, her phone began to vibrate. It was Zhang again. This time she decided to answer, reminding herself, before she did, that she was in London, and that London was eight hours behind Shanghai.

If Naemi ended the call abruptly, it was because she had glimpsed a movement in the corner of her eye. Mad Dog had lurched to his feet. As he paid for his beer, tossing a few coins onto the table, she eased off the bench and hid behind a parked car. Mad Dog came to a standstill outside the restaurant, by the door. He was feeling for something in his pocket. Why had she answered the second time Zhang called? She supposed that she couldn't resist the chance to hear his voice. She had been missing him. But what if he had recognized the sound of Shanghai in the background? What if it occurred to him that she might not be in London at all—that the work trip she had mentioned was a fabrication? She shook her head. She had taken such a risk. Still, it seemed she might have got away with it. In the meantime, Mad Dog was having trouble guiding the flame of the lighter towards the end of his cigarette. Finally, he managed it. Inhaling deeply, he muttered something to himself and moved off along the pavement. She waited a few moments, then crossed the street.

As she followed Mad Dog, she thought he was more unsteady than before. The beer must have gone straight to his head. She stared at his hunched back with such intensity it was a wonder he didn't sense her presence. She was thinking of the night she met him, at Yu Yin Tang. There had been a few moments when she was alone with him, on the terrace. She had been gazing out into the park when he said something to her, but he was already drunk and slurring his words and she hadn't understood. Then he said it again, more clearly this time. *You're not welcome here.* She told him she had been invited. She was Zhang's guest. He looked at her quickly, as if looking was hazardous, then lowered his eyes. *I know what you are.*

Arriving at a roundabout with a single, solitary tree in the middle, she watched Mad Dog take the first turning on the left, which curved off between run-down, two-story houses. She didn't think she could delay much longer. Switching to the other side of the road, she walked faster. She kept her head down, but glanced sideways every now and then to make sure he hadn't vanished into a building or an alley. She couldn't afford to lose him, not now. From behind a steel roll-door came the clucking and squabbling of chickens, shut in for the night.

Once she was some distance ahead of him, she took off her wool hat and shook out her hair, then crossed the road again. He was still fifty meters away, but moving in her direction. She stood on the pavement, facing him.

He didn't notice her until the last moment, when he was only a few feet away. Lifting his eyes from the ground, he came to a standstill and swayed a little, mouth gaping.

"What are *you* doing here?"

"I couldn't sleep," she said. "I live nearby. Just over there." She gestured vaguely to the west.

The noise he made in the back of his throat suggested either that he didn't believe her or that he couldn't care less. Pushing past her, he moved on up the street. She turned and followed. He was leaning forwards, teeth gritted, like a man walking into a headwind.

"What is it that you have against me?" she asked.

He kept walking and said nothing. Though tired and drunk, he seemed intent on getting home. She was struck by his determination. His will. She remembered Zhang telling her that Mad Dog was indestructible. Walking next to him, she felt that indestructibility.

"I said, what have you got against me?"

He whirled around. "I'm not talking to you." His hands were up in front of him, palms facing out. He was breathing through his mouth. They had stopped next to a shop where you could get keys cut.

"Do you think I'm a threat to Zhang Guo Xing?" she said. "Is that what's bothering you?"

"You shouldn't be with him."

"It's only for a short time. Then I'll be gone."

"A short time is already too long."

She took hold of his sleeve. "Why are you being so difficult?"

"Let go." He shook her off. "You're not real," he said. "You're a ghost. You don't exist."

"A *ghost*? What does that even mean?"

Once again, he pushed past her. Once again, she followed.

They were walking away from the crossroads, away from the lights. Every now and then, between the darkened shop fronts, there was a gate made of upright metal bars that opened onto a network of alleys and passageways. The houses were old and poorly built and crammed together. Soon he would turn in through one of these gates, and then it would be too late. She moved in front of him, blocking his path, not yet knowing what she would do.

"I'm not telling you again," he snarled, his spit landing on her cheek. "Leave me alone—"

"Or what?" she said.

He swung a fist at her, and light exploded at the edge of her field of vision, bright as a camera flash. Though he had knocked her to the ground, she picked herself up quickly. He came at her again. This time she was ready. Stepping inside the next punch he threw, she placed a hand on his chest and pushed with all her strength. As he staggered backwards, his heel caught on the raised lip of a paving stone, and he toppled into a dark space that appeared, just then, to have opened up behind him. She stood quite still. There was a gap in the railings, and three shallow steps led down to a small flat area. Mad Dog was lying slumped against the front wall of a brick building. She looked left and right. There were no people about. No cars. The street was dimly lit, trees overhead.

Approaching the gap in the railings, she saw that Mad Dog's eyes were open, and he was breathing. He didn't seem to be hurt—and even if he was he wouldn't feel it, she thought, not with all that alcohol inside him. To his right, the steps led down again, but much more steeply. At the bottom was the padlocked entrance to a basement.

She leaned over him. "Are you all right?"

His lips moved, but she couldn't hear what he was saying. She leaned closer.

"Go to hell," he said.

Straightening up, she twisted her hair into a loose bun and pulled on her black wool hat, then she turned around. The stucco building opposite looked derelict, its ground-floor windows boarded up. It must once have been a warehouse or a factory. She decided not to go back the way she had come. At the crossroads, there were shops that were still open. There was also a man selling street food from a stall. She didn't want to give anyone a second chance to see her or remember her. Leaving Mad Dog where he was, she set off in the other direction. Her left eye was beginning to swell up, and there was a steady buzzing in her ear. She had hoped he might listen to her, and that they might reach some kind of accommodation. A temporary truce, at least. But she had been naïve. She should have realized that his black view of her was un-shakable, and that nothing she could say would make the slightest difference. After all, there was a sense in which he was right about her. He was wrong, but he was also right.

Near Linping Road metro station, she saw a taxi with its green light on. Climbing in, she sat behind the driver, out of range of his rearview mirror. She told him to take her to the Broadway Mansions Hotel. She didn't want him knowing where she lived. She didn't want anybody know-ing. The taxi rocked and swayed through the dark streets. Whenever they slowed down or stopped, the vicious chat-ter of cicadas forced its way through the half-open window.

11

ON MONDAY NIGHT, at nine o'clock, Zhang was following the path that led to his building when he noticed a woman standing beneath one of the streetlamps that were placed at regular intervals throughout the grounds. The brightness of the light falling on her from above heightened the chalky pallor of her limbs and the red of her shift dress. Her black hair had an eerie sheen, as if it was in a display case, under glass. When he drew close, he saw that she had been crying.

"Are you all right?" he said.

She jerked, then touched her fingertips to the skin under her eyes. "Mr. Zhang?"

It was his turn to be startled. "Ling Ling? Is that you?"

She nodded.

"I didn't recognize you," he said.

He had only met her once or twice, and then only briefly. She'd not made much of an impression.

"I tried to call you," she said.

"You didn't leave a message," he said. "I checked my voice mail a few minutes ago."

"It's about Gong Shen."

"What about him?"

"He didn't come home. After he went to meet you."

"But that was two days ago—" He stared at her. "You haven't seen him since Saturday?"

"No." She began to cry again, soundlessly, one hand over her eyes.

Zhang suggested they talk indoors.

Once in his apartment, Ling Ling stood in the middle of the living room. Her dress was cheap and poorly made, and the shape of her toes showed through the thin fabric of her shoes. He led her to the sofa, where she sat upright with her knees together and her hands on either side of her thighs. She reminded him of someone sitting on the edge of a swimming pool, prior to getting in. He offered her a glass of water. She shook her head.

"Where's your daughter?" he asked.

"I left her with my mother."

"Good."

He told her what he knew—that he and Mad Dog had left the bar on Beijing East Road at the same time, that they had walked together for an hour or so, and that when he said he was catching a taxi Mad Dog had refused the offer of a lift. This was in the early hours of Sunday morning, he said. About one thirty.

"He'd been drinking," Ling Ling said.

Zhang nodded. "He always has a few drinks after a practice session. We all do."

"He usually shouts at me when he gets home." She looked at Zhang with no expression.

He asked if she had called the police.

"I thought I would come to you first," she said. "You're his closest friend."

This came as a surprise to Zhang, but he concealed it. He told Ling Ling that he would contact the police himself. He would do everything he could. In the meantime, she should go home and look after her daughter. He reminded her that Mad Dog often had trouble getting home. The time he was hit by a moped, for instance.

Ling Ling sat on the sofa without moving, and he had the feeling she hadn't heard a word he had said.

After a few long moments, her eyes lifted slowly to his, and he felt something unexpected pass between them. It was fear. She wasn't frightened for Mad Dog, though, or for herself. She was frightened for him.

"In the last few days, he talked about you all the time," she said. "He thought you were in danger."

"I know," Zhang said. "He told me."

Ling Ling was still looking at him with that oddly expressionless face. "I knew something was going to happen," she said slowly, "but I thought it would happen to you."

Later, when she had gone, Zhang stood by the window. Mad Dog was out there somewhere—lost, or hurt, or ill. He wondered what Ling Ling was thinking. His skin prickled as he recalled what she had said. *I knew something was going to happen, but I thought it would happen to you.* She had *hoped* it would happen to him—rather than to Mad Dog, anyway. It amounted to a kind of curse.

He took out his phone and called the deputy commissioner of police. When the deputy commissioner answered, he apologized for disturbing him at such a late hour.

"No problem." The deputy commissioner spoke in a voice made gravelly by years of drinking *baijiu* and smoking untipped cigarettes. "How's that nephew of mine?"

"He's hardworking and responsible—a real credit to his family," Zhang said. "I foresee a promotion in the near future."

"I'm glad he's proving of some use to you, Mr. Zhang. But why are you calling? Is there something I can help you with?"

"I'm sorry to bother you with this, but a friend of mine has been missing for nearly forty-eight hours, and I'm beginning to worry."

He gave the deputy commissioner Mad Dog's home address and a physical description, and he pinpointed the junction where he and Mad Dog had parted in the early hours of Sunday morning. Whatever had happened, he said, must have happened somewhere between the two locations. The deputy commissioner promised to look into the matter personally. After thanking him and wishing him a good evening, Zhang ended the call, then he picked up his keys and wallet and left the apartment.

There was a taxi parked on the street near the main entrance to the compound. The driver had fallen asleep. His head was tipped back, and he was breathing through his mouth. Zhang tapped on the window. The driver's eyes slid open. He yawned and wound the window down. Cold air from inside the car pushed softly against Zhang's face.

"Tanggu Road," he said.

Half an hour later, the taxi dropped him at the place where he and Mad Dog had said goodbye. No young couples dancing tonight, just an empty paved area, and leaves shifting on the enormous, overhanging trees. As he set off up Tanggu Road, he remembered how he had found Ling Ling, standing beneath the streetlamp. At first, he had thought she was some kind of apparition. Then he thought that perhaps a woman who was disturbed had strayed into the grounds. He remembered how Ling Ling sat on the sofa, not saying anything, her face quite blank. He didn't think it was anxiety or nervousness. It was how she was—naturally. He had often teased Mad Dog about having a girlfriend half his age, but now he saw that she might not be so easy to live with. Could that explain why Mad Dog always turned down the offer of a lift? It wasn't stubbornness or pride. It might just be that he was in no great hurry to get home.

Zhang came to a row of shops and restaurants, only two or three of them still open. Beyond him, the road stretched away into darkness, balls of fuzzy yellow light where the streetlamps were. A man in sunglasses walked past with a white dog on a lead. There was a grating of cicadas, a burst of almost wooden sound that rose to a crescendo and then died away again for no apparent reason. It seemed hotter now than when he had got out of the taxi, even though it was already after midnight.

If Mad Dog had wanted to avoid going home, he might have stopped for something to eat or drink. He might have stopped at any one of these places. Zhang walked into the first restaurant he came to, which was empty. The young waitress was practicing with a rainbow-colored Hula-Hoop, her eyes fixed on a TV high up on the wall.

"Miss?"

She let the Hula-Hoop drop to the floor with a clatter and then stepped over it. Zhang described Mad Dog and asked if she had seen him on Saturday night. She shook her head.

Zhang tried a massage parlor, a shop selling air conditioning, and an estate agent, but nobody could tell him anything. As he walked on, he thought of how he first met Mad Dog. One Thursday night, not long after he moved to Shanghai, he called in at the House of Blues and Jazz, and sometime in the early hours of Friday morning a three-piece band took the stage. Two white Americans were playing the guitar and drums, but the man on the double bass was Chinese. Afterwards, Zhang went up to Mad Dog and told him how much he had enjoyed the set. Buy me a drink, was Mad Dog's response. Zhang smiled. Some things never change. They started talking, and there came a point when Zhang told Mad Dog that he should be playing with musicians who were at least as good as he was. Like who? Mad Dog wanted to know. Like me, Zhang said. Mad Dog's eyebrows lifted, and he looked Zhang up and down, but he agreed to meet a few days later, and after their first session together he grudgingly admitted that Zhang wasn't a total disaster.

Zhang had reached a creek that ran under the road. Tractors stood on the north bank. On the other side was a row of wooden shacks with lights on in their windows. Shadowy figures moved through the squares of yellow. Next to the bridge was a simple noodle place. Four or five people stood about while a middle-aged woman tipped a bucket of slops into the gutter. Walking over, Zhang asked if any of them had noticed an old man passing by on Saturday night.

"No shortage of old men round here," the woman said.

"He's got shoulder-length gray hair," Zhang said. "He was wearing a suit."

The woman grunted.

"He'd had a few drinks," Zhang added.

The people exchanged a glance, but no one volunteered any information. A little girl kept kicking a pink plastic ball into the air with the side of her foot.

Moving back to the road, Zhang leaned on a wall that overlooked the creek. To the east, above a jumble of dark rooftops, he could see the high-rise building that housed the Park Hyatt, its sheer sides outlined in blue neon. That was where he and Naemi had spent their first night together. Another world. Once again, he pictured her on the plane to London, hard-edged and golden, and everyone around her sleeping. Why did he find that image so unnerving? Behind him, a car sped past. A rush of air, then nothing. He was aware of one set of concerns shadowing another. Parallel uncertainties.

He began to walk again. On the left side of the road was a dreary, brightly lit restaurant, its seats covered with purple fabric. He went in and told the man behind the counter that he was looking for a friend who had gone missing.

"This place is on his way home," Zhang said. "It's possible he came in here on Saturday."

The man sucked on his teeth. "I wasn't here on Saturday."

Someone tugged at Zhang's sleeve, and he turned to see a wiry man with bloodshot eyes.

"I was," the man said.

"My friend was wearing a gray suit and a green shirt," Zhang said. "He's about seventy, with long gray hair."

"No," the man said. "I don't remember anyone like that."

Zhang left the restaurant and moved on.

Hanyang Road was quiet, but whenever he came across a business that was open he stopped and asked about his friend. Nobody remembered him. Nobody. Perhaps, after all, Mad Dog had taken a different route home—or perhaps he had gone somewhere else entirely. The possibilities were infinite. Zhang was tiring, and he felt he had lost the scent—if he had ever *had* the scent, that is—but since he was close to where Mad Dog lived he resolved to keep going. Then at least he could tell himself that he had covered the ground.

He came to a crossroads near Mad Dog's house. Positioned diagonally across from each other were two 24-hour convenience stores. He thought he should try them both.

The girl behind the counter in Quik wore glasses with thick black frames. Her hair was long on top and shaved at the sides, and a snake tattoo coiled round her left forearm.

"Were you here on Saturday night," Zhang said, "at about this time?"

She stared at him with hard, unblinking eyes. "I'm here every night."

He described Mad Dog. "Did you see anyone like that?" He saw her hesitate. "It's all right. I'm a friend of his."

"Gray suit, you said?"

Zhang nodded. "And a green shirt."

"I think I saw him. But it was earlier than this—about one in the morning."

"How do you know?"

"Because I'd just got off the phone with my pain-in-the-ass boss. He asked how business was going, and I said it was slow. He said it was down to me. He thinks I put people off."

"Where was my friend when you saw him?"

The girl came out from behind the counter and moved over to a glass-topped freezer cabinet. "I was standing here, checking the plug. The connection's faulty, and the ice creams keep melting. At some point, I looked out of the window. That was when I noticed him."

"Where?"

She pointed. "Over there, by the shop where they cut keys. He was talking to a blonde woman."

Zhang stared at the girl. All of a sudden, his heart was beating high up in his throat. "You're sure?"

The girl nodded firmly. "It was the woman I saw first. I probably wouldn't have noticed him otherwise."

"And they were talking?"

"Yes—but it was strange. They didn't look like people who would know each other. It wasn't just that she was foreign. It was like they came from two completely different worlds." She gazed through the window. "The woman was amazing-looking, like a comic-book character or a superhero, and he was just an old man in a suit, you know?"

"Do you remember anything else?"

The girl screwed up her eyes, thinking. "The *way* they were talking was strange too. She seemed to be trying to explain something to him, or plead with him, but he wasn't interested." She paused. "You'd think it would have been the other way round—him bothering her..."

"Then what happened?"

"The phone rang, and I went to answer it. Next time I looked out of the window they were gone, and there were some foreign guys outside with skateboards and beer."

"Thank you. You've been very helpful." At the door, Zhang paused and turned back. "You know something? You're wasted in this place. You should be a detective."

The girl's face lost all its hardness. "I'd *love* that," she said.

Zhang crossed the road and stared into the darkened window of the key-cutting shop. Mad Dog had been standing here. Right here. He had been talking to a blonde woman, who had been trying to explain something to him. He was only a couple of minutes' walk from where he lived, and yet he hadn't made it home.

A blonde woman...

He had instantly thought of Naemi, of course. The woman sounded just like her. But it couldn't be. She was thousands of kilometers away, in London... Fragments of recent conversation circled inside his head. First Naemi: *He doesn't like me, does he.* Then Mad Dog: *I'd have nothing to do with her. I'd run a mile.* Then Naemi again: *He should be careful.* A taxi came along, but Zhang made no attempt to flag it down. Instead, he watched the taillights sink into the murk, then he crossed the road again and stood where the skateboarders had stood, with his back to the convenience store. Looking towards the key-cutting shop, it wasn't an old man and a blonde woman he saw. It was Mad Dog and Naemi, and they were involved in some kind of altercation. Another taxi passed. Still he didn't lift a hand.

He should be careful.

At the time, he had taken this remark of hers for solicitude. Now he thought about it, though, it sounded like a threat—and hadn't Mad Dog talked of threats, the night he appeared unexpectedly in Pudong, the night they saw the owl?

It was approaching two in the morning, but Zhang felt an urge to complete the journey. He walked away from the crossroads and turned into the narrow alleyway where Mad Dog lived. An old man in a white under-shirt and plaid shorts was watering his plants. He looked at Zhang vacantly as he passed by. Zhang stopped outside Mad Dog's house. The wooden gate was open, and light from the house fell across the yard. He could see the corrugated-plastic lean-to, and the outdoor sink, and the Formica table where they had eaten lunch. On the shelf above the sink was an ashtray full of butts. One of Mad Dog's shoes stood upright next to a small round cactus in a pale green pot. The light was coming from the kitchen window. Someone was awake. Perhaps, after all, Mad Dog had finally returned. Perhaps he had been on a two-day drinking binge, or perhaps he had been with a woman. Perhaps he and Ling Ling were arguing—though Zhang couldn't imagine Ling Ling arguing, or even raising her voice. Perhaps she was telling him, in low tones, that she was leaving him, and he was telling her not to be ridiculous. Perhaps he was telling her he loved her. Zhang hoped all this was true.

He eased through the gate and closed it behind him, then he swiftly and silently crossed the yard. Positioning himself just to one side of the light, he moved his head until he could see into the room. Ling Ling was sitting at the kitchen table, and she had both hands over her face, like a child counting to one hundred while her friends ran off and hid. One look at her, and it was obvious Mad Dog had not come home. Zhang stepped back from the window, darkness closing round his heart.

The night was hot and wet, like a night in July or August, and Zhang was driving. His heart was light as a balloon, and seemed to drift inside his body, as if he was on his way to meet somebody new. His mind was cool and fluent, no thoughts as such, just the low-level fizzle of anticipation. He pulled up outside a club. A valet opened the car door for him and took his keys. Mauve neon spilled across the pavement. The rain was warm.

He walked past the line of people waiting. In the foyer, a girl stamped the inside of his wrist with the symbol of a fingerprint, which glowed in the ultraviolet. He passed through the crowd and on into the bar area. Everybody in the place was beautiful. Crossing the dance floor, he could feel the bass notes pushing against the soles of his shoes. Faces spun past, seemingly hurled at him and glancing off.

Then he was in a corridor, the music behind him now, and muffled. He was looking for someone. He wasn't sure who. His heart felt heavier, hemmed in. He found it hard to catch his breath. He stepped sideways, through a half-open door. There were six or seven young people in the room. The girls all wore short skirts. One of them had dyed blue hair—or perhaps it was a wig. The men had taken off their shirts. They had gold chains round their necks. Their jeans were black.

One of the girls bent over a glass table and snorted white powder through a straw. Straightening up again, she pushed her hair back and pinched her nose, then she handed him the straw and reached for a microphone. On the screen behind her was a blown-up photographic image of green foliage and dappled sunlight. She began to sing. She had chosen a heavy metal track about lust and killing. Somebody tapped him on the shoulder. One of the men. The tattoo of a rope coiled around his upper body, encircling his neck. He jerked his head towards the white lines on the table. Zhang bent down and snorted.

His nostril burned. He gave the straw to the man with the rope tattoo and left the room.

At the end of the corridor was a black door, and the light that oozed around its edges was a fuzzy gold. He was soaring inside his head, all the giddiness and claustrophobia gone. Someone took his arm. It was the girl who had been singing. Blood trickled from her nose, but she was smiling. Her black T-shirt was tight over her breasts. You were good, he told her. I never expected you to be so good. She tilted her face towards his, offering her lips. They kissed. She opened the black door and started up the stairs. He followed. There was no effort involved. He could have climbed those stairs forever. Time seemed to have unraveled. Space too. The idea that there might be another world outside the club seemed far-fetched, unbelievable. Even the night drive through the city. Even his car keys glinting in the valet's hand...

It was dark in the room, and there was a steady roar, like air conditioning. The girl told him this was the Golden Lounge. The small man in the pale blue suit was sitting at a table in the corner with a drink. There you are, Zhang said. He felt excited. Everything made sense. The man said nothing, though. He was studying his fingernails. Zhang wanted to know where the little suitcase was. Lifting his eyes, the man slowly shook his head. He seemed disappointed, and disdainful, but also resigned. When you think of all the questions you could have asked, he said.

Zhang looked upwards. There was no ceiling, only a brown night sky. Rain splashed down into the room. He watched the drops sink into the carpet, one after another. The small man and the girl were gone—

He woke up covered with sweat, a damp sheet tangled round his body. *When you think of all the questions you could have asked...* He switched on the bedside light and looked at the soles of his feet. No little marks or holes. No sensitivity. He drank some water from the glass next to his bed, then reached for his phone. It was ten to five. Switching off the light again, he lay down and closed his eyes. Moments later, seemingly, his alarm went off. Leaving his bed, he walked into the kitchen and made a pot of yellow leaf tea.

He had been trying to speak to his sister for several days, but she wasn't answering the phone. She didn't return his calls either. That afternoon, he told Chun Tao to drive him to Huaihai Road, where Qi Jing worked. The city was sunk in a dirty white fog, like a moth wrapped in a cocoon. All the cars had their headlights on, even though dusk was still an hour away.

When the Jaguar pulled up outside Qi Jing's high-fashion clothes shop, she was in the window, adjusting the leather jacket on a shop dummy. He crossed the pavement and pushed the door open. Though he was sure she had seen him approaching, she didn't look round.

"You've been ignoring my calls," he said.

She stepped out of the window and onto the shop floor. "What were you calling about?" She seemed cold, indifferent. Her face looked stiff.

"I just wanted to see how you were doing."

"I'm doing fine."

Qi Jing's assistant appeared from a back room with a number of silk scarves. Qi Jing asked her to leave them on the counter and take a half-hour break. She needed some time alone with her brother, she said.

When the young woman had left the shop, Qi Jing turned the sign on the door so it would read CLOSED to anyone who might be standing on the pavement, then she swung round.

"Was it your idea to set me up with Laser?"

He shook his head. Sometimes she was more perceptive than he gave her credit for. "Why?" he said. "Didn't you like him?"

"That's not the point."

"In the text you sent me you seemed to like him. You said he was cute."

"You set me up. You manipulated me."

"I had no idea you'd sleep with him. All I did was ask you to come out for a drink."

"I don't believe you."

He shrugged, then began to look through the dresses hanging on a clothes rail by the wall. He might find a gift for Naemi.

"Did you hear what I said?"

He looked round.

Qi Jing was standing in the middle of the shop, her feet apart, her left hand on her hip with the thumb pointing forwards. This was something she did when she was in a rage. The hand on the hip. The thumb. She had done it even as a child.

"How *dare* you fuck with my life?"

Her fury was intense and colorless, like the sun concentrated into a small hot circle on a piece of paper by a magnifying glass.

"You not only set me up with your drummer," she went on. "You also sabotaged my relationship with Chu En Li."

Zhang affected a blank look.

"You had him sent to the Philippines, didn't you." She came and stood in front of him, her flushed face close to his. "Don't pretend you don't know what I'm talking about."

Oddly enough—and even though Qi Jing's accusations were wholly justified—her anger sparked a corresponding anger in him. "I've got more important things to think about," he said, "than some affair you were having that didn't work out."

"Oh really?" Her tone was withering. "Like what?"

"A friend of mine's gone missing." He saw something shift in her. He had caught her off guard. "You met him the other night, in the bar."

"The old man, you mean?"

He nodded. "No one's seen him in three days."

"I'm sorry." She looked at the floor, then lifted her eyes to him again. "But that doesn't change how I feel."

He moved to the door of the shop and peered out. The fog still hadn't lifted. He could see his Jaguar parked on the street, Chun Tao with his earbuds in, listening to music.

"I know it was you," Qi Jing was saying. "Chu En Li told me. You're friends with his boss, apparently. He saw you together."

In the noodle place, Zhang thought. In Yangpu district.

He turned to face his sister again. Some of her fury had burned off, leaving a residue of bitterness or scorn. "Chu En Li," he said. "Was he the one you were with in that bar on the Bund?"

"What do *you* think?"

"The way he behaved that night." He let out a laugh that was dismissive, contemptuous. "He seemed to think he was some kind of gangster."

"Maybe you should be worried then."

He stared at his sister. "Why should I be worried?"

She gave him a look that was provocative, almost flirtatious, then she pushed past him and opened the door.

"I'd like you to go now," she said.

"What have I got to be worried about?"

"Just go."

He sighed and shook his head and then he left.

That evening, on his way back from a dinner with Sebastian, Zhang called Johnny Yu.

"How's the head?" he asked.

"I went to the hospital," Johnny said. "Five stitches."

"And the apartment?"

"I had to buy a new kitchen door, and new glass for one of the windows. She broke a lamp. The TV too. All in all, it cost me close to 15,000 RMB."

"Expensive argument."

"She's fiery, but you know..." Johnny paused. "It has its advantages."

"There's something I need you to do," Zhang said.

"What is it this time?" Johnny said. "Something else that's beneath me?"

Zhang smiled. "Can you meet me at the Dark Horse tomorrow afternoon?"

"I could meet you now, if you like."

"No," Zhang said. "It's been a long day. I need to get to bed."

"*Who are the companions sitting alone at the bright window? / I and my shadow—the two of us.*" Johnny paused again. "Hsiang Kao. A minor writer, of whose life nothing is known."

"Good night, Johnny."

For once, the lines Johnny had quoted had spoken to him directly. It was Golden Week, and he could have been in London with Naemi, but she had told him she was busy, so here he was in Shanghai, on his own...He called his wife's number. She didn't answer. He called his son, Hai Long, but he didn't pick up either. It was late, and they were probably asleep. Or perhaps they had gone away, like everybody else.

Up ahead, he could see the mouth of the Dalian Road Tunnel.

He leaned his head against the headrest. White lights slid up the windscreen, then a metal grille clanged twice beneath the wheels, and they emerged into the wide, empty avenues of Pudong.

The following afternoon, Zhang arrived at the Dark Horse five minutes early. He ordered a beer and sat at a table by the wall. The two young women who ran the bar were playing pool, but they weren't taking the game seriously, potting balls out of turn and putting each other off. It was just a way of killing time until the place filled up.

While he was waiting for Johnny, he rang Ling Ling and asked if Mad Dog had appeared yet. She said he hadn't. It was quiet behind her voice. Though he knew where she lived, and what the inside of the house looked like, he saw her in isolation, against a blank blue screen, like an actor shooting a scene with CGI.

"I'm sure he'll turn up," he said. "He always does."

It was several seconds before Ling Ling spoke, a silence that was filled by the click of pool balls and the laughter of the girls.

"I don't think I'll ever see him again," she said at last.

He told her about the call he had put in to the deputy commissioner. She simply absorbed the information. Nothing came back. He didn't mention his attempt to follow in Mad Dog's footsteps, or his encounter with the tattooed girl in Quik. Perhaps he felt incapable of altering Ling Ling's state of mind—or perhaps he was finding it difficult to work out what significance any of it had. The fact was, no one had seen Mad Dog in almost four days.

"Let me know if you hear something," he said. "Call me any time of day or night."

She hung up.

I don't think I'll ever see him again.

He could no longer imagine what Mad Dog might be doing. Every time he thought of Mad Dog, he saw the same thing: the old man walking away, the back of his hand showing above his shoulder, youngsters dancing in couples under huge, dark trees—

The door opened, and Johnny appeared, his suit dark blue, his shirt a muddy brown. His porkpie hat perched on top of a bandage that covered his five stitches. He signaled for a beer, then pulled out a chair, sat down, and lit a cigarette.

"*We wish to keep our youth, and wait for wealth and honor / But wealth and honor do not come, and youth departs.*"

"I recognize that," Zhang said.

"Maybe I quoted it before." Johnny tapped a few flakes of ash into the ashtray. "Po Chu-I. A T'ang poet. Very popular."

"Why so gloomy?"

Johnny shrugged. "The girlfriend."

"More arguments?"

Johnny's beer arrived. He drank, then put the bottle down. "You know what she said to my uncle recently? 'He makes me angry. Every day, he makes me angry.'"

"Maybe you'd be better off apart."

"Thing is, I'm fond of her." Johnny looked down at the table. "She's a good girl, really. She's just got a temper, that's all."

Zhang slid the photo of Chu En Li across the table.

"Who's this?" Johnny asked.

Zhang told him.

"He's supposed to have left for Manila," he said. "Can you make sure he's not still here, in Shanghai?"

"That shouldn't be a problem."

For the next two days, Zhang hardly had a moment. Though it was Golden Week, Jun Wei had scheduled wall-to-wall meetings—the Iran deal seemed imminent—and Zhang's evenings were taken up by long, elaborate dinners with Jun Wei and his associates. His anxieties were temporarily pushed to the far reaches of his mind, where they could not be felt. He didn't hear from Ling Ling, or from Johnny. On Thursday night, though, as Chun Tao drove him back from a function in Hongqiao, he looked off to the left and saw a white neon sign that said WHERE ARE YOU. They were on the Yan'an elevated highway, not far from People's Square. Like a love song when you're in love, the sign appeared to be aimed specifically at him.

He asked Chun Tao if he had seen the sign.

Chun Tao tilted his head back without taking his eyes off the road. They were traveling at 150 kilometers an hour. "What sign was that, Mr. Zhang?"

"It was in English. On the roof of a building—" Zhang looked to his left again, but it was already behind them.

"I didn't see any English signs," Chun Tao said.

Zhang sat back. "Never mind."

"I forgot to tell you," Chun Tao said after a few moments. "That advice you gave me really worked."

"What advice?"

"I took my girlfriend to dinner and asked her if she would marry me. Her face lit up, just like you said it would."

"Did she say yes?"

"Not exactly. She's planning to do a six-month business course in Beijing, and she wants me to use that time to think about the future. She wants me to be sure I'm ready."

"She sounds very wise."

Chun Tao smiled. "She is."

"And if you ask her again in six months' time will she say yes?"

"She told me the answer wasn't in doubt. Only the question was in doubt."

"There's an alternative after all," Zhang said, "just as you hoped."

Later, when he remembered this brief exchange, he felt it had some bearing on his own predicament, and though he couldn't establish the precise connection the feeling stayed with him for several hours.

On Friday night, Zhang attended a family dinner at a Hong Kong–style restaurant near Xujiahui metro station. His father had booked a private room on the third floor.

There were twelve of them in all—an uncle Zhang hadn't seen in years, and various cousins with their teenage children. Qi Jing had stayed at home, claiming she had flu. This was almost certainly a lie. It seemed more likely that she had heard he was coming, and wanted to avoid him. She still hadn't forgiven him for interfering in her life, but she would, he thought, in time.

Towards the end of the evening, his father took him aside.

"You seem distracted," his father said.

"I'm fine," Zhang said.

"How's my grandson?"

"He's well."

"When did you last see him?"

"It's been a while," Zhang said. "We speak most weeks, though, on the phone."

His father studied him with his usual mixture of dissatisfaction and disappointment, then he poured himself a cognac and stood by the window, looking at the heavy traffic on Hongqiao Road.

"What about your mother?" he said. "Have you visited at all?"

"I'll be going in the second week of October," Zhang said. "How is she?"

"The same."

Zhang nodded, then drank. An ambulance was stuck in the traffic, its blue light whirling uselessly.

"At least Qi Jing seems to have seen the error of her ways," his father said after a long silence.

Zhang allowed himself a smile. This, he knew, was as close as his father would get to thanking him.

"The trouble is," he said, "I'm not sure how long it will last."

"What's that supposed to mean?"

"She likes younger men."

"Don't be vulgar."

Zhang let out a sigh, then glanced at his watch. "I should go. I have some work to catch up on."

As he turned away to say his goodbyes, his father caught him by the arm, his grip surprisingly strong. "Something you should not forget."

Zhang looked at him. "What's that?"

"Family," his father said. "It's all there is."

The following day, as Zhang was leaving the Athens Palace, after his usual Saturday-afternoon massage, his phone rang. It was the deputy commissioner of police.

"Bad news," he said.

Mad Dog's body had been found at the bottom of a steep flight of steps that led down to the basement of a building. His injuries were consistent with a fall. There were no signs of a struggle. Toxicology had revealed extremely high levels of alcohol in the blood. It was being treated as death by misadventure. A tragic accident, in other words.

Zhang had come to a standstill in the middle of the lobby, and was staring at the ivory-colored grand piano. "Where was he found?"

The deputy commissioner named a small street that was no more than a minute's walk from where Mad Dog lived. This, Zhang realized, was his chance to mention what the girl in Quik had told him, but he didn't. He wasn't sure why.

"I'm sorry," the deputy commissioner said.

"Has his partner been informed?"

"I believe she has."

Zhang thanked the deputy commissioner for all he had done, and for letting him know, then he ended the call.

Half an hour later, a taxi dropped him at the Bamboo Lounge. He climbed the stairs and pushed through the wooden Wild West–style swinging doors. The same girl was working behind the bar.

She smiled when she saw him. "It's been a while."

He nodded. She was wearing a raspberry-colored dress whose fabric had been worked with a fine silver filigree. Her hair hung down her back, reaching almost to her waist.

"Have you come to tell me about your life?" she asked.

He couldn't answer. He felt bewildered. Desolate.

"Give me a large whiskey," he said.

"Of course." She poured the whiskey and put it on a paper coaster in front of him.

"I'm sorry," he said. "A friend of mine just died."

He wondered if he should have mentioned it. It wasn't a story he could tell—at least, not in its entirety. There were a few hard facts, and the rest was speculation. But perhaps that was why he had come. It would be safer if he unburdened himself to a well-meaning stranger. He might even learn something. Certain truths can only be arrived at by thinking out loud.

"It was a close friend?" she asked.

"We were in a band together."

"You're a musician? I wouldn't have guessed."

"We play the blues."

A puzzled look appeared on her face. Obviously, the blues meant nothing to her.

He didn't know that much about his friend, he went on, even though they had played together for fifteen years. They seldom talked about anything personal. It had been a friendship sustained almost exclusively by music.

"But perhaps that is also a kind of talking," the girl said. "Perhaps you know him better than you think you do."

"Perhaps." Zhang finished his whiskey. "All his viciousness left him when he played. All his cynicism too. It was like getting access to a pure version of the man. But his life also found its way into his playing, if that doesn't sound contradictory. I could hear it. The reason why he was the way he was."

"It sounds like you were actually quite close."

What had Ling Ling said? *You're his closest friend.* Zhang pushed his empty glass towards the girl. "Same again." He saw her hesitate. "Don't worry, I won't get drunk—or if I do, it won't be here."

She poured him another large whiskey and set it down before him.

"It might sound cruel," he went on, "but I don't think there are many people who will miss him. He was always making enemies."

"Who will miss him, then," the girl said, "apart from you?"

"His girlfriend, Ling Ling. Maybe Ling Ling's daughter. Our drummer..." He shrugged and drank.

"The child was his?"

"No." He turned his glass slowly on the bar. "She's only five. In a few years, she probably won't even remember him."

The girl adjusted the position of the bottles on the back wall. Her face, reflected in the mirror tiles, was sober, composed, and seemingly unaware that he was watching her.

"So now I know you a little," she said eventually.

She seemed to appreciate the fact that he had repaid her confidences with confidences of his own, yet she expected nothing from him. He found this relaxing. He was different when he was talking to her. He was more considerate, and more vulnerable. He was a musician. He had no name.

Finishing his drink, he asked for the check.

"You have to go?" she said.

He nodded.

"Will you be back?"

"I don't think this place would survive without me," he said.

She was smiling as he turned and left.

Out on the street he hailed a taxi. As he headed north, towards Anguo Road, he found that he had accepted the official version of the story. Mad Dog had drunk too much, and he had fallen down and hit his head, as alcoholics often do. It was tragic, as the deputy commissioner had said, but it was also predictable. To tell the truth, it was a wonder that it hadn't happened before. As for the tattooed girl in Quik, her evidence was circumstantial. Was it *really* Mad Dog who she had seen? After all, Shanghai was full of old men, as the woman outside the noodle place on Monday night had said. And the blonde? Well, Naemi was hardly the only fair-haired woman in the city—and anyway, she had an alibi: she was halfway round the world, in London. Only one thing was certain. Mad Dog was gone. He had been a man of many accomplishments, some of which— the scholarship, the writing—he had hidden, even from his friends. Zhang wondered if Mad Dog's sour nature might not have been his way of disguising feelings of shyness and self-doubt. Like lemon juice, it had added a zest to things, and as a musician he was second to none, his playing of the double bass both rich and minimal. There would be no replacing him.

In the alley, the old man was watering his plants again, and he gave Zhang the same unblinking look. Zhang opened the gate to Mad Dog's yard. The kitchen light was on, as usual. When he knocked, Ling Ling came to the door.

"Mr. Zhang," she said. "Come in."

He followed her into the kitchen, where she offered him a glass of tea. He had the strange sensation, sitting at the table, that there was another version of himself outside the window, looking in. He remembered Mad Dog telling him that, for ghosts, the past could bleed into the present, and it seemed believable to Zhang just then. He looked at Ling Ling. Though she wasn't crying, her eyes were swollen. He told her he was very sorry for her loss. It was his loss too, of course, he said.

"It's better to know," she said. "The not-knowing—that was difficult." Her voice was uninflected, monotonous, like a landscape drained of color by the moon.

"How long were you together?"

"Five years."

"You have a daughter—"

"She wasn't his, but he grew to love her as if she was." Ling Ling paused. "I think he was happy to have a daughter."

"I don't think I ever saw him happy," Zhang said. "I can't really imagine it."

"He saw it as a form of weakness. But sometimes he gave in to it." Ling Ling rose from the table. "Would you like more tea?"

Through the open doorway, Zhang could see into the next room, where Mad Dog's spare double bass leaned against a green wall. In its hard case, which gleamed in the half-light, it reminded him of a huge insect, wings folded for the night. Before Ling Ling moved in, Zhang had often called round with his guitar, and the two of them had jammed together, sometimes for hours.

"What was it like to live with a man who was so much older?" he asked.

"I never thought about it." She brought the tea to the table and sat down. "I'm not someone who thinks very far ahead."

"That's probably a good way to live."

"I don't know any other way."

They fell quiet.

Ling Ling went to check on her daughter, who was asleep in the bedroom. Zhang bent over his tea and blew on it. As he lifted his eyes, he noticed a bookshelf on the far wall, beyond the double bass. He got up from the table and threaded his way through pieces of furniture, cardboard boxes, and piles of neatly ironed clothing. While scanning the shelves, he came across something unexpected. The book had a matte-black cover, and red characters on the front and down the spine. Its title was *A Handbook of Ghost Culture in China, from Ancient Times to the Present Day*. Inside was a photograph of the author, Mad Dog as a much younger man. He still had the same sour curl to his top lip, but his hair was cut short and showed no trace of gray.

"You can have that, if you like."

He turned to see Ling Ling in the doorway behind him, her arms folded.

"Are you sure?" he said.

"I don't have any use for it."

Thanking her, he took the book back to the kitchen with him, and they sat down again.

"You were the last person to see him," Ling Ling said.

He nodded. "So far as we know."

He told her that when he and Mad Dog left the bar, Mad Dog seemed to want company.

"Was that unusual?" she asked.

"Yes," he said. "Normally, he would insist on walking home alone."

"But this time he wanted you to walk with him?"

"Yes."

"Why would he do that?"

"I don't know. Perhaps he was a bit drunker than usual. Perhaps he felt unsteady."

Ling Ling stared down into her tea.

"It was so unlike him to ask for something," Zhang said. "He never asked for anything, not in all the years I knew him. He didn't want to be in debt to anyone, not even his friends. He was his own man. I respected that."

"Perhaps it was selfishness," Ling Ling said.

Zhang looked at her.

"Not allowing people to do things for you," Ling Ling went on. "Not allowing them to feel good."

"I never thought of it like that."

They fell quiet again. Outside, in the yard, a cat let out a low and mournful howl.

"He was drunker than usual, though, you think," Ling Ling said at last.

"It's hard to say." Zhang finished his tea. "I feel bad. Maybe I should have forced him to get into the taxi. Maybe I shouldn't have given him a choice."

Ling Ling looked at him, but said nothing.

"We had walked for about an hour," Zhang went on. "I felt tired suddenly. It had been a long week, and it was late. When a taxi stopped for me, I offered him a lift, but he wasn't interested. He said he preferred to continue on foot, and that the night air would do him good." He paused. "That was the last thing I heard him say—"

A dizziness came over him, and he felt for a moment that he might faint. He asked if he could use the toilet.

"Do you remember where it is?"

He shook his head.

She led him down a narrow corridor. In the yard, there was a concrete outhouse with a weak bare bulb, electric wires dangling. He pulled the door half shut behind him and turned on the tap. Tepid water trickled out. It didn't smell too clean. He brought the water up to his face a few times, then turned the tap off again and stood with his hands braced on the edge of the sink and his head lowered. The stray cat howled again, closer this time. The swirling sensation passed. He returned to the kitchen, where Ling Ling was sitting at the table, as before.

"Tell the funeral people to contact me," he said. "I'll take care of everything." He put his business card on the table.

She seemed to have become immobilized, as she had been in the grounds outside his building, and on the sofa in his apartment. His card lay in front of her, untouched. He couldn't imagine the kinds of thoughts that were going through her mind. Maybe none. He picked up Mad Dog's book on ghosts and left.

In the taxi, it occurred to him that Ling Ling might see his offer to pay for the funeral as an attempt to buy her silence. He knew more about Mad Dog's death than he was letting on. He was implicated, somehow—or even guilty. She might see it as the sort of grand gesture a person only makes if he has something to atone for.

Did he have something to atone for?

He woke at half past five in the morning. Sleep was all around him, sticky as cobwebs, heavy as clay, and he had to fight his way free of it. He forced his eyes open. Was that his alarm? No, the sound was wrong. He reached for his phone. Someone was calling.

"Mr. Zhang?"

"Yes—" The word came out strangled. He cleared his throat.

"It's Torben Gulsvig."

Zhang put his feet on the floor and sat with the phone pressed to his right ear.

"I'm sorry to be calling so early," Gulsvig said. "I couldn't wait any longer."

Gulsvig told him that although there was some evidence to suggest that Nina had studied in England—the University of London had a record of her enrollment—he could find no trace of her in Finland. No trace whatsoever. She wasn't currently registered as a voter. In fact, she never had been. She didn't have a social security number or a driving license. She had never paid tax. He hadn't even been able to find a birth certificate for her—or a death certificate, for that matter.

"I'm utterly bewildered," Gulsvig concluded. "It's as if she didn't exist outside my knowledge of her, and that makes me feel like I imagined her. Like I imagined the whole thing."

The darkness in Zhang's bedroom pulsed and prickled. Dawn was still half an hour away.

"Last time we spoke," he said, "you told me Nina's boyfriend died."

"What about it?" Gulsvig said.

"I don't know." Zhang was still trying to think. "In all the time you knew her, did you ever feel you might be in danger?"

There was a silence on the other end.

"In danger," Gulsvig said at last, and slowly, as if to taste the words, or test their relevance. "From her, you mean?"

"Yes."

"Why do you ask?"

"A friend of mine warned me against Naemi," Zhang said, "and now he's dead."

Another silence.

"It was an accident," Zhang said. "He fell."

"But Mr. Zhang," Gulsvig said, "Nina and Naemi are two completely different people."

"I know. But there seem to be certain—*similarities*..."

"You think they're connected in some way?"

"I don't know. I can't prove anything." Zhang paused. "But you didn't answer my question. Did you ever feel you might be in danger?"

"Actually, there was one time," Gulsvig said.

At the end of their second year at university, he and Nina had flown back to Helsinki for the summer holidays. Not long after they arrived, a friend hosted a party at his parents' villa, which was on a small island on the outskirts of the city. Like everyone that evening, he drank too much. Towards midnight, he found himself sitting on a wooden jetty, looking out over the Gulf of Finland. Since he was some distance from the house, he assumed he was alone, but then a movement in the half-light had him glancing to his left. A blonde girl in a white top stood at the water's edge. His heart rose up inside him, and he called out to her.

"Nina?"

Her face turned in his direction. "Torben? Is that you?"

She came along the beach and climbed up onto the jetty and sat down next to him, her legs dangling over the water. The night seemed to sharpen into focus, and he had the sudden, keen sense that he was at the heart of things, the very center of the world. This was all her doing. He wondered what it would be like to have that kind of power.

"Sorry if I interrupted," he said. "Did you want to be alone?"

"It's all right." She looked at him sideways, through her hair. "What are you doing out here?"

"Sometimes things get a bit much for me and I have to get away."

"I know that feeling." She was wearing a miniskirt, and her hands gripped the edge of the jetty, on either side of her bare legs. "But I often feel lonely too. I can't seem to get the balance right."

"How are things with Peter?" He felt he had to ask. He would not be a proper friend to her if there were parts of her life that he refused to address, or even countenance.

"*Peter.*" Her voice was amused, but also despairing.

"Do you miss him?"

"Sometimes." She peered down into the water. "The sex is good—when he's not too stoned, that is."

Listening to her talk about her love life was the most hateful part of the role he had devised for himself, but he was her confidant, and her adviser. It was the price he had to pay.

"He wants too much from me," she said.

"How do you mean?"

"He can't seem to get close enough. Sometimes it's as if he wants to climb inside my skin." She gave a little shudder.

Torben found Peter arrogant and condescending—Peter came from an aristocratic English family—and he was secretly hoping that the relationship might soon be over, though he was aware that there would be other Peters, and aware also that he would never be among them. But perhaps he could find some satisfaction in the thought that he might outlast one of her lovers, and that he might even, in his own modest way, outlast them all.

"I spoke to him earlier, on the phone," Nina was saying. "He wants to know where I am, and who I'm with. He wants me to be with him all the time."

"Sounds claustrophobic," Torben said—though he could imagine wanting exactly the same thing.

"It makes me wish he was out of the way." She turned to him for the first time since she had sat down. Her eyes were black and silver, and there was a smell of carrion suddenly, as if something was decaying nearby. "Have you ever had the feeling that someone is so close," she went on, "that you might have to kill that person just so you can breathe?"

Kill that person.

The night stepped back. In that moment, it seemed to him that she wasn't a human being at all. She was an animal, pretending to be human. He didn't know where the idea had come from, only that it was there, and it was so vivid, so *present*, that he felt at risk. Like prey. She must have seen something in his face because she spoke again.

"I'm sorry, Torben. Did I frighten you?"

"A little, yes." It was probably a gamble to admit it, but somehow he had to tell the truth.

She gazed out across the water. Though it was the middle of the night, the sky above the horizon was a pale blue that had some green in it, like the flames in a gas fire. She looked so sad just then that he wished he could put an arm round her, but he was worried she might misinterpret it.

"Don't stop being my friend," she said in a low voice.

"I'll never stop," he said. "I couldn't."

She faced him again, and whatever had seemed inhuman or primeval was gone. "I have this secret. I can't tell you what it is. I can't tell anyone." She glanced over her shoulder, towards the house, as if to make sure nobody was listening. "Some people sense it. They become curious. 'Tell me your secret,' they say. 'I'll keep it to myself. I promise.' And I'm tempted, I'm so tempted—it would be such a weight off me—but I can't. The consequences would be—well, it doesn't bear thinking about. There would be no going back, in any case. And so I'm forced to do things I don't want to do. To protect myself." She sighed, then looked down into her lap. "There's no peace."

She wouldn't say any more. In fact, he suspected that she felt she might already have said too much. It was in the calculating glance she gave him. What she had told him was so vague, though, that he couldn't make any sense of it, and he put it down to the anarchic, off-kilter atmosphere of those long, white summer nights in Finland. People would do and say the most extraordinary things.

"I'll always be there for you," he told her. "You can tell me as much or as little as you like. It's up to you."

"You're a good friend," she said. "I don't deserve you." She reached out and ruffled his hair, then she jumped to her feet. "We should go back to the party, don't you think?"

Zhang moved his phone from one ear to the other. Outside, it was beginning to get light. Gulsvig had talked for fifteen minutes without a break.

"To return to your question," Gulsvig went on, "I wasn't in danger exactly, but I did sense a kind of threat. There were borders and limits, and I knew I couldn't step over them. Maybe other people had, though—in the past."

"You think that's what happened to Peter?"

"Who can say? Whatever the truth of it, her wish was granted. It wasn't long before he was out of the way." Gulsvig paused once more, and when he spoke again he sounded different. Shaken, or even haunted. "When she told me, a year later, that Peter had died, it felt like something she had prepared me for. Warned me about."

"How do you mean?"

"People died around her. Perhaps that was what she'd been trying to tell me."

Zhang stood up and walked to the window. A chill October rain was falling on the city. "You're sure there's no record of her in Finland?"

"Not that I can find."

"Well, if you learn anything new—"

"Of course," Gulsvig said. "Mr. Zhang, I'm sorry, but it's after midnight here. I should go to bed."

"Sleep well, Professor," Zhang said. "And thank you for calling."

Aware that Naemi would soon be returning to Shanghai—she had already been gone for seven days—he kept replaying his phone call with Gulsvig. He would like to have dismissed the story as an instance of midsummer madness, as Gulsvig had, but almost everything the professor had told him had found some correlation in his own recent experience. The young woman Gulsvig had described was a young woman Zhang recognized. She was Nina, but she was also, somehow, Naemi. How could two women from completely different eras have so much in common? Why did they share the same preoccupations, the same anxieties? And why did they express themselves in such a similar way? Those words—*protect myself*—were eerily familiar. Could they be mother and daughter after all? Naemi had told him her mother was dead, but Gulsvig had said there was no death certificate for Nina. What had happened to her, then? How was it possible for somebody to leave so little trace of herself? Could Naemi have had a hand in her disappearance? Perhaps there had been some terrible accident or tragedy. Perhaps there had even been a crime. *People died around her.* Was this the secret she carried with her, the secret she could not reveal?

12

THE PHILIPPINE AIRLINES FLIGHT TO MANILA was only half full, and Naemi had three seats to herself. She put her headphones on and sat back with her eyes closed, pretending to be asleep. *Go to hell.* They were the last words she had heard Mad Dog say. Once again, she saw him slumped against a brick wall in Hongkou district. As soon as she walked away, she had known what it would mean. She would have to leave the city. The country too, probably. When she returned to her apartment, she fast-tracked an order for new documents. She needed to prepare for another life. But there was something she wanted to look into first. It had to do with Zhang's sister's lover, Chu En Li.

On the night of the Business Awards dinner, Zhang's friend Wang Jun Wei had started talking to her. His face was flushed, and his movements were slow and fumbling, like a lobster in a tank. He had been drinking heavily.

He began to boast about a special favor he had done for Zhang. Something to do with Zhang's sister. He leaned in close, his breathing arduous, as though he had been running. She had been sleeping with his driver, Chu En Li, he said. It had become a problem for Zhang's family, especially his father, but he, Jun Wei, had found a solution.

"What kind of solution?" she asked.

He leaned closer still, and spoke into her ear. "I sent him to Manila."

"Oh," she said. "I thought it might be something more—I don't know—*extreme*."

Straightening up, he looked at her steadily. "Like what?"

"Life is much more fragile than we think."

His gaze lasted a moment longer, then he tipped his head back, his mouth wide open, his eyes squeezed shut. She realized that he was laughing.

Later that same night, in an attempt to follow up on what she had learned, she searched Zhang's apartment while he was asleep. In the pocket of his suit jacket, she found a picture of the man she had seen with Qi Jing in the Glamour Bar. Assuming this was Chu En Li, she took a photo of the picture with her phone. The following evening, back in her own apartment, she spent several hours on WeChat, hacking into a number of different accounts, including that of Zhang's sister. Qi Jing had posted photos of herself and Chu En Li together. She had also referred to their recent, cruel separation. She had used emojis: a face with a down-turned mouth, a heart broken into jagged pieces, a spray of tears...

Once in Manila, it only took Naemi a day to track Chu En Li down to a modest hotel in the city center, not far from Luneta Park. He was renting a room on the third floor, facing the street. Half hidden by the trees on the other side of the road, she had watched his plate-glass window slide open. Naked to the waist, he stood on the narrow balcony next to an air-conditioning unit, smoking a cigarette.

On her second evening in the city, she followed him to a nightclub on the waterfront. He was accompanied by two Filipino women. He had zigzag lightning strikes carved into his close-cropped hair, and wore a pale gray suit that had a sheen to it. She left the three of them at the edge of the dance floor and walked out onto the terrace, where the music was less insistent. There were sets of sofas facing each other, with low glass tables in between. There was the usual view of high-rise buildings. Off to the right, she could see cargo boats at anchor in the enormous blackness of Manila Bay. She took a seat in the middle of the terrace. Sometimes she would long for a place that was far from everything—a place where it was quiet, and nothing happened. A few years ago, she had flown over Guatemala at night. She remembered how the dark was almost uninterrupted, just the occasional tight sprinkle of dim lights to signify a town. Well, perhaps she had all that to look forward to, in the not-too-distant future...

She had been sitting outside for about half an hour when Chu En Li appeared, as she had suspected he might. The women walked on either side of him, leaning into him, their tight-fitting dresses patterned with big tropical flowers, his arms around their shoulders. He was moving past her, towards the end of the terrace, when his head turned. His eyes stopped on her face.

"I know you," he said.

She looked up at him, but didn't speak.

"I saw you in Shanghai," he went on, "in that fancy bar on the Bund. You were with my girlfriend's brother."

"I'm sorry. I don't remember you." She paused. "I meet a lot of people."

Since he had recognized her, she could pretend she didn't know who he was. That way, he wouldn't suspect that she had engineered the encounter. It was important that he saw it as a coincidence.

He signaled to the two women with a jerk of his head. They smiled and turned away and went inside.

"You were with Zhang Guo Xing." He sat down opposite her, his arms spread along the back of the sofa, his legs wide apart.

She watched him watching her. Up close, he looked cheaper and more venal than she had expected. There was a spider tattoo on the web of skin between the thumb and forefinger of his right hand.

"You don't have a drink," he said.

He stopped a passing waitress and ordered two cocktails. She noticed that he didn't bother to ask her what she wanted. Not that she cared. She wasn't going to drink it anyway.

"So what are *you* doing in this shithole?" he asked when the waitress had gone.

"You don't like Manila?"

He shrugged. "It's not Shanghai, is it."

"Why are you here, then?"

Still leaning back, he kept his eyes on her. "You know why."

She met his gaze, but didn't say anything.

"Your boyfriend sent me here," he went on. "Apparently, he didn't like me seeing his sister." There was no hurt in his face, and no embarrassment, only a veneer of disgust.

The drinks arrived—pink cocktails in tall glasses, the rims cluttered with fruit. She watched as he picked off the bright wedges and tossed them on the table.

"Zhang has nothing against you," she said at last. "It was his father who disapproved."

Chu En Li was watching her again. Something stubborn in his face told her he was unconvinced. She would have to try harder.

"He was acting on behalf of his family," she went on. "Doing their bidding." She paused. "You can hardly blame him for that."

Picking up his drink, Chu En Li sucked down half of it, then he put it back on the table and leaned forwards, his elbows on his thighs, his hands dangling between his knees.

"I'm beginning to get the picture," he said.

"Sorry?"

"I know why you came."

"I work for a gallery. I'm here on business."

He smiled, as if he knew better. "You want to fuck me."

"I'm already with someone," she said. "You know that."

"Do you like rough sex?"

"What?"

He touched a finger to the corner of his left eye, indicating the place where Mad Dog's punch had landed. "You have a bruise."

"I got out of a taxi too fast. I hit my head."

Smirking, he finished his drink and then sat back, his arms spread out on either side of him again, his black shirt pulled tight across his chest. "So you're not going to fuck me?"

"I already told you. I'm with someone." She glanced sideways, towards the club's strobe-lit interior. "In any case, it seems you have that side of things taken care of."

"Those girls?" He smoothed a hand over his hair. "They're nothing."

"They're very pretty—"

"They're not you."

Shaking her head, she looked off into the dark.

"You don't think I'm good enough for you," she heard him say after a while. "I can see it in your face."

She lit a cigarette.

"But Zhang Guo Xing," he went on in the same sour voice, "*he's* good enough..."

The mere mention of Zhang's name, even in the mouth of this third-rate gangster, aroused a longing in her, and though she knew it was ill-advised, given everything that had happened, she determined in that moment that she would spend another night with him. Just one more night.

"You haven't touched your drink," Chu En Li said.

"I didn't ask for it."

"You talk very tough," he said, "for someone who looks the way you do."

He seemed to want to make her the subject of the conversation, but she hadn't flown two thousand kilometers to talk about herself. She decided to have one last attempt.

"If you want to be angry with someone," she said, "be angry with Qi Jing's father. Or with your employer, Wang Jun Wei."

Leaning forwards, she crushed out her cigarette, half smoked, then she stood up and wished him a good evening. As she turned away, he called out after her, but she paid no attention.

The two young Filipino women were sitting at the bar. They also had pink drinks.

"Maybe you should leave," she said, "while you can."

They smiled and waved at her with their fingers as she moved on.

Once she was downstairs, on the street, her stomach seemed to rise towards her throat. In a back alley behind the club, among restaurant dumpsters and empty cardboard boxes, she bent over and retched. Nothing came up.

13

AFTER WORK ON MONDAY NIGHT, Zhang joined Jun Wei at a newly opened KTV club in Putuo district. Like most high-end karaoke places, the decor was extravagant and overblown. With its marble floors, its mirror-paneled walls, and its lavish use of gold, it reminded him of a Saudi palace. A lift took him to a room where Jun Wei and several members of his inner circle were lounging on golden sofas, each of which must have been at least ten meters long. Hennessy X.O was being served by three or four pretty girls in short black dresses.

When Jun Wei saw him, his face opened wide. "You came!"

He made it sound as if Zhang had surmounted unbelievable odds to be with him.

"You're my brother," Zhang said. "Of course I came."

Jun Wei motioned to one of the girls, and she poured

Zhang a cognac on the rocks in a balloon glass and passed it to him using both her hands.

"How long have we known each other?" Jun Wei asked.

"Twenty-eight years."

Jun Wei nodded slowly. "It's a long time, and we have done well for ourselves." He sipped his drink. "Without you, though, none of it would have been possible."

"That's an exaggeration," Zhang said. "You would have succeeded—with or without me."

"You think?"

One of Jun Wei's inner circle—a cousin—stood up, took hold of the microphone, and, putting out his cigarette, began to sing a romantic song.

"Life wouldn't be life if it was smooth all the way," Jun Wei said.

Zhang looked at him. "Is something the matter?"

"The Iran deal fell through."

"I'm sorry." But Zhang felt a small burst of relief. He hadn't wanted to be involved in the first place.

"We had to work all through Golden Week," Jun Wei said, "for nothing."

"Maybe we can salvage it."

"No." Jun Wei shook his head several times, firmly.

"There will be other deals," Zhang said.

"It's of no great consequence to you, I suppose—the man who has everything." Jun Wei looked out across the room.

The man who has everything. Zhang was sure the phrase was intended as a piece of gentle mockery, but he was troubled by the bitterness that seemed to coat the words. Perhaps Jun Wei had sensed Zhang's relief—or his indifference, at least. He had always had an instinct for such things.

"How's the new girlfriend?" Jun Wei asked after a few moments.

"She's been in London. She's due back tonight."

Jun Wei looked at Zhang with sleepy eyes. His gaze had a weight that was uncomfortable, and unfamiliar.

"What?" Zhang said.

Jun Wei shook his head again, then handed his empty glass to one of the pretty girls, who replenished it. "She and I had a little talk," he said, "on the night of the banquet..."

Zhang remembered.

"I think she forgave me for my crass remark." Jun Wei swirled the cognac in his glass. "How was I supposed to know she spoke Chinese?"

Zhang smiled, but said nothing.

Reaching into his cognac with finger and thumb, Jun Wei pulled out a cube of ice, put it in his mouth and began to chew on it. He seemed to relish the splintering and cracking sounds it made. His cousin finally came to the end of his dreary, sentimental song, and Jun Wei and Zhang applauded.

Zhang's phone rang. It was Naemi.

"I have to take this," he said.

Jun Wei nodded.

Standing up, Zhang pressed Accept, then he crossed the room and sat down on a sofa that wasn't occupied.

"Are you back?" he asked.

"I just landed," she said. "Can I see you?"

Zhang watched as Jun Wei took hold of the microphone and began to sing "Don't Say You Don't Care About My Tears," which was the song he always sang. The collapse of the Iran deal had upset him. To see him performing, though, you would never have guessed. He seemed his usual affable self.

"Zhang? Are you there?"

"I can't tonight," he said. "I'm with some people."

"You can't get away?"

"Not really."

He was still watching Jun Wei. On high or heartfelt notes, his friend would move the mic away from his mouth and then back again, as pop stars often do, but there was really no need, since his voice was weak, almost effeminate.

"I'm actually pretty tired," Naemi said. "It was a long flight."

"You should get some rest." He had adopted a distant, soothing tone, as if they were at a completely different stage in their relationship. A much later stage. He could easily have made his excuses and left. He wasn't quite sure why he hadn't.

"You remember Kung Lan," she was saying, "the artist I told you about? His opening's tomorrow night, at the gallery. Why don't you come along? We could go out afterwards."

"Text me the details," Zhang said.

"All right." She paused. "I can't wait to see you, Zhang. It's been ages."

"I can't wait to see you either."

He ended the call and rejoined Jun Wei, who was sitting down again.

"Your singing hasn't improved," he said.

Jun Wei grinned, then reached for his cigarettes and looked around. "Do you like this place?"

"It's better than the place on Dapu Road."

"There are women here. On another floor." Jun Wei's smile was sudden, unnerving.

"I'm sure," Zhang said.

"Do you want a woman? Do you want two?"

"You know what? I think I'll get an early night." Zhang rose to his feet. "Thanks for the drink."

Jun Wei stood up and put a heavy arm round Zhang's shoulders. "You're sure you don't want a woman? You seem a bit tense. It might relax you."

"I already have a woman."

"She's not here, though."

Zhang looked at the floor and smiled and shook his head. Jun Wei was always trying to push you into doing something you didn't want to do. It was as if he knew best. And if you didn't give in, if you didn't go along with what he was proposing, you were made to feel you were questioning his powers of persuasion, or even his judgment. In resisting him, you were insulting him.

"And anyway," Jun Wei went on, "it never stopped you before."

"This is different," Zhang said.

"If you say so, my friend. If you say so." Jun Wei stood back and slid his hands into his trouser pockets. "But perhaps everything isn't as straightforward as you think."

Zhang smiled.

When he reached the doorway, he stopped and looked back. Jun Wei was sitting on the sofa again. He had scooped up a handful of peanuts and was lobbing them, one by one, towards an empty glass. The first three missed. The fourth bounced off the rim. The fifth landed inside. Smiling to himself, Jun Wei tossed the rest of the nuts into his mouth. There was always a moment in the evening when he tried to lob peanuts into a glass, usually when he was by himself and he thought nobody was paying attention. But he was Wang Jun Wei. There was always somebody paying attention.

As Chun Tao drove him home, Zhang reflected on Jun Wei's state of mind that evening. His friend had seemed prickly and distracted, and there had been a pointed aspect to many of his remarks. The man who has everything, he had said—and yet he was far wealthier than Zhang would ever be...Did he blame Zhang for the collapse of the Iran deal? Had he realized that Zhang's heart had not been in it? Or did it have to do with Chu En Li? Implicit in Zhang's concern about Chu En Li's relationship with his sister was the feeling that Chu En Li was beneath her, and it was possible Jun Wei had taken that personally. After all, Chu En Li was somebody he had worked with, somebody he had hired. Jun Wei could be thin-skinned at times, and Zhang suspected him of feeling slighted, or harboring a grudge. Was it something he had done, or something he had failed to do? Had he been insensitive? His thoughts kept circling the subject without ever arriving at an answer.

The following evening, a low-voltage yellow glow colored the tops of the buildings as Chun Tao drove Zhang across the city. At street level, though, it was already dusk, and the snack booths and the shops selling rice noodles had their lights on. The pavements were filled with the silhouettes of people walking home from work. Two text messages came in, one after the other. The first was from his secretary, letting him know that she had booked him on the ten a.m. flight to Beijing. He had meetings in the capital, and would also be seeing his family. His wife, his son. His mother. He would be back in time for Mad Dog's funeral, on Tuesday. In the second text, Johnny Yu told him that Chu En Li had flown to Manila the week before. He was living in a three-star hotel not far from the waterfront. Zhang nodded, then put his phone away.

At half past six, they turned into Moganshan Road, passing graffiti-covered walls and a middle-aged woman with a hosepipe washing a car. Art Island was located on the third floor of a building at the rear of the complex. Zhang climbed several flights of wooden stairs that had been painted red and entered a room with high white walls and skylights. Though he was early, the gallery was already packed, and since he couldn't see Naemi anywhere he began to look at the work. As she had told him previously, the show was called *Modern Madonnas*. He stopped in front of a larger-than-life picture of a Chinese girl in her early twenties. Dressed in a scarlet blouse, she was leaning against part of a bus shelter. It was evening, and the light filtering down from a streetlamp overhead made the gritty concrete wall behind her look yellow. The expression on her face was demure and yet delighted, and it wasn't hard to imagine that she was gazing not at a phone but at a baby. Her expression worked for both. He thought the image was exquisite—the primary colors, the glossy-magazine glamour—but it was scathing too. In capturing the way in which people worshipped their devices, Kung Lan was implying that social media was the new religion. What's more, since all the women photographed were on their own, since they were isolated figures in an urban landscape, he was also positing the idea that virtual interaction was beginning to supersede its human equivalent. Only the day before, Zhang had read an article about two teenage girls in Shanghai who had run into each other on the street by chance. They wanted to talk, but weren't able to find a place they were both happy with. In the end, they decided to return to their respective homes and communicate online, as usual.

"Zhang!"

He turned to see Naemi standing at his shoulder in a simple, tight-fitting black dress. There was the trace of a bruise near her left eye, and he wondered if she'd had another of her fainting fits.

"Did you notice anything unusual?" she asked.

He smiled. "Like what?"

She took his hand and led him through the crowd to the far end of the gallery. There, on the back wall, was an enormous photograph of her. It seemed that she, too, was part of the exhibition.

"What do you think?" she said.

Like all the other women, she was looking at her phone, and though he suspected that she knew she was being photographed the image had a certain spontaneity about it. Her expression—a fond half smile, as if she was watching a child take its first steps—felt entirely natural. The fake-fur jacket she was wearing echoed the tones of gold and honey in her hair. The sky behind was a deep midnight blue, the shapes of trees low down in the frame, as brittle and black-edged as burnt paper.

"Where was it taken?" he asked.

"Hong Kong. In a park."

He nodded.

"You know the funny thing?" she said. "I was reading a text—from you."

"Really?"

"Yes." She considered the photograph again. "When he first asked me to do it I didn't want to, but he kept on at me, and now I'm kind of glad I did."

"It's beautiful," Zhang said. "You look modern, but also—I don't know—eternal."

Something flashed across her face and was gone, too fast for him to be able to interpret it.

"Kung Lan would like that. You should tell him." She looked past him and nodded, and he realized they were about to be interrupted.

"You have to work," he said. "Are we still seeing each other afterwards?"

"Absolutely."

"If I'm not here, I'll be outside in the car." He kissed her on the lips, then turned away.

————

After spending an hour in the gallery, Zhang returned to the Jaguar and opened his copy of Mad Dog's book on ghost culture. He picked up where he had left off—a chapter about blood-drinking ghosts, also known as *jiangshi*. Mad Dog's style, which was dry, spare, and elastic, not unlike his bass playing, was highly readable. Since blood-drinking ghosts had no flexibility—their limbs were stiff, as if with rigor mortis—they hopped rather than walked, usually with their arms outstretched. Their hair was long and white, and their skin had a greenish tinge, a reference to the mold that appears on things that are old or dead. What's more, their bodies were often covered with white fur, like that of a snow weasel. They were frightened of mirrors, and peach wood, and the cock's crow, and if you wanted to distract them you simply dropped rice or sand on the ground, as they would feel compelled to count every last grain. Zhang had been carrying the peach twig on him ever since Mad Dog had given it to him, along with the tin-backed mirror and the red envelope containing orange peel, but they didn't seem to have affected Naemi in the slightest. Shaking his head, he skipped a few pages, then started reading again.

When people died in ancient China, Mad Dog wrote, their souls traveled across a bridge to the afterlife, but they could not set off until the appropriate funeral services and burials had taken place. Also, certain customs or rituals had to be observed. If any part of this process was mismanaged or overlooked, the souls of the deceased would lack the sense of peace required for their journey. Instead, they would return to the earth and bother those who were still alive. Generally speaking, this would be their families. Their loved ones. Ghosts were a reality, Mad Dog argued, whether you believed in them or not. As phenomena, they might seem abnormal and disturbing, but they should be viewed as natural, not *super*natural, since they were emanations of qi, the psychophysical energy that constitutes the essence of every object and being in the universe. As Feng Menglong wrote, "The dark netherworld and the clear world of the living blend into each other, as water melts into water." In other words, the border between the two worlds was porous. The dead could visit the living, and vice versa—

Sensing somebody approaching the car, Zhang looked up and saw Naemi crossing the pavement. He closed the book quickly and slid it beneath the seat in front of him.

"Sorry I was so long," she said when she got in. "Kung Lan wouldn't let me go."

"Well, it's his night," Zhang said.

She leaned over and kissed him. "The look on your face when you saw that photograph of me..."

"Actually, I bought it."

She stared at him. "What?"

"I bought it," he said. "It wasn't cheap, but I'm told that Kung Lan's work is really beginning to take off. I think it's probably a good investment."

His deadpan answer made her smile, though he sensed that his purchase had shocked her, and made her uneasy. It wasn't a straightforward response.

As they drove across the city, he decided to change the subject.

"How was London?"

"It was lovely." She sighed. "The air had that autumn smell already—fireworks and dead leaves. There were dead leaves everywhere." She glanced at him, the blue neon passing through the inside of the car making her blonde hair look cold. "Have you been?"

"Once or twice," he said, "but never at this time of year." He looked out through the window and saw an office building with all its lights on, no one sitting at any of the desks. "Tell me about your mother."

"My mother?" she said. "Where did that come from?"

He shrugged. "I don't know. I'm curious."

"She was restless. Quite wild. She was a Sami. I think I mentioned that before."

"Did she look like you?"

"Not really. She was about my height, but she had black hair. Her eyes were blue."

"When did she die?"

"Years ago." Naemi stared straight ahead. "I loved her very much. I miss her."

Black hair, blue eyes. If what Naemi was telling him was true, it put paid to his theory that she was the daughter of Nina, the girl Gulsvig had known.

He tried another angle. "Did she ever go to university?"

"My mother?" Naemi laughed. "I told you. My parents were country people. I grew up in the middle of nowhere."

"It seems so unlikely," he said, "you being the child of country people."

"That's me. Unlikely."

Some minutes later, Chun Tao pulled up on the north side of People's Square. The Shanghai Museum stood in the middle, rounded and glowing, like an interplanetary craft that had just landed.

"I want to show you something," Zhang said.

Naemi contemplated the floodlit museum for a few

moments, then turned to look at him. "Are you sure about this?"

"I'm sure."

They entered the museum by the side entrance and climbed the steps to the second floor. As always, the building housed a grainy silence. When they reached the ceramics gallery, he led her to an ivory-colored vase with a round body and a long neck. The small white card below it said: *T'ang: 618–907.* The vase was almost defiant in its plainness and its simplicity, and yet it carried with it a sense of all the years that it had lived through. All the centuries. He glanced at Naemi, and saw a new stillness in her face. He didn't ask her what she was thinking. She would speak if she wanted to. There was no need, in fact, to speak at all. Like meditation, it was an experience that transcended words.

"About the photograph," he said. "Did you mind me buying it?"

"No, of course not. It's just—" She cut herself off, unwilling to go further.

"Just what?"

But she wouldn't say anything else.

They moved on round the gallery. Most of the pieces had the same qualities of elegance and blankness. She was drawn to a celadon jar or bowl that stood in a glass case of its own in the middle of a room. Made in the early eighteenth century, during the reign of Yongzheng, it had a pale green glaze, and was decorated with an embossed design of mingling clouds and dragons.

"This doesn't feel quite as calm as the others," she said.

"If the others are ascetics or holy men," he said, "this one's a kind of warrior."

"Yes. Exactly."

"The people who made these pieces were channeling something much bigger than they were. They were real masters of their craft, but they were servants too. They weren't entirely in control."

"They were vessels," she said. "Vessels making vessels."

"That's clever—and true." Slipping an arm round her waist, he drew her close and kissed her.

Later, when they were outside again, he told her that he always felt different afterwards. "Cleaner than before, somehow, and capable of anything. Or nothing."

Her eyes on the ground, she nodded and smiled.

As they walked back to the car, he suggested they sit for a few moments. She sank down onto a bench and looked up into the trees. The night was warm and damp. Leaning sideways, he took a little dark green box out of his jacket pocket.

"Here," he said.

"What's this?" she asked.

"A gift."

She shook her head, a movement so small that it was almost imperceptible. He couldn't tell if she was disapproving or overwhelmed.

"Why don't you open it?" he said.

She undid the catch and lifted the hinged lid. Inside was an antique ring he had bought for her earlier that day, a single oblong piece of jade in a setting of carved gold. Her lips parted, and her black eyes seemed to be emitting light.

"Try it on," he said.

She did as he asked. The milky green stone was precisely the same width as her ring finger. She didn't speak. A breeze pushed through the branches overhead.

"The moment I saw it," he said, "I thought of you. The way the beauty of the gold combined and yet contrasted with the mystery of the jade." He took hold of her hand and looked down at the ring. "We have a saying here in China. Perhaps you know it: *Gold has a value, but jade is priceless*."

"I don't think I've heard that before," she murmured.

"People think jade wards off evil spirits, and that it brings good fortune. They also think it stands for longevity. I don't know whether you believe in any of that. I'm not sure I do." He smiled faintly. "In any case, it can't do any harm."

"Longevity?" She gave him a furtive look, almost as if she were guilty of something.

"Isn't that what everybody wants?"

She didn't say anything else.

On the way back to his apartment, she rested her head against his shoulder. Her hair smelled of frankincense. *The Sacred Tears of Thebes.* He should forget about what she might or might not have done. Who she might or might not be. He should forget about what people said. He had only been seeing her for a few weeks, and it seemed doubtful that it would last. The affair would burn itself out, like all the others. Why not make the most of things in the little time that they had left? He felt his heart expand, as it had expanded in the nightclub dream, but there were no girls in tight black tops and no golden lounges, and the small man in the pale blue suit wasn't a metaphor for anything, or an oracle. He was just one of life's many enigmas. Not every question had an answer.

Once Chun Tao had dropped them outside Zhang's building, they hurried through the revolving doors and across the lobby. The concierge said good evening, but they didn't stop. In the lift, they stood against opposing walls, their eyes on the illuminated numbers above the door. Their desire for each other was so powerful that they didn't know what to do with it. They couldn't look at each other, or even speak.

Then they were in his apartment and stumbling towards the bed, undressing each other as they went, no time to turn on any of the lights, just the city's brownish-yellow glow filling the room like a liquid, slowing them down. She clutched at him as if afraid of being cut loose—or perhaps he was the one who was adrift, and she was trying to rescue him. Sometimes he felt she was stronger than he was, but then she would startle him with a moment of defenselessness or vulnerability, the one seemingly rooted in the other in a way he could never grasp. He remembered Gulsvig telling him about Nina. That night at the party, on the outskirts of Helsinki. *I have this secret. I can't tell you what it is.* That sounded just like the woman he was with. Waves took him, luminous and supple. He gave himself to them. It didn't matter. Nothing mattered. No world but this world, no moment but this moment. She came first, which made him come, then she appeared to come again, her cries and shudders impossible to separate from his . . .

At last, they fell back, breathing hard, his left hand behind his head, her right arm across his belly, a cold place where the ring was.

"I had something engraved on the inside," he said.

"The inside of what?" Her voice was drowsy.

"The ring."

She propped herself on one elbow. "What does it say?"

"You can look."

"Why don't you tell me?"

"All right. It says: *My heart is like the pine and cypress / But what is your heart like?*"

She didn't speak. There was just the silver glitter of her eyes.

"They're not my words," he said. "They were written by Li Po, a great T'ang poet. The same era as the vases we saw earlier."

Li Po had traveled widely, and had a reputation for heavy drinking and general irresponsibility. *What would Li Po have done?* This was something Johnny Yu would often say, when he found himself in a dilemma, and the Li Po option was always the most reckless and attractive of those on offer.

"It's from one of the Wu songs," Zhang went on. "He would take song structures and write poems to fit them.

The poems were intended to be lighthearted and playful. They were very popular at the time."

"If your heart is like the pine and cypress," Naemi said, "I imagine your feelings must be steadfast and true."

"Yes," he said, "I'm not known for that."

She smiled. "Have you changed? Did I change you?"

He didn't answer.

"You feel something for me which is constant," she went on. "That's what the ring is saying?"

"Yes."

"But you want to know what I'm feeling…"

"It's Li Po talking, remember? It's not serious. Constancy is the one thing he can't manage." He paused. "*Do you love me?* People ask that a lot. But it's the wrong question."

She was nodding. "I agree."

There was a silence, and he must have fallen asleep because when he reached for her she wasn't there. Sometimes, when he woke, he thought he had only dreamed that he was with her, but there she would be, reading on the chair in the corner, under the lamp, or standing beside the bed, reaching back to fasten the clip on her bra, or leaning against the window, looking at the view…Lying still, he thought he heard the shower running. He dozed again. Next time he looked, she was in the bedroom, already dressed, strands of fair hair tumbling across her face as she bent down to zip up a boot. Watching her through narrowed eyes, he was struck by her litheness and her grace. *An animal, pretending to be human...*

"Are you awake?" she said.

He opened his eyes and stretched. "Just about."

She placed the ring on the bedside table. "I loved wearing it, even for twelve hours, but I'm afraid I can't accept it."

"Why not?"

"It has come at the wrong time." She sat down on the edge of the bed. "You came too close. You asked too many questions." She paused. "I think I fell for you."

He watched her, but said nothing.

"It was supposed to be casual," she went on, "something we could walk into. Walk away from. Intense, but momentary, like a shaft of sunlight reaching down into a forest." She laughed softly, mocking herself for being so poetic. "I thought you'd be capable of that. I thought it would come naturally to you."

He took her hand. "The ring is a gift. I'm not holding you to anything."

"I know. But it's too much."

From far below came the ghostly wail of a siren.

"You told me once that you had to protect yourself," he said. "What are you protecting yourself from?"

She looked away from him, towards the window. Outside, day was breaking. No sign of the sun, just a gradually encroaching grayness.

"It's something I can't imagine, isn't it," he said.

"This is what I mean," she said, "by asking too many questions."

He was silent, thinking. Remembering.

"I forgot to tell you," he said. "Mad Dog died."

She stiffened, then removed her hand from his. "What happened?"

He told her about the drinks in the bar, the late-night walk. He told her Mad Dog had fallen down a flight of steps and hit his head. He said he was the last person to have seen him.

She moved from the bed to the window and stood facing away from him. "I'm sorry. He was your friend." She seemed affected by the news, more than he would have expected.

"I don't know why I'm telling you," he said. "You only met him once. You hardly knew him."

"I heard him play..."

"He was good, wasn't he."

"Yes, he was."

He was about to say something else when his phone rang. It was the concierge. Wang Jun Wei was in the lobby. Zhang glanced at his watch. It was a few minutes after six. Probably Jun Wei had been out all night.

"Should I send him up?" the concierge asked.

"Tell him to wait," Zhang said. "I'll come down." He ended the call and saw that Naemi was by the window, watching him. "It's Wang Jun Wei. He's in the lobby."

"I'd rather he didn't see me."

Zhang nodded. "I'll show you out the back way."

He pulled on a T-shirt and trousers, then took her hand and led her through the living room and the kitchen and on into the utility room. There was a door he rarely used, which opened onto the service lift and the emergency stairs. He pressed the call button and heard the lift grind into motion somewhere deep down in the building.

"When will I see you?" he asked.

"I'm not sure," she said.

The lift arrived. He kept his finger on the button to prevent the door from closing on her as she stepped inside. She turned to face him. The fluorescent strip light in the ceiling lit her gold-blonde hair and her smooth forehead. Her eyes were in shadow. As she stood on the gouged and battered metal floor in her dark clothes, the harsh white light splashing down on her, he remembered what the girl in Quik had said. *She was amazing-looking, like a comic-book character or a superhero.* In that moment, with his finger still pressing the button and the door of the lift still open, the realization hit him. There wasn't anyone who looked like her—not in Shanghai, not anywhere. There wasn't anyone who even came close. It had to have been her.

"Is something wrong?" she asked.

"You never went to London," he said, "did you."

She stared at him, her blonde hair gleaming, her eyes shadow-black, unreadable.

"It was you." His voice was calm. A sense of dream or wonderment. "You killed him."

He had taken his finger off the button, and the door was sliding shut, but he could still see her through the small, smeared window. The light above her head began to flicker on and off. Rapid, flashed glimpses of her. Her face a maze of cracks and wrinkles. Her hair all white. Flecks of blood flew at the glass, like paint flicked from a brush. He stepped back, his heart beating so hard he felt his whole body was being shaken.

Then she dropped out of sight.

For a few long moments he didn't move. He couldn't. He wasn't sure what he had seen.

When the lift jolted to a halt at ground level, and the cables had fallen still, he backed into the utility room and locked the door and leaned against it, looking towards the kitchen but not seeing it, a hissing in his head, like tinnitus, his throat parched and dry. He closed his eyes and felt the cool painted wood beneath his hands. He remembered Jun Wei, who would be waiting in the lobby. At least ten minutes had gone by since the concierge had called. Opening his eyes again, he pushed away from the door and fetched his phone from the bedside table. When the concierge answered, he asked to speak to Wang Jun Wei.

"He just left," the concierge said.

Zhang called Jun Wei's number, but there was no reply. He sent a text instead. *Sorry to miss you. Flying to Beijing this morning. Back on Monday.* After showering and getting dressed, he packed a small bag, picked up a set of car keys from the kitchen counter, and left the apartment. Once in the lift, he pressed B for basement. His mind seemed to have closed down. There were no thoughts. Only practicalities.

In the car park under the building, Chun Tao was already waiting.

"Change of plan," Zhang said. "I'm going to drive myself to the airport. I won't need you again till after the weekend."

In the far corner of the car park was a black Mercedes, which he kept for private use. He watched Chun Tao depart, then he walked over to the Mercedes and got in. Putting on his dark glasses, he drove up the ramp and out into the daylight. When he stopped at the security barrier, he glanced in the rearview mirror. The road behind him was empty. He wasn't sure what he had expected to see.

At the first red light, he called his wife. They had arranged to meet the following day, he reminded her, but he would also like to have time with his son. She told him that Sunday would be best. He drove towards the Yan'an Road Tunnel, which would take him west, to the airport in Hongqiao. Though it was the second week of October, a kind of summer had returned. It wasn't the Autumn Tiger, when the weather was unseasonably hot and dry. This was something else. Something humid. Clammy. Something that didn't have a name.

The curved silver edge of a CD was protruding from the CD player. He pushed it all the way in. It was a Howlin' Wolf album called *Killing Floor*, and the title song had never seemed more apt. *I shoulda quit you / A long time ago*...For years, he had assumed that "killing floor" referred to the Chicago slaughterhouses, where so many black men ended up working when they fled the Deep South, and he wasn't necessarily wrong, but then he had read an interview with the Wolf's guitarist, Hubert Sumlin, which had cast a new light on the lyric. Sumlin explained that the Wolf's wife had suspected him of being unfaithful to her while he was away on tour. The day he returned, she opened fire on him from the front window of their house. The Wolf was picking buckshot out of himself for weeks after. On the killing floor, Sumlin said. It's when a relationship brings you down so low you wish you were dead.

Zhang drove towards Hongqiao, with Howlin' Wolf's abrasive voice scouring the inside of the car. Every now and then, he checked his rearview mirror. He still didn't know what he was looking for. Probably he felt dogged or poisoned by what he had witnessed, and was struggling to shake it off.

Five days later, on Monday morning, his plane touched down in Shanghai. The trip to Beijing had not been a success. When he met Xuan Xuan, she had done nothing but complain about money—she needed a new car, among other things—and he had agreed to increase the limit on her credit cards. The next day, he visited his mother in the nursing home. As usual, she didn't speak or move. It seemed unlikely that she knew who he was, or even that he was there. Her eyes were misty. Blind-looking. He sat with her for an hour, then kissed her on the forehead and left. That evening, he took Hai Long out to dinner, but the fifteen-year-old spent most of the time on his phone. He responded to Zhang's questions with a kind of distant courtesy, as if they had no relevance to him whatsoever and he was simply providing answers that he imagined might be appropriate. Zhang sensed boredom and contempt beneath the politeness, and perhaps that was only to be expected. All things considered, he had not been much of a father.

He collected his Mercedes from the short-stay car park and drove back into the city. A truck had crashed on the Yan'an elevated highway, and dozens of glossy pale green cabbages were scattered across the road, some of them crushed flat, others so unmarked that people were getting out of their cars to pick them up. It took Zhang an hour and a half to reach the complex of galleries and studios on Moganshan Road. He parked outside and sat with his hands on the steering wheel. It was still early, not even ten o'clock, and the street was empty except for a security guard on duty by the main entrance. The air was tense and gray. Why had he come? What did he hope to achieve? He had told Naemi that she was responsible for Mad Dog's death, something he could neither justify nor prove, and he wished he had never opened his mouth. At the same time, he had been unable to forget what had happened during the moments that followed his accusation. Had he perceived some truth about her, or had his mind been bent out of shape by Mad Dog's unrelenting talk of ghosts and demons? Had he, too, begun to see things that weren't there? That would amount to a kind of derangement. But if sanity meant he had to believe what he had seen, perhaps he would rather not be sane. As a child, he had always run towards his fear. It was something his father had taught him. If you're afraid of heights, his father said, look for a high building or a precipice. If the darkness scares you, turn off all the lights. Nothing had ever frightened Zhang more than the face he had glimpsed in the split second before the service lift dropped out of sight. But it was that face that he had come to see.

He entered the complex and climbed the red stairs to the gallery where the opening had taken place the previous Wednesday. At the far end of the space was a two-story glass cube where several gallery employees sat at desks, their faces lit by computer screens. A woman emerged as he approached. She was in her forties or fifties, and her face had the pallor and consistency of wax. She wore glasses with oblong lenses and severe black frames. Her jacket and trousers were also black.

"I'm looking for Naemi Kuusela," he said.

"She left."

"When will she be back?"

The woman shook her head. "You don't understand. She no longer works here. Friday was her last day."

He stared at her. "Has she got a new job?"

"I suppose so."

"Where?"

"She didn't tell me."

He was still staring. "Are you in charge here?"

"I'm the director."

"And she didn't tell you where she was going?"

"Why should she? It's none of my business." The woman examined him through her designer glasses. Her default expression was that of somebody conducting an experiment. Measured, impassive. Scientific. "Now, if you'll excuse me—"

"Wait."

The other people in the gallery looked up from their computers. He had raised his voice.

"She told me she was leaving China," the woman said. "She had been here for long enough. There comes a time, she said, when you just know. But she didn't say where she was going, or what she might be doing in the future."

Leaving China? Zhang looked down at the polished concrete floor. He was thinking of Nina again. Gulsvig's Nina. He remembered Gulsvig talking of her abrupt and unforeseen departure for New York. He imagined she would have left New York too, eventually, and with similar abruptness. And whenever she disappeared, she would leave a death in her wake. In London, it had been her boyfriend, Peter. In New York, he thought, there would also have been an unexpected death. She cast off people as a snake casts off its skin. Places too. Things that had been important to her, crucial even, suddenly became superfluous, disposable. Gulsvig's actual words came back to him, Gulsvig recalling something Nina had said about her English boyfriend. *He can't seem to get close enough.* Naemi had said very nearly the same thing to him, early on Thursday morning, when she returned the jade ring he had given her. Was that a coincidence? If so, what kind of coincidence? Once again, the two young women, born forty years apart, appeared to merge, to overlap, but the link between them remained as obscure and mysterious as ever.

"I was sorry to lose her," the director said. "Her knowledge was remarkable—especially for someone so young."

Zhang nodded to himself. "And you really have no idea where she might have gone?"

"She was always very discreet. Very private." The director looked past him, towards the entrance to the gallery. "I had the impression that it wasn't just China that she was leaving. She was leaving the art world too. There were other avenues she wanted to explore. She is one of those people who can turn their hand to almost anything. Perhaps I was lucky she stayed as long as she did." She shook her head in admiration, and also, Zhang thought, in disbelief.

He thanked the woman, and was just moving away when she asked him for his name. He looked at her over his shoulder.

"So I can tell her that you asked for her," the woman said, "when she gets in touch."

"She won't," he said. "You'll never hear from her again."

The woman blinked.

On his way back down the stairs, Zhang checked his phone. Just work e-mails. He would deal with them later. When he reached the road, he stopped and looked around. The sky was darker, greener. There was going to be a storm. The rain would fall with such force that it would bounce off the pavement. The temperature would drop.

"You want to buy a gift?"

He turned. The street vendor had arrived with his wooden cart and his trinkets.

"What about a nice piece of jade," the vendor said, "for luck?"

Zhang took out his car keys and pressed Unlock. "You look like you could use it more than me."

"There isn't a person in the world who doesn't need a bit of luck from time to time." Shaking his head, the vendor adjusted the position of an old cracked teakettle. "This weather. Everybody's out of sorts."

Zhang selected a couple of notes from his wallet and laid them on the handcart.

The vendor looked at the money. "What's that for?"

Zhang shrugged.

Once in the car, he put in a call to Johnny Yu.

"Naemi's disappeared," he said.

"*After the parting I know not if she is far or near / What meets the eye is bleak and doleful.*" There was a quick rasping sound as Johnny lit a cigarette. "That's Ou-Yang Hsiu. A Confucian master."

"I think she left the country," Zhang said.

"You want me to find out what's going on?"

"I'm not sure..."

He remembered how relief had mingled with regret when he said goodbye to Naemi outside the private members' club on the night of their first meeting. At the time, he had found his relief bewildering. It had seemed out of character, and out of place. He hadn't understood why he should be feeling such a thing. Now, though, it occurred to him that he might have had some sort of premonition. Perhaps, after all, relief was appropriate, and valid. Perhaps he should simply let her go. And yet...

As he stared through the windscreen at the street vendor, the air began to look busy, almost pixelated. The rain was coming down, just as he had predicted. In a matter of seconds, it became torrential. The vendor was no longer visible.

"Johnny?" he said.

"Yes?"

"There is one thing you could do."

———

Mist rose off the road, and he drove through it, the rain loud on the roof of the car, a constant, brutal roar. He felt slightly sick, as though he had eaten something that was past its sell-by date. On reaching the Embankment Building, he parked directly opposite and sat behind the wheel, staring straight ahead. Gradually, the rain began to slacken off. He switched on the radio and listened to the news.

He had been waiting for about twenty minutes when he saw a bulky, middle-aged woman in gray overalls trudging up the street, head lowered. She had a toolbox in one hand and a company logo stitched above her breast pocket. He got out of the car and hurried over the road.

"Did Mr. Yu send you?" he asked.

She looked at him. "You locked yourself out, apparently." Her hair was plastered flat against her head, and water dripped from her eyebrows and the tip of her blunt nose.

He led her through the lobby, noting the letters EB set into the floor in charcoal gray. To the left was a makeshift wood-and-glass structure that housed the concierge. There was a CCTV camera on the top, but it seemed unlikely that it worked—and even if it did work he would have been prepared to bet that nobody ever so much as glanced at the footage. It was a huge building, with hundreds of tenants. People came and went unchecked all the time.

They took a lift to the seventh floor. When the door opened, he was faced with a corridor that stretched away in both directions. The walls were painted a dull institutional green, and the air smelled of stale food and dust. Fat silver heating pipes clung to the ceiling. Which way should he go? When he was lying on his back in bed a few weeks before and imagined coming to the building, he had been unable to locate Naemi's apartment, and there was part of him that wondered if it even existed, but he chose to walk to the right, and there, after a few paces, was number 710. Stopping in front of the solid matte-black door, he noticed that it was fitted with two expensive-looking locks. Something about the feeling of anonymity and the enhanced nature of the security measures confirmed the fact that this was Naemi's apartment. The locksmith put down her toolbox and examined the locks from close-up.

"State-of-the-art, these are," she said.

Since the door was set deep in the wall, she was able to work without being seen, but Zhang stood guard, just in case. If someone came along, he would use the story he had told Johnny to use: he was looking after the apartment while his friend was away, and he had mislaid his keys. There was no reason why anyone would think to question that. The locksmith hadn't. If someone who actually knew Naemi happened to pass by, he had no idea what he would say.

But nobody appeared.

It took another half an hour to dismantle and replace the locks, but at last the door was open. The locksmith gave him a new set of keys, then put her tools back in the box. He counted out some notes and handed them to her. She counted them again, the tip of her tongue showing in the corner of her mouth, then she nodded to herself. Turning away, she started back towards the lift.

When she had gone, he entered the apartment, pulling the door shut behind him. From the small, square hallway, with its row of coat hooks, he walked into a room that had the dimensions of a loft. The walls were the same matte-black as the front door. So were the pillars that supported the ceiling. The floorboards had been painted with a deep red Chinese lacquer, and the traditional wood furniture was upholstered in stiff slub silks and dark brocades. Probably it had come with the apartment. The effect of the somber palette used throughout—even the

cushions on the sofa were plum- or damson-colored—
was to create a kind of hush. He moved on into the center
of the room. There were windows all along one side, the
view of the city simplified by the mist, its trees and buildings reduced to soft gray shapes.

He began to look around. Naemi's departure may
have been sudden, but it had obviously been planned.
He sensed the calmness and efficiency of somebody
for whom the severing of all connections was familiar.
Would that be overstating it? He thought not. He moved
on, looking for clues as to where she might have gone,
but everything he found belonged to a present that was
already past—a Flying Pigeon bicycle with a yellow
frame, a shelf of Art Island catalogues, a large-scale street
map of Shanghai. Gradually, though, he realized that he
was learning something after all. The kitchen, which was
built into the back wall, and separated from the main
living area by a granite-topped counter or breakfast bar,
looked brand-new, as if it had been fitted only days ago.
He ran a finger along the inside of the oven door. There
wasn't even a suggestion of grease. He opened the fridge.
Not just empty, but pristine. It wasn't that the appliances
were clean. They had never been used. He had heard
of people who didn't like their apartments to smell of

cooking. Perhaps she was particular in that way, preferring to eat out—though, come to think of it, he couldn't remember seeing her eat anything at all. It was in the bedroom, however, that he made the discovery that puzzled him the most. Like the rest of the apartment, it had been painted black. There was no bed, though. If the apartment had been rented furnished, surely there ought to have been a bed. As he crossed the room with his head lowered, deep in thought, he became aware of something gritty underneath his shoes. Squatting down, he touched the varnished floorboards. Tiny particles of earth stuck to his fingertips. It looked as if somebody had tried to sweep it up, but he still found traces in every part of the room, as if, at some point, the entire floor had been covered with it. It didn't look like the kind of earth that might collect on your shoes if you went for a walk in the country, the kind of earth you might accidentally track into your home. It was more like soil. The soil you found in potted plants. But why was it scattered all over the floor? A chill went through him, and he stood up quickly, rubbing one hand against the other.

He returned to the living room. As he stood in the middle of the vast space, his phone began to ring. He looked at the screen. *Unknown.* If this had happened a week earlier, he would have assumed it was Naemi. Now, though, he wasn't so sure. He had the sudden conviction that if he answered, he would be allowing something harmful into his life, just as the opening of an attachment can admit a virus. He pressed Decline. It was only midday, but the light had faded, and as he looked towards the bank of windows the whole apartment seemed to shudder and leap sideways, shadows appearing, then disappearing, the floorboards bright as glass. There was a thick silence, as if the walls were padded, then thunder exploded overhead. On the street below, a car alarm went off. He remained quite still, skin prickling. He had sensed something behind him. He turned slowly. There she was, in the bedroom doorway. She was wearing a black shift dress. Her arms and legs were bare. There was blood around her mouth, and blood had spilled down her front, shiny and wet, dark stains on the darkness. More thunder rolled across the roof.

"Naemi?"

His voice was dry and brittle as a dead rose. One touch, and it would crumble.

"I thought you'd left," he murmured.

She smiled. There was blood on her teeth.

"When I was with you," she said, "I tried to inhabit the part of me that would excite you. The part that you would love. The rest, I hid away. I'm used to that. But you were more open than I expected you to be. More curious." She looked past him, towards the window. "I thought it would just be sex. I thought you were that kind of man."

"I am that kind of man," he said.

Lightning darted through the apartment. In the silvery glare, the walls seemed dusty, but her eyes were blacker than ever. The thunder was like rocks tipped off a truck.

"So is it true?" he said. "Are you a ghost?"

Stepping close to him, she put her lips to his. They were cold and sticky.

"I can't tell you that," she murmured.

"The blood," he said.

"Yes..."

"What happens?"

"I don't hurt anyone." She looked at him. "The blood is mine."

She turned away, passing through the doorway that led into the bedroom. When he reached the doorway, she was already disappearing behind the freestanding wall at the far end of the room. He followed her and found himself in the bathroom. On the marble surface, next to the sink, was a flat wooden box with metal catches. It was the kind of box that might once have held dusted pink cubes of Turkish delight, or Cuban cigars in tightly packed rows—or even, perhaps, a gun. He lifted the lid and saw the cannula and the syringes she had ordered from the medical supplies place. There was also a slim bottle of white spirit, a roll of surgical tape, some cotton wool, and two neatly coiled lengths of tubing. He looked at himself in the mirror. There was blood on his lower lip. Turning on the cold tap, he bent over the sink and washed it off. He didn't ask himself any questions. He knew the answers were beyond him.

Later, as he was on the point of leaving the apartment, he stopped and took one last look round. In years to come, if he was ever asked about Naemi, it would be tempting to say that he had been ill. He had been suffering from hallucinations. He had descended into a kind of temporary madness. He felt how Gulsvig must have felt when he walked into the breakfast room at the Park Hyatt, or when he researched the young woman he had known and loved and found precisely nothing. It was as if she had never been. Others had seen her, of course—Wang Jun Wei, Chun Tao, Laser—but if a forensics team were to be called to the apartment he doubted they would find any trace of a Naemi Vieno Kuusela. Like a master criminal, she would have thoroughly erased herself. He didn't understand who she was—not really. There was the young woman with blonde hair, black eyes, and the body of a dancer, and then there was the ancient hag, the nightmare apparition. If Mad Dog was to be believed, though, there was another woman hidden underneath them both, *inside* them both—a succubus craving a host, an unquiet soul, a murderer...

Out on the street, there was the sound of water everywhere, rushing through drains and gutters, dripping off the trees. The creek looked swollen. All the colors were muted—shades of brown and gray, of mud and metal, nothing primary or garish. He thought of the red blood trickling from her mouth. He thought of that last kiss. But he had imagined that. He had imagined *her*. She would already be far away, in another country. Another world.

He opened the door of his Mercedes and climbed in. Should he have brought the wooden box with him, as proof of something, as evidence? As he sat behind the wheel, not moving, his phone rang. He expected it to say *Unknown* again, but it was Ling Ling, her daughter crying in the background.

"Mr. Zhang," she said. "I wanted to remind you. The funeral's tomorrow."

"I hadn't forgotten," he said.

If they failed to observe the proper rituals, he thought, would Mad Dog come back to haunt them? Or would he haunt them anyway? After all, his life had been cut short in a brutal manner, and his death would almost certainly have caught him unprepared. What had Mad Dog told him on the night they saw the owl? *A ghost is a manifestation of something that is incomplete.* He didn't look forward to being visited by Mad Dog. He had been bitter enough when he was alive. Imagine how bitter he would be now he was dead.

"I'd like to thank you for helping us," Ling Ling was saying.

"Don't mention it," Zhang said.

He fingered the bill for the funeral, which was in a folded envelope in his jacket pocket. How would Mad Dog have reacted if he knew who was paying? He imagined the old man's lips twisting as he framed some typically caustic remark—

But another call was coming in, and he had to cut Ling Ling off. It was Johnny Yu, asking if the locksmith had shown up. Zhang said she had.

"Were you satisfied with the job she did?" Johnny asked.

"I was. Very."

"And how did Beijing go?"

Zhang sighed.

"As bad as that?" Johnny said.

"Not good."

"I have something interesting for you—something a bit different."

"Go ahead."

"*Tell me again about the day you turned your back / on everything dear and took the stony track / that led away from your house and hearth—the death / of the old without sight of the new.*"

"It sounds foreign," Zhang said.

"It was written by an Englishman." Johnny paused. "His name is Harsent. He's still alive."

Zhang had both his hands on the steering wheel, but he still hadn't turned the key in the ignition, or switched on the windscreen wipers. The world outside looked bleary, blurred. It was quiet where he was.

The death of the old without sight of the new.

The English poet had described him to perfection.

It took more than an hour to drive to Kangqiao, the roads covered with sheets of water after the downpour, the traffic moving slowly. The skies were clearing, though, and by the time he pulled into the car park of the Holiday Inn at just after two o'clock a weak and colorless sun had broken through.

The young woman at reception asked how long he would be staying.

"A few hours," he said.

Once in his room on the twenty-first floor, he sat on the bed, facing a window that framed a square of empty grayish yellow sky. He remembered the white neon sign that said WHERE ARE YOU, its loneliness and desperation made keener by the absence of a question mark. He took out his phone and sent Naemi a text. In all probability, she would never receive it, but he couldn't help himself. He had not imagined that his life could be so disrupted, or that he could be so shaken. The end of one affair usually signified the beginning of another. He wasn't accustomed to feeling agitation or regret. Rather, he would be grateful for what had happened, and grateful that it had not gone on too long. He would be excited by the prospect of what lay ahead. Not this time, though. He saw her as he had seen her last, her dark dress stained darker still with blood. Obviously, she had not been real, and yet the apparition had been so detailed that it felt believable and true. Her actual presence, by contrast, had often seemed like a fantasy. The tangled gold-blonde hair, the heavenly skin...

He looked around. It was indistinguishable from the room where they had made love in September. The same neutral, inoffensive pastel colors. The same drab art. Taking off his shoes, he placed them side by side next to the bed, then he removed his suit and hung it on a hanger in the cupboard. He hung his shirt on a hanger too. He slipped out of his underwear and his socks and laid them, folded, on a shelf beneath his suit and shirt. In the same cupboard, he found a white toweling bathrobe and a pair of white hotel slippers. He put them on. Pushing his key into the pocket of the robe, he left the room and set off towards the lifts. As he passed down the corridor, he heard a burst of laughter from a TV, and then applause. Later, the murmur of a woman talking on her phone. A damp, swampy smell rose off the carpet. It was a Monday in October, three in the afternoon. How had it come to this?

He reached the lifts and pressed the call button. Almost immediately, one of the lifts arrived, and a man in a shiny, pale gray suit stepped out. He seemed to hesitate, but Zhang stepped past him without looking and pressed 24. The doors slid shut. The lift ascended. He had a sudden urge to call Torben Gulsvig and tell him what he had seen in the Embankment Building—not his vision of Naemi, but the matte-black walls, the traces of loose earth on the bedroom floor, the wooden box ... He wanted to know whether any of it sounded familiar to Gulsvig, and if so what he made of it. He would put in a call after his swim. He should also call his son, Hai Long. He wanted to ask him to come and spend a weekend in Shanghai.

He entered the pool area and showed his room key to a girl in a gray-and-orange uniform.

She gave him a long look. "You were here before."

"You have a good memory," he said.

"Not really." She glanced beyond him, towards the pool. "It's strange, but not too many people use this place. Sometimes a whole day goes by, and nobody comes in at all."

"You don't get bored," he said, "or lonely?"

She shrugged, then smiled.

He asked if he could rent or buy a pair of swimming trunks and some goggles. She had trunks and goggles in Lost Property, she said, and he was welcome to borrow them. He thanked her. She fetched the trunks and goggles, and handed him a towel as well, then she returned to her station by the door, next to the cash register.

He stood by the silver sculpture with its sleek curves, its vaguely shell-like shapes. Since the last third of the pool had been conceived as an overhang, with glass walls and a glass ceiling, the water made a fourth wall that was seemingly built from the same ambiguous gray-blue material. There was the conviction, difficult to dispel, that if he stepped into the water he would also be stepping into the sky, a world that was limitless and dizzying, and offered no way back.

He pulled on the trunks, which were too big for him, then took off the robe and laid it on a plastic lounger. Stepping out of his hotel slippers, he walked to the vertical ladder at the shallow end and climbed down into water that felt surprisingly cool. A shiver shook him. He moistened the goggles and fitted them over his eyes, then pushed away from the tiled edge. He was swimming breaststroke, and the water parted before him in an inverted V, small waves peeling away on either side. The water that lay ahead was still smooth, so smooth it was hard not to think of it as solid. He was swimming towards a kind of precipice that he couldn't see, but this time he didn't feel any fear. He was looking forward to the feeling of suspension, of being afloat twice over, once in water, once in air. One stroke, and then another. His head above the surface, then beneath it. Then above it once again.

As he approached the glass panes, the place where the bottom of the pool became a window, he was aware of a movement in the corner of his eye, and he thought it must be the girl in the gray-and-orange uniform, she had come to tell him something, there was something he should know, but before he could turn properly and look there was a loud flat sound, a sort of crash, as if somebody had dropped a metal dustbin lid, and he was pushed sideways with great force, and the water and the sky both vanished, and all he could see was a blackness flecked with silver, like a memory of fireworks when he was a child in Beijing, his hand in his mother's hand, his father somewhere else, abroad perhaps, but then the blackness began to shrink, and he was shrinking with it, and he knew he wasn't going to make it to the end—

EPILOGUE

SHE STOOD AT HER LIVING-ROOM WINDOW, a small suitcase on the floor behind her. Her throat ached, and there was blood on her top lip. She was thinking about her last night with Zhang. She had been worried that he might ask why she had fought with Mad Dog, and why she had pretended to be in London, but his mind seemed to be on other things. He had even asked her what London had been like! Was it possible that Mad Dog hadn't said anything? By the time they reached the Shanghai Museum, she found she was beginning to relax. Then, in the early morning, he came out with it. *I forgot to tell you. Mad Dog died.* She had been startled by the news. This wasn't an outcome she had ever imagined. How could it have happened? Mad Dog had been alive when she left. He must have tried to get to his feet and then lost his balance and fallen down the steps . . . Within minutes, she received a second shock. As she stood in Zhang's service lift, about to say goodbye, a look of horror rose on to his face. *You killed him. It was you.* There was a violent detonation in her head. Everything flattened, wrecked. Then a numb feeling. The lift dropped slowly through the dark, the light in the ceiling fizzing, blinking. A wire had come loose. She had no memory of what came next. No memory of leaving the building, or walking through the grounds, which would have been deserted at that hour. No memory of flagging down a taxi, or traveling across the city, or arriving at her apartment, though she supposed she must have done all those things. Because she found herself standing at the window in her living room, as she was now. Her brain tingling as the life stole back into it. Like pins and needles. *It was you.* How could he think such a thing? He was distraught about the death of his friend. He wasn't seeing straight. And it was clear to her then, if it wasn't clear before, that she could never set eyes on him again, not ever . . .

Earlier, it had rained so hard that the Shanghai skyline had disappeared. Now, the rain had eased. Just a drifting curtain between her and the view. A Monday morning in the middle of October. An ordinary day. But not one she would forget. She wiped the blood from her mouth, then turned from the window and left the apartment, pulling the case behind her.

Out on the street she hailed a taxi.

"Longyang Road," she said. "The station."

The driver eyed her in his rearview mirror. "You going on a trip?"

"I don't want to talk," she said.

Shrugging, the driver turned up the volume on his radio and pulled away from the curb. He waited for a black Mercedes to pass, then he turned right, onto a bridge that spanned the creek.

She stared through the window as they bumped down into one of the narrow streets that ran behind the Bund. The traffic slowed, then stopped. A young man in a chef's apron sat on a doorstep outside a restaurant, shelling prawns. His T-shirt said ATTITUDE ADJUSTMENT. She let out a laugh that was scarcely a laugh at all, just a short sharp exhalation. She found it hard to believe that her years in Shanghai were over. The ache in her throat wasn't an infection. It was regret.

Zhang Guo Xing.

When she arrived at the bar in the Park Hyatt, she was able to approach him without him knowing. She saw him first, just as she had in the club on the night they met. His head was lowered. He seemed lost in thought. He wasn't scanning the bar for her, as men she was meeting normally did. He wasn't apprehensive, or predatory. He might almost have forgotten that she was coming. She liked this about him. He mirrored her desire for an intimacy that would be more profound because it sprang from confidence, not need or lack. She stood by the table for a few seconds, watching him. Then, finally, she spoke. *Have you been waiting long?* He glanced up and saw her. Once again, he surprised her, since he didn't have the look of a man who wanted something from her. It was more as if the sight of her gladdened his heart. She felt, oddly, like the view from a high window—miles and miles of wooded hills and valleys unfolding into a distance that was hazy, blue.

Have a seat. What can I get you?

The taxi dropped her at Longyang Road station, and she took an escalator up to the concourse, where she bought a one-way ticket to Pudong airport. The woman told her the Maglev would be leaving in thirteen minutes. She stepped onto a second escalator that led up to the platform. Once she had boarded the train, she sat down and stared out of the window. Not long afterwards, a middle-aged man in a New York baseball cap sat nearby. He looked Taiwanese, or possibly Malaysian. A camera with a long lens hung around his neck.

When she lay down with Zhang in the Chairman Suite on that first night, everything that he did felt right.

He touched her body as if he was already familiar with it. He knew when words were needed, and when they were not. How often did that happen? She wondered briefly if he had also lived more than one life—if she had been with him before...But no, he was too young in himself. Too new. It was instinct on his part. It was her good fortune. Even then, though, she had registered a flicker of anxiety, scarcely detectible, yet catastrophic, like the discarded cigarette that starts a forest fire. If he knew how to touch her, what else did he know? What would he sense in her? How would she conceal what she needed to conceal? She had wanted to sleep with him the moment she saw him. She was someone who responded quickly. But she seemed drawn to the very people who endangered her. The intuitive, the curious—and sometimes, also, the malevolent. How long could she give him? A week? A month? Or should she remove herself immediately? As she gazed at the top of the Jinmao Tower, the china animals motionless behind her on their artificial grass, she was torn between self-indulgence and self-denial. They were both powerful, both painful. That was what her life was like. Raids on the sublime tended to be followed by rapid withdrawals. *I don't love you. Forget me. I was never here.*

In hindsight, one thing was certain. She should have ended it before she met Mad Dog. She should have ended it as soon as Torben appeared. That was a sign, if ever there was one—the past floating up into the present and capsizing it. What did the fishermen in Finnmark used to say? *The wave that sinks you is the wave you never see.* It should have been a one-night stand—an assignation that couldn't be repeated. The exotic stranger, the deluxe hotel. Nothing wrong with that. But she had been un-disciplined, and greedy. She'd allowed herself to become involved...

As the train slid out of the station, there were an-nouncements in a number of different languages. The air-port was thirty kilometers southeast of Shanghai, and the journey would take just over seven minutes. They would be traveling at speeds of up to 430 kilometers an hour. Something about the shortness of time it would take to reach the airport undid her. She began to tremble, tears spilling from her eyes.

"Are you all right?" The man in the baseball cap was leaning towards her, across the aisle.

She held up a hand to ward him off. "I'm fine—"

"Can I help?"

"No," she said. "Thank you—"

The train gathered speed, tilting on its rails. A digital screen at the far end of the carriage showed how fast they were going: 180 kmh. 190 kmh. 210 kmh. The man in the baseball cap was on his feet in the aisle, taking photographs of the screen.

The flat land outside the window was a blur.

She remembered dancing with Zhang in his apartment late at night. They had ended up pressed against each other, barely moving, the music Spanish, sentimental. *Pero tengo que ser / Tengo que ser como soy*... In that moment, she would willingly have traded all her many lifetimes for a single life with him, but as the song suggested she couldn't get away from who she was.

430 kmh. 431 kmh. 430 kmh.

The train had reached its optimum speed. Had she loved him? She thought she had.

The tears kept coming.

The Maglev slowed and stopped. As she left the train, the man in the baseball cap asked once again if he could help in any way. She thanked him, then said she was feeling better. Though she was several hours early for her flight, she headed straight to Security. She handed the uniformed official her passport and boarding card. He studied her name, the name that was about to become obsolete. It was a pity. She had grown to like it. But this was her last day as Naemi Vieno Kuusela. The official lifted his eyes and was looking at her steadily. Perhaps he could tell she had been crying. But there was nothing unusual or suspicious about that. People were always crying in airports. At last, he stamped her passport and handed it back to her. This, too, would become obsolete as soon as she cleared Customs and Immigration in Frankfurt.

Since her flight wasn't due to leave until the evening, she decided to check into the hourly rate hotel. A manager with a badge that said ANGELA escorted her to reception on the seventh floor of an annex, where she was given a simple, uncluttered room. Switching on the TV, she took off her coat and shoes and lay down on the bed. Her tears had left her feeling shaky, weak. This moment, when it came, never felt good. There was usually somebody she cared for, or somebody she had to leave—somebody whose silence she had to secure if she was going to survive. Sometimes her hands were dirty, sometimes not, but her heart was seldom clean. Through the sealed window, she saw dark clouds massing to the northwest. It looked as if a thunderstorm had descended on Shanghai.

She remembered the day her English boyfriend Peter died. After calling the police—she had used a public phone box, and had chosen to remain anonymous— she ran to the halls of residence where Torben lived and knocked on the door of his room. She was crying and shaking. Torben didn't know what to say. He hadn't liked Peter. He had never thought Peter was good enough for her. Then again, he wouldn't have thought anyone was good enough for her, and he was sufficiently self-aware to realize that, and to be able to laugh at himself. He put his arms around her and held her until she calmed down, then he made her a cup of Nescafé and rolled her a cigarette.

"I told him the drugs would kill him," she said, "but he didn't listen to me."

"He didn't listen to anyone." Torben paused. "Sometimes, when we were talking, I'd think of that line in *The Tale of the Heike*: '*The arrogant do not long endure.*'" He looked at her. "I feel bad about that now."

She nodded slowly.

"What are you going to do?" he asked.

"I don't know," she said.

She did, though. It was the end of her time in London. She wasn't a suspect in Peter's death, but she couldn't afford to allow herself to be questioned by his family, or by the police. Her life wouldn't stand up to scrutiny. There were too many inconsistencies, too many blanks. She had already visited a travel agency and booked a flight to New York. She would be leaving the following day, in the evening. She knew disappearing would make her look guilty, as if she had something to hide, but she also knew she didn't have a choice.

They sat on the floor, cross-legged, in the dim yellow glow of a single lamp, and Torben put on *Blue* by Joni Mitchell. He had played it for her before, hoping she would appreciate its significance and beauty. She never had. That night, though, for the first time, the songs made sense to her. They rushed forwards, as driven and breathless as her life, the lines constantly merging, one into another. The voice was thin, almost nervous, but it had a strange strength too, like wire. Each time the needle reached the end of the side, they turned the record over. They must have listened to it half a dozen times.

At five thirty in the morning, she stretched her arms into the air above her head and told him she should go.

"Already?" Torben grinned.

She stood up and looked around. His posters of Hendrix and Che Guevara, his stereo with its wooden speakers. The dead branch he had brought back from a long walk over Hampstead Heath. Some words from one of the Joni Mitchell songs had lodged in her head: *Let's not talk about fare-thee-wells now / The night is a starry dome*...He didn't realize their friendship was over, and she couldn't tell him either. It seemed so cruel. But there was no other way.

This moment, when it came—and it always came...

She glanced at the TV. Breaking news. A headline had appeared at the bottom of the screen. MAN SHOT IN SHANGHAI HOTEL. There was some jerky footage of journalists and photographers crowding round a stretcher, pushing and shoving, as it was wheeled across a patch of tarmac and loaded into a waiting ambulance. Then the camera pulled back to reveal the front of the hotel. It was the Holiday Inn, in Kangqiao. Her mind jammed. The breath stalled in her throat. She grabbed the remote and turned up the sound. The incident had taken place in the hotel pool, the reporter was saying. The victim's identity had yet to be confirmed, and the motive for the shooting was unclear.

Zhang.

Was he alive? The reporter didn't say.

She pictured herself on the pavement looking up at the hotel, the pool protruding from the side of the building, its four glass windows clearly visible. Zhang's body was floating in the deep end, the cloud of blood standing out, red against the white clouds in the sky. His clothes would be laid out in his room. His Prada suit, his sunglasses. His phone—

The smell of his skin came back to her. You only had to look at him to know he would smell good. Something sharp and clean, like freshly cut timber. Once again, she thought of the night they had spent together, after the opening. She had known this was the last she would ever see of him. Perhaps that explained the dull ache in her belly, the desperate grasping at sensation... She lay with her face close to his, breathing in as he was breathing out. She inhaled the air that came from his mouth so that it flowed straight from the inside of his body to the inside of hers. She watched him sleep. She listened to him dream. How strange that people felt they could afford all these hours of unconsciousness. How strange to let time slip through your fingers when you had so very little of it. This was the complacency—the sense of ease—that she had lost.

That night, she took pictures of him without him knowing. She didn't use the flash, but she could see the outline of his face, blue-silver light tracing the straight line of his nose, the subtle M-shape of his upper lip, the smooth curve of his jaw. *You're very beautiful. So are you.* He murmured something and turned away from her, his right arm reaching out beyond the edge of the bed, his fingers curled in towards his palm. He slept on. She stayed awake, as always. She had been with him longer than he had been with her. She had loved him as much as she knew how. Her surroundings blurred. She was crying again, even harder than before...

A photo had flashed up on to the TV screen. A twenty-six-year-old man had been arrested, the reporter was saying. He was a suspect in the shooting.

It was Chu En Li.

Her hand over her mouth, she left the bed. She leaned against the window, looking out. Her legs felt too brittle to hold her up. She remembered how he sat facing her on the nightclub terrace, his black shirt stretched tight across his chest, a chain of gold links gleaming in the spaces between the buttonholes. Somewhere deep in her bones, she had sensed that he might pose a threat, and she had flown to Manila in order to defuse it, but she had not been sufficiently sensitive or diplomatic. She had allowed him to see how much Zhang meant to her. She had ended up provoking him. Her hand moved to her forehead, which was damp. Everything was jumbled up, the wrong way round. It was Chu En Li, not Mad Dog, who should have died. It was Chu En Li who should have been removed from the equation. Zhang had needed her protection. Instead, she had only succeeded in putting his life in jeopardy.

Why was this always happening to her?

Outside, it was growing dark, the orange fading into brown. A chill rose off the glass. She could see planes coming in to land, small clusters of lights stacked up in the sky.

Her phone vibrated on the bedside table. Probably the airline, with an update. She glanced at the screen. The text had come from Zhang, and it was in English. *The death of the old without sight of the new.* That was all it said. But how could he be writing to her if he had been shot? Some mechanism inside her seemed to slow down and stop. Her hands suddenly felt cold. Then she realized. There must have been a problem with the server, or with the coverage. He would have sent the message hours ago. Even so, it was eerie. She wished she could find out if he was all right, but she knew she couldn't. She slid the phone into her pocket, then she switched off the TV, put on her shoes and coat, and left the room.

At reception, she placed her key on the counter.

"Did you manage to get some rest?" the receptionist asked with a smile.

"Yes," Naemi said. "Thank you."

The bill was 300 RMB.

Ten minutes later, she was standing in Departures. She looked at Zhang's text again. It was almost as if he understood what she was doing. As if he had traveled with her, in spirit form. This was why she had been drawn to him, and why she'd had to bring the whole thing to an end. She sat on an orange plastic seat, took out her phone, and scrolled through her recent photographs. Zhang lying on his back with a hand on his belly and his face turned to one side, the crumpled sheet pushed down to his waist. Zhang at half three in the morning, lost to the world . . . He slept deeply for a man in his forties. It was the sleep of someone half his age.

Switching her phone off, she removed the SIM card and snapped it in half, then she hid the phone and the broken card inside a copy of the *Shanghai Daily* that she was carrying and dropped it in a nearby bin. All the messages from him gone. All the photos. Gone. She reached into her coat pocket and took out her brand-new passport. She had checked it when it first arrived, and also before she left her apartment, but now she opened it and checked it again. Nicola Viktorija Krstulovic. Born in Riga, Latvia, on February 19, 1991.

"Nicola," she murmured.

This was the name she would answer to the moment she walked out of Frankfurt airport. This was her new identity.

Though Frankfurt was her immediate destination, she wasn't planning to spend more than a day or two in the city. She was thinking of returning to her roots. She hadn't been to the north of Finland for many years, and no one there would know her. After Shanghai, she needed a quiet, uneventful life. She needed a place where she could fit in. Lie low. Long dark winters. The short mad blaze of summer...She glanced at the screen that listed all the departing flights. Her gate number had flashed up. She closed her passport and rose to her feet.

Some minutes later, she was on a travelator, making for her gate, when she saw a familiar figure coming the other way. It was the man Zhang had talked about when they first met. The man was dressed in the same pale blue suit, and he was pulling the same blue case behind him. As they drew level with each other, he looked at her and winked. There was no time to respond. He had already passed beyond her. All she could do was watch him over her shoulder as he moved towards Arrivals. He hadn't even broken his stride, and the gap between them was widening with every second. Slowly, she faced front again, and smiled to herself. She had just realized what he was carrying in his luggage. Outside, beyond the plate-glass window, it was night.

She passed another screen listing departures. A single word had appeared next to her gate number.

Boarding.

Temple Drake lives in London.